A History of Magic

The Last Great Hero
Book 2

Scott J. Robinson

All characters and events portrayed
in this book are fictional,
and any resemblance to real people
or incidents is coincidental.

Copyright © 2018
Scott Robinson

1st Edition

ISBN-13: 978-0-9943355-4-8

For more information visit
www.tengama.com
or email
scott@tengama.com

Please help support
independent writers and publishers.
Your money is wonderful.
So are your reviews,
comments, mentions, tweets,
emails, blogs, likes,
and deliveries of chocolate.

A History of Magic

Wensday

RAWK, THE LAST OF THE GREAT HEROES, wondered how long he should wait.

He'd been standing under the tree for at least half an hour, a rock amidst the surge and swirl of the market but, after having met with Maris twice previously, he was starting to get the impression that she was always late. So he stayed where he was, eating a long curl of sticky pastry he'd bought from a cock-eyed hawker, and gazed around. There were noticeably less people than there had been a while ago. The serious morning shoppers were done for the day and the more casual lunch crowd had not yet materialized.

Licking his fingers a few minutes later, he was surprised that nobody had yet come to talk to him, requesting a story, or just looking for a story they could tell their friends later on. They did it often enough, complete strangers acting as if his fame somehow made it all right to bother him and make demands of his time. Not so long ago he was happy with the arrangement, but it seemed that recently he was seeking out more moments to call his own. Perhaps standing in the market was not the best location to find one of those, but still...

Eventually he turned to a hawker and paid for another of the pastries. While he waited for the man to stash the money he turned to look up at Theron Tower. The clock at the top said that it was almost fifteen minutes past ten. Though it was the oldest in the city, and notoriously unreliable, he decided that if he waited much longer even the late breakfasts would be over and it would be lunchtime. Just as he was really starting to wonder if Maris had changed her mind, she came into view, strolling along one of the alleyways between stalls. Once she made it into the relatively clear space under the tree, she paused and looked around, brushing hair from her eyes. She smiled when she saw him and, for a moment, Rawk thought it was a smile of relief, as if she thought he might not be there.

He took a couple of steps towards her, favoring his injured knee.

"Sorry I'm late," she said. "Were you waiting long?"

"No. I was a bit late myself."

"Oh, that's good. I had trouble finding my earrings."

The items in question seemed to be ivory hoops carved with intricate patterns. Rawk wasn't sure if they were worth the effort; they were a bit gaudy for his taste.

"They're nice," he said. "I was doing my hair." He rubbed his hand over his bald scalp.

Maris laughed softly.

"Here ya go, Rawk," the hawker said, appearing suddenly at his elbow. He looked at both Rawk with one eye and Maris with the other. "I think three may be a record for anyone."

Rawk took the pastry. The third one he'd had; so much for having just arrived. But if Maris noticed the inconsistencies in his story, she didn't say anything.

A scream ended the chance for any further conversation. Then another scream, louder than the first, and people were running everywhere, streaming along between the stalls, pushing and shoving. They were like a drift of flowers caught in a wild, surging stream. Noisy, rude flowers. But it seemed that most didn't know what they were running from. Or where they were running to.

The noise of shouting and mass movement grew like an approaching storm.

Trying to get his bearings, Rawk headed for where the craziness was at its most intense. He pushed against the tide, shouldering people aside, stalking between the stalls. He paused at a corner. The smell of a candle maker's tent, heavy with spices and perfumes, assaulted him. He kept going, and the smell trailed him almost all the way to the far side.

The crowd was thinning now. Everyone had decided where they were going and had gone. Rawk kept walking straight ahead, past a pickler and into the fresh food section of the market. And in the farthest corner he found an exot.

The creature looked a lot like a watermelon with six crab-legs and a tuft of yellow hair. It might almost have been funny, except its long teeth were obviously made for tearing and it had the growl of a cornered bear. A starving, injured, late-for-work, cornered bear. It also had two short, muscular arms. In one hand it had a 'sword', no bigger than a dagger for a human, and in the other was a club. The sword was much used; it had a bent tip and a notch taken out of the edge.

And beyond it was a dark geometric delta of blood on the street, following the cobbles as it spread away from a dead washerwoman.

Rawk wanted to finish his pastry. It was very good, but now half of it was a squashed mess in his hand and the other half was back behind him somewhere. Or he could just go to a cafe like he and Maris had planned and have breakfast. Or lunch. Or whatever it was. He thought that, or something similar, every time he came against an exot these days. Perhaps his stomach was trying to tell him something. He looked around and saw that quite a crowd had gathered, moving in behind him when they realized who he was. They were too close. They wouldn't all be able to get away if the thing decided they looked like a better target than Rawk. Perhaps they couldn't see the dead woman. They obviously thought Rawk would win, because he always did. Except one day he wouldn't.

Rawk swore under his breath. He dropped the pastry and wiped his hand on his breeches. He drew his sword with sticky fingers and raised it above his head so the crowd could cheer. Then stayed where he was as he tried to think. Not long ago he would have charged, but he was starting to realize that could be a terrible idea. He wasn't as young as he had once been and the sudden increase in exots coming to Katamood— he'd killed at least a dozen in the last week— had been exhausting.

"If you aren't going to kill it, old man, I will." A tall, slim woman was standing at the edge of the crowd. She had her sword drawn and was wearing dented black armor like she knew how to use it.

It took Rawk a moment to recognize her. "Josey? Is that you? It's been years."

The woman nodded. "You're getting old."

"That didn't concern you last time."

"You weren't so old then."

Rawk couldn't argue with that. "What are you doing here?"

"I was drawn here."

"Was I really that good?"

She smiled but said, "Everyone is being drawn here, Rawk. Katamood is the center of the world again."

"Well, I don't need any help." He could see at least three other Heroes in the crowd as well, all waiting for the opportunity to jump in. One of them was inching slowly forward.

Josey raised an eyebrow. "Really? Then go and make the claim before I do. Manners will only hold me so long."

For a moment, Rawk considered letting her take the claim, but apparently he still wasn't ready to go that far, not with a crowd watching anyway. So he started slowly forward as the creature came to meet him on scuttling legs. It clattered across the cobbles, slashing at his leg with the sword. Rawk blocked but almost had his kneecap shattered by the club. He took the blow in his shin, hobbling back a step, as he knocked aside another attack.

Rawk reassessed and held his ground, using his longer reach to keep the creature away. Keeping it away from his legs was relatively easy once he had its measure. Until the exot leapt up to head height and almost took out an eye with a quick, vicious jab. And that moment when Rawk almost died gave him the chance to finish the fight. He swung *Dabaneera* upwards, anticipated the block, twisted.

And the creature disappeared with the sound of breaking glass and a faint whiff of... rosemary.

There was a moment of silence, then the crowd started to cheer. Rawk looked at his sword. He cleared his throat and turned to look at Josey. She raised her eyebrows.

Rawk took a deep breath. And the breath was knocked out of him as Maris dashed from amongst the stalls and threw herself into his arms.

"That was amazing," she said in his ear. He could barely hear her over the cheering. "Don't do it again. Ever."

"I'm Rawk; I have to." He turned to the crowd to acknowledge the cheers.

At that moment there was a pop and a bright flash of light. The crowd didn't seem to notice, or at least they didn't care, but Josey had dropped to a fighting crouch.

"What was that?" Rawk pushed Maris aside and readied *Dabaneera*. He blinked and rubbed his eyes, trying to see. "Did you see who it was, Josey? Was it magic?"

The woman shook her head as she straightened. "It was a dwarf, I think."

"Are you sure?"

"Does the phrase 'I think' lead you to believe I am sure?" She looked around. "Nobody else seems to be worried."

Dwarves could not do magic, so Rawk started to relax as well. He cleared his throat and rubbed his eyes some more.

Maris was looking a bit offended. "What was it?"

"Didn't you see it? Or hear it?"

She shook her head.

Josey motioned towards the crowd. "Well, the little bugger has gone now, anyway," she said walking slowly to Rawk's side as she sheathed her blade. "And speaking of magic..."

Rawk didn't reply. He examined his blade instead.

"Is that a magical sword? It doesn't look all that special."

"It's just a sword," Rawk muttered.

"You didn't hit the thing, did you?"

"Didn't get close, really."

"That's what I thought. I won't say anything, but people might get a bit suspicious if it comes back."

"There could be lots of them."

"Perhaps. I know one thing, there's lots of magic going on around here, even if neither you nor that dwarf are the ones doing it."

"Why do you say that?"

"All the exots appearing around here haven't been hiding under people's back porches. They're coming from somewhere else."

"The forest maybe," Rawk said. They weren't coming from the forest; they were appearing all over the city, not just to the west; but even if they were, magic was probably still involved.

Josey shook her head. "Well, you go look in the forest. I'll just stay here and get my claims without all the walking." She patted Rawk on the shoulder and sauntered away.

"What do you mean you didn't hit it?" Maris asked.

Rawk cleared his throat and looked at his sword again. "The creature disappeared when the sword was about two inches away from it."

"Oh. So it isn't dead?" She looked around as if the creature might suddenly reappear.

Rawk knew of no reason why it *couldn't* reappear. "I have no idea." There was no evidence to suggest where it had gone. The only thing he really saw was the dead washerwoman, though her hood covered her face. Was she screaming when she died or had she been surprised? Rawk couldn't see any wounds. The flow of blood across the cobbles had stopped

Blinking, he looked around. The crowd was still clapping and cheering. Some of them were talking amongst themselves, as if they had just watched a particularly good piece of theatre. None of them seemed to take any notice of the dead woman, even when the City Guard turned up and started to organize for the body to be taken away. Waydin arrived with a pair of dwarves pulling the cleaning wagon. The soldier took a moment to talk to Rawk.

"Did you get the claim, Rawk?"

He nodded.

"Was it big?"

"No. Just an animated watermelon."

"Well, you can let Weaver know at lunch."

"Today? Really?"

Waydin smiled and gave him the name of the tavern and the alias Weaver would be using.

"But I haven't even had breakfast yet."

The soldier shrugged. "Then you'd better hurry up." He went to make sure nobody disturbed the dwarves at their work

Rawk watched for a few minutes as the woman's body was carefully placed in the wagon and the pavers were scrubbed. The crowd was still there, watching the final act. "Let's go and get something to eat before someone starts throwing walnuts."

"What?"

"Come on."

"Oh, don't worry, I'll be sticking close to you."

The crowd cheered as they started to shuffle back out of the way.

"Path bless you, Rawk," someone shouted. The little woman held up two fingers in the sign of the god.

"Thank you." But he didn't care about Path; Path had let the woman die. He made his way through the crowd, trying not to hobble. He just wanted to sit down and have something to eat.

Maris directed him to a cafe back the way they had come. There were tables and chairs set up on the sidewalk outside the small building with flowers on the table to drown out the smell of the river.

A waiter rushed out as soon as they sat down.

"I'll have an ale, please," Rawk said. It was going to taste horrible but he needed *something*. "And a..."

"I imagine Maris will have an cherry wine." The waiter smiled at her and she nodded.

Then he scurried away, collecting dirty crockery from as table as he went.

"So, you come here a lot?" Rawk said in the lengthening silence. The place didn't seem all that special.

"Yes. The manager is a friend."

"It's nice. I've never been here before."

The cafe was just fifty yards from Dragon Bridge. The sound of sailors and wharf hands competed with the din of the market, which was just starting to find its rhythm again.

Maris nodded. "I like it. No matter what's going on, it always seems to be quiet here. I feel calmer when I sit down."

Calm? Rawk cleared his throat. Calm would have been nice. He was nervous every time he saw Maris. He didn't know what to say or do so he bumbled along, feeling like a fool. Feeling like a boy again. He had seen her twice since first taking her for a late night sugar—stick and he still wasn't quite sure how to act. He'd never been in that situation before. Normally he saw a woman once, slept with her, then didn't see her again, or spent considerable effort avoiding her. Occasionally he saw her a second time, but that usually involved sex as well. But the topic of sex had not come up with Maris, and Rawk found that he didn't mind at all.

The waiter returned and set the drinks on the table. "Are you ready to order?"

Maris gave a small nod then looked at Rawk. "I know what I want. The gasa is excellent." But he felt her hand on his leg under the table and came to the conclusion that she wasn't interested in breakfast at all. Or lunch.

Rawk cleared his throat. He fumbled with the menu, pulling it from amidst the flower arrangement.

When he spun it around, it took a moment for his eyes to focus. He coughed as Maris started to rub his leg. "I don't like gasa all that much, I think it's the sultanas. Have you just got some type of stew?"

"We have lamb casserole with Makavian spices and mashed potato."

That sounded a bit fancy; Weaver would be horrified. "That sounds perfect."

Maris smiled. "You seem like a man who stands by his convictions."

"Well, I can't understand why you would want to ruin a perfectly good grape."

"I suppose you prefer them squashed and fermented."

Rawk smiled. "Something like that." Though he didn't like wine all that much more than he liked ale. He just liked eating grapes. And as he took his bone handled knife and fork from the pouch on his belt he wondered why he hadn't just said that. He was still playing the part of the Hero, being the person that was expected. "I actually—"

"The food is all cooked fresh, here. It may take a while for it to arrive." She moved her hand away from his leg and took his hand instead.

–O–

Rawk smiled to himself as he watched Maris make her way up the steps into the Veterans' Club. And when she was gone he stayed there a while longer to contemplate the trudge around the side of the hill to the *Rusted Hammer*. It wasn't actually all that far at all, but knowing that didn't help at all. He couldn't stand there all day; there was a team of dwarves working on the sewers just down the hill and by the end of they day they'd probably be telling stories about him moping around like a love struck youth. So, with a sigh that probably suited the dwarves' narrative, he started to walk.

As usual it was a slow journey with people stopping to shake his hand and wish him well. Three people waved the Y symbol of the Great Path at him and a group of children followed him for a block before asking for a story. And he actually didn't mind at all because it was all a good excuse for his slow pace. By the time he made it to the front of the *Hammer* the last of the morning had slipped away.

Prince Weaver was sitting on the front porch of the tavern, feet up on the rail, ale in hand. "Halloo, friend Rawk. It hath been a long time since I saw you last."

Rawk sighed again. "Gavin? Is that you?" Gavin was one of the prince's favorite disguises. He'd used it several times before.

"Course it is. Who else would it be?" The accent was still as terrible as ever.

Rawk climbed up the stairs and sat down by Weaver's side. He looked around and saw several guards trying to look inconspicuous.

"Let me buy ya some lunch."

"Not today, thanks. I only just finished breakfast."

"You hath only just risen? You hath a need to vacate this city and do some real Hero work."

"I'll be fine here, thanks. There are more than enough exots turning up around here theses days."

"Really?"

"Yes. I've killed three this week. One of them was this morning, which was the reason for my delayed breakfast." That wasn't a *complete* lie.

"Really?"

"Yes. Waydin had some dwarves cleaning up the mess when I left."

Weaver looked around, checking for listeners. Satisfied they were unobserved, he leaned over and whispered, "I think there must be sorcerers hiding in Katamood, Rawk."

"Why do you say that?"

"It is always sorcerers opening portals to let exots through. Always. I am going to have to send out the Guard, I think. I will have them search door to door until I find the culprits."

Rawk nodded slowly as he tried to think. "Aren't you over-reacting a bit?" Sylvia was one of the 'culprits' that would most likely be found. If some guards started asking questions her name was bound to come up.

"I don't think so. I'll start south of the river, because that's where they'll be, I'm sure."

Rawk nodded some more. "Perhaps." Sylvia was right near the top of Mount Grace, so it would be a while before any search got to her place, but still... "I thought you wanted exots for me to kill. The good old days, remember?"

"But you don't want the good old days. You said so. And exots are one thing. Sorcerers are quite another."

"I know. But... What will the people say if they think you don't have everything under control?"

"If I don't uphold the law..." His eyes narrowed. "Why are you protecting sorcerers?"

"I'm not protecting sorcerers."

"It sounds like you are."

"Well, just because I don't want to take part in the good old days myself, doesn't mean I don't like the excitement of being around when others do it."

Weaver sat back in his seat. "Huh," he said, forgetting his accent. "I told you so. Give it a few more weeks and you'll be out there hunting for the exots. But that's beside the point, anyway." He looked around again and leaned in close. "I can't have sorcerers wandering around the city."

"How much will these searches cost you?"

"Well..."

Rawk knew he'd found the right argument. "Just hold off for a while and let me see what I can find for you."

Weaver pursed his lips. "You would do that? I don't want the people to panic. Very well. I will give you a week, no more. And then every spare man will be out looking. That will show the people of Katamood who's in charge."

"I'm sure it will."

Weaver gave a nod, as if it was all sorted out. "Now, what did you say you wanted for lunch?"

Rawk sighed. "Potato stew, of course."

Weaver smiled. "Excellent. Let's go inside and order."

They found a table, though that was probably because a guard came in first and suggested that somebody move. Rawk sat down but didn't even have a chance to take his cutlery from the pouch on his belt. He saw Ramaner standing in the doorway, looking even more angry than normal.

"What have I done this time?" he muttered.

"Pardon?"

Rawk didn't say anything, merely motioning to the general. Weaver turned to look.

"Ramaner, what do you want?" Rawk asked when the small precession arrived beside the table.

The general sneered but turned to look at Weaver. He cleared his throat and glanced around the room. "Gavin Tuug, of Tharpin?"

Weaver was looking confused. "Yes."

"You are under arrest."

He looked even more confused. "What for?"

Ramaner took a moment to think of something. Something that would require him to come down from the palace instead of just sending some cheaper men. "Conspiracy to commit treason."

Weaver obviously didn't understand that Ramaner wanted to talk to him but was trying to let the prince keep his cover. "I didn't do anything," he said.

Rawk smiled. "You know Gavin is from Tharpin, right?"

Now *Ramaner* was confused. "Yes."

"So, he cannot actually commit treason against Katamood. The charges would have to be something about espionage, I imagine."

"Shut up, Rawk."

"I'm just saying."

Ramaner leaned in close. His eyes were full of hatred, dark and heavy like a storm. "Just be thankful I'm not arresting you as well. You could well be one of the people he is conspiring with."

"You know as well as I do that Prince Weaver wouldn't let you get away with that."

Ramaner didn't take his eyes off Rawk as he spoke to Weaver. "Get up now, *Gavin*, before I decide you are too much trouble and skip the judge."

"I'm not sure you are allowed to do that," Rawk said, watching the other man carefully.

Ramaner's eye twitched. His gripped the hilt of his sword a little bit tighter than was necessary, turning his knuckles white. He leaned in close and whispered. "One day, Weaver won't be around to protect you, Rawk."

Rawk smiled. "Perhaps you should go with him, Gavin. Get this mess cleared up."

He watched as Weaver was marched from the now silent common room and waved when Ramaner glanced back. When the guards and their prisoner had left, the conversation picked up in the room once more. In normal circumstances Gavin of Tharpin would have been the main topic of conversation, but seeing nobody fell for the disguise the whole incident was quickly forgotten. And as the noise swelled, Rawk was pleased to realize he was all alone and no food had been ordered, so he could leave any time he liked.

"That went rather well," he said. He clapped his hands on the table and rose to his feet. The walk up the hill to the *Hero's Rest* didn't seem so bad.

−O−

There was a fiddle player in the corner of the taproom working as hard as he could, but the man could hardly be heard above the din. Thin notes darted about the room, looking for others to join in some kind of melody. The smell of spices filled the gaps.

"Rawk?"

Rawk looked around. "Travis. Good crowd." He gestured to the musician. "Is that Lika Olend?"

Travis nodded.

"He's supposed to be pretty good." Rawk tried to listen again, but it was useless.

"So they say."

"Shame we can't actually hear him."

"Yes."

"Bit of a waste of money, really."

Travis shrugged. "Well, you can't have your cake and eat it too."

"What's that supposed to mean?"

"Well, you can't have a musician that draws a crowd and then complain about the crowd."

"You can hear the musicians at The Armory."

"Yes, but the music is the point there. Here the point is the ale and the food."

Rawk nodded slowly. "You're right. Can you come down stairs when you have a couple of minutes? I had an idea earlier and I need your help."

"An idea?" His eyes narrowed. "I don't like the sound of that."

"Just come downstairs."

"Very well."

Rawk headed out the back door and went down the stairs. It wasn't often anyone went down there. Not that he knew of anyway. It was dark at the bottom. He groped at the wall for a moment until he located a torch, then took the flint and striker from a pouch on his belt and put them to use. The dancing, orange light showed a hallway. It was five yards from where he stood to a closed door at the far end and there were doors on either side, halfway along. One of them gave access to the private stairs that led all the way up to his rooms. Taking the torch, he went to the final door and managed to shoulder it open, but didn't go any further. Beyond wasn't nearly as impressive or exciting as he remembered.

The room was filled with weapons. Swords, maces, crossbows, flails, shields, armor. There were racks and shelves, hooks and drawers. There were piles in the corners and overflowing barrels. Forty years of loot filling the room from wall to wall with just a narrow walkway leading to the back wall and the two doors that occupied it. Once, Rawk had been able to tell the story behind each and every piece of equipment. He might still remember them if pushed. A sword given to him by the King of Keplamar. He'd killed a rebeth to earn it. A shield he'd scooped up while fighting the Fezen Champion on the battlefield of Dorn. Forty years. His history. His life. And every story was pretty much the same. Death. It was always about death. Not his, yet, but the day would come. He wondered who would have his sword when that happened.

Once it had been easy to keep the room neat and tidy but it looked as if Travis had long since given up. It was possible he hadn't even been down here for years, because Rawk was paid in gold more than anything else these days and didn't go around collecting trophies.

Travis arrived a few minutes later.

"This had better be good, I have work to do."

Rawk smiled. "You normally spend more time running around after me than anything else."

Travis sighed. "How did I end up working for you again?"

"Luck, I guess."

"Yeah, *bad* luck. So, what are we doing down here?"

"I'm going to clean all this up and..."

"Wait, surely you mean *I'm* going to clean up."

"No, Rawk the Invincible is going to battle the mess. You, noble friend, are going shopping." He hung the torch just inside the door.

"Are you all right?"

His arm ached a lot this afternoon. His knee ached. And the chair at the cafe had been terrible and the kitchen bench... he had a kink in his back that made it painful to twist. He shrugged.

"Well, you could have sent me shopping from upstairs, surely. And can't someone else do it, anyway? I'll help here or... Or do the work I'm actually paid for."

"You're paid to do whatever I want, Travis; you should know that by now."

"Well, there may be limits to what I'm willing to do, you know."

"I have a horrible feeling that we will find out very soon." Rawk turned to look at his friend. "It won't be today though, Travis. I just need you to go out and buy some books for me."

"Books? Now I *know* you're unwell."

"I know. What's the world coming to, right?"

"So, out with it then."

"It's all these exots."

"You're buying books for them to read? Keep them busy?"

"No. The point is, I can't keep up. My arm is going to fall off soon. Or I'll find one that I can't beat. All the new Heroes turning up can't keep up either. It only takes a minute for innocent people to be killed."

"Still don't know what you're after."

"Magic, Travis. And that's why I couldn't tell you upstairs, in case someone heard." Rawk leaned against the doorframe and rubbed his face. "These creatures must be coming through portals and someone must be opening them."

"Right."

"And now Weaver has got it into his head that he's going to send the guard out into the city to find whoever's doing it."

"And you want to beat them to it?"

"Exactly. I need the money. So, go and buy me some books about magic."

"Books on magic?"

"Yes, and books about exots. As many as you can find. There's a bookshop just west of Mount Cheese. Go and talk to Juskin first."

"You know the owner of a bookshop by name?"

"Yes. Shut up."

Travis shook his head. "And what if I get caught?"

"Then I'll sort it out. Just don't get caught."

Travis sighed but went to do as he was asked and Rawk turned to his own task.

He followed the path to the back of the room and lit another torch before opening the first of the doors. Wrong one. The room was filled with clothes. Silks and brocades, dresses and pantaloons. Garments from all around the world, most of them never worn. Most of them he wouldn't be seen dead in, though Weaver would have had endless fun organizing his disguises. He grunted and closed the door.

The other room was slightly larger and had a couple a chests full of gold in the back corner and a scattering of other things— valuables and crates and chests that had once held even more gold. Once, it had been full of the stuff. Chests and bags and barrels full to overflowing. Slippery, glinting mountains of the stuff. Coins, goblets, bowls, candelabra, serving platters. Gold and silver and gems. A fortune to rival the nobles' who swanned through he streets of Katamood as if they owned them. Not any more. He remembered the term Yardi had used. A 'diversified portfolio.' Or something like that. There was still enough gold there for him to live comfortably for the rest of his life, if he wanted but now, it was just in the way. It would take too long to move and his knee would not like it at all. He left the full chests and moved anything that was worth money into a pile close by. Then he gathered some of the other things into a big crate and dragged it into the weapons room. He tried to make it a bit tidy, but that was silly when nothing else in the room was neat. So he cleared a spot for it and slid it out of the way and piled more stuff on top. Then he went back for more.

Half an hour later, sweating and aching in so many places he nearly forgot about his knee and his shoulder and all his usual aches, he decided the cleaning was done. Relieved, he grabbed the torch as he made his way into the hallway and down to the door at the far end. Beyond was the largest room in the cellar complex. It was easily as large as the taproom and crammed full of everything that wasn't weapons or clothes or treasure. Some, like the high-backed Mindor saddle, was loot, but a lot was just stuff he had somehow accumulated. There were artworks, rugs, cooking pots, bags of spice from around the world— he should let Kalesie know about those, if they were still any good— and maps. And in the corner, right across the other side of the room of course, was furniture, hardly more than hulking black beasts in the flickering darkness.

Rawk followed a snaking trail through the mess, kicking stuff out of the way as he went, choking on the heavy clouds of dust that roiled around him, to see what he could see. There were a couple of shelves that might be handy. And a desk he could definitely use. *I never thought I'd have to say something like that.* He gave a grunt of amusement.

While he waited for Travis to return, Rawk looked around in the dancing light of the torch. There was an old ledger in the top drawer of the desk. It contained line after line of small neat text. As far as Rawk could tell, it had something to do with the importation of animal skins from Tharpin. It was twenty years old but the prices were very good. In the next drawer there was an inkpot with flaking, redolent black ink lining the inside.

There was a square of material on a bookshelf that might have been torn from a flag or pennant. Behind a pile of chairs, none of which were any good, was an old chest with rusting hinges and a broken lock. There was a ceramic vase on the floor and he propped the torch up inside so he could flip open the lid of the chest and look inside. There were some scraps of paper and what looked like the remains of a cushion. He almost moved on but crouched down and picked up some of the paper. Most of the writing had faded away to almost nothing. Rawk managed to decipher something about flushing cheeks and coy looks so he was glad he couldn't read any more.

Beneath the papers and the snowdrift of feathers, hardly visible in the dust and shadows, was a bag and inside the bag was... Rawk didn't know what it was at first. He pulled it out and it still took him a moment to realize it was a drum. The same type of drum that Grint used when he played in the Armory with Celeste. The light colored timber frame was shot through with swirls of grain. One of the little double–headed sticks was clipped onto the inside. The skin was stiff and dark and smelled of... something.

Rawk pulled to stick out and gave an experimental tap. Remembering how the dwarf played the drum, he tried to do the same. Apparently it wasn't as easy as it looked. Grint made music that didn't seem possible with just one simple drum while his own efforts sounded like a stampede of cattle. He stopped with a pained wince. "Maybe not."

"Maybe not, what?"

Rawk almost dropped the drum as he spun about. Travis was standing in the doorway with an armload of books clutched precariously under one arm. In his other hand was a lamp. A real lamp with a bright, steady white light.

"Maybe I shouldn't try playing the drum."

"What?"

Rawk held up the offending object. "I found this."

"Oh. Well, I could have told you not to try."

"Why's that?"

"You like music, I like music; we wouldn't want to spoil it."

"Thanks for your vote of confidence."

"That's all right. Now, what do you want me to do with these? They're a bit heavy."

Rawk looked at the books. "There's only six of them."

"They're pretty big though. And I think they're every book in the city. So, where can I put these?"

"Oh, sorry, just in the gold room." Rawk waved in the general direction then followed when Travis went out into the hall.

Travis was standing in the doorway to the weapon room when Rawk arrived. "You know this doesn't count as tidying up, right. You have to lessen the mess, not just move it somewhere else."

"Well, why didn't you tell me that before? I think it's the first time I've ever tried to tidy anything; it's trickier than it looks."

"I suppose it's pretty good for your first try." Travis made his way through the increased clutter to the gold room and put the books on the floor near the wall, just inside the door.

Rawk went to have a look. Blinking at the spines, stretching out his arm, he read the titles. *"Magic of the Old Ways. A Witches Guide to Portals. Fire Magic. Bedlam's Book of Spells and Potions. Natural Energy. Convergence."* He sniffed. "That's it? Did you see Juskin?"

"Yes. He's the one who gave me those last two. I wouldn't have known they were about magic otherwise."

"And this is all you can find?"

"Sorcery and magic isn't encouraged around here, remember? Who would want to buy the books?"

"Well, I guess they'll have to do for now. I want you to go out a couple of times a week and see what you can find though."

"Do I have to?"

"Yes. You'll enjoy that more than what I have planned for now."

"And what's that?"

"I need to get some furniture in here."

Travis groaned.

"Exactly."

A couple of hours later, Rawk sighed and sat down. It had been a long time since he'd done that much work all in one day. That much *real* work. The last time would have been back on the docks when he was a boy. It wasn't as bad as he remembered. There were three mismatched bookshelves along one wall, which was a bit of over kill seeing he only had six books, all of which were still sitting on the desk, but he hoped to have more soon. And the wall really should have been swept down first, but it was too late now. There were also two tables, with colorful foreign tablecloths, or something, hiding the chests of gold in the corner. And the desk. It wasn't quite as big as a barge, but it weighed as much, he was sure. It wasn't fond of doorways.

"You've got an office," Travis said. He sat on the floor and leaned against the wall.

"I know. I'm not quite sure how I feel about that." He looked around and wondered what else he needed. He tried to think of what Yardi had in her office at *Keeto Alata,* though she did real work there, so it probably wasn't a really good comparison.

"I think it looks good on you."

"You're just saying that."

"No. You could do something like run a tavern from here. If you had one to run."

"Speaking of which, how much do I pay you?"

"Not enough."

Rawk grunted. "How would you feel about a change of jobs?"

Travis' eyes narrowed. "I'm not cooking anything."

"No. You can be a full time manager and my assistant."

"So, I'd officially be doing what I'm already doing?"

"Pretty much. You could get yourself an office and hire an extra person to take your place in the taproom."

"Maybe."

"Give yourself a fifty percent pay rise."

"Do you actually have *any* idea how much I get paid?"

"None. But I know how much profit the *Rest* is making and that's all I need to know. And I know there's still a pile of gold in the corner."

"I'll think about it."

"Right, in the mean time, can you get me some hot water so I can have some tea." He took a little satchel of the aromatic leaves from a pouch on his belt and threw them to Travis. "And stop talking to me, I've got work to do and I've only got a week to do it." He picked up a book at random and started flipping through the pages.

"Where are you even going to start?"

Rawk closed the book for a moment and squinted at the title. *Convergence.* He had no idea what that was even about. He put it back and chose another. "I'm going to start with *A Witch's Guide to Portals,*" he said. But he knew it wasn't much more that a stab in the dark, even if it was the right topic.

"You're trying to do yourself out of a job, you know?" Travis said.

"I don't have a job, I'm retired."

As Travis left, Rawk sat back and tapped the book. He actually thought he already knew where the exots were coming from and finding out for sure would probably be a whole heap easier than reading an entire book, or six. So, a job for tomorrow, and that meant tonight was free. He smiled and put the book back down.

–O–

Rawk sat near the front of the Armory in his usual spot. It was standing room only down the back these days, so he always made sure he arrived early.

"This is a strange place for listening to music," Maris said. She had to lean in close to be heard as the crowd was already growing.

Rawk thought it was a strange thing to say. She worked at the Veteran's Club and was the one who decided to put the musicians in here. It was almost as if she'd never actually seen the room before. He gestured to the crowd. "Surely you'll have to move them to the main hall soon."

As the room filled he dragged his package closer with his foot. He nodded to another of the regulars but didn't really notice the comings and going of the rest of the crowd. He could smell them, and that was more than enough information.

"I normally don't like music all that much. I like to watch the fencing tournaments over near the barracks."

"This isn't just music…"

"Have you ever fought in the tournaments?"

Rawk gave a laugh.

"What's so funny?"

He realized she was serious. He cleared his throat. "That's sport, it isn't real fighting. I'd likely cut someone's arm off and get in trouble."

"It looks real." Maris looked a bit offended.

"There are rules for everything. You can't counter attack during a laganaree. You can't…"

"During a what?"

Rawk waved it away. Apparently it would all be meaningless to her anyway, despite the fact that she liked the sport enough to go and watch. "The point is, in real fighting the only rule is come out the other side alive."

Celeste and Grint slipped into the room. It looked like they were trying to hide, as if they didn't want anyone to notice. Perhaps they were shy. Or perhaps this was just how they were when on the north side of the river, where neither dwarves nor fermi were really welcome. Both of them were both, fermi and dwarf, though it was hard to tell. Despite their stealth, the crowd did notice. Those who had been there before fell silent, anticipating what was to come. And soon the rest followed suite.

By the time the two performers had settled themselves there was no noise at all in the room. And Grint started to play his drum. The dwarf used his double-ended stick to beat an intricate rhythm that danced around the room, like the heartbeat of a mountain stream. His free hand was inside, touching the skin to change pitch. Rawk still couldn't believe the music that could be made by the simple instrument. He could have spent the night listening to the dwarf play but, after a few minutes, Celeste started to play her mandolin and her clear, soft voice joined in as well.

Rawk glanced at Maris. She took a drink of ale and shifted in her seat and he couldn't spare her any more of his attention. He looked back at the performers and hardly moved for the next two hours as the music swirled around him. They played some tunes he didn't know and even the ones that were familiar sounded different, as if they'd had new life breathed into them.

When the music stopped, Rawk blinked back to the real world and reached out to take up his forgotten drink. "Wasn't that amazing?" He set his tankard down without having a drink and turned to Maris.

"What? Oh, yes." It looked as if she was just waking up. "I suppose so."

Rawk grunted and took a drink as the crowd continued to drift away. He hardly even noticed that it was ale. Soon just a couple of snoring drunks, the performers and the bartender remained in the room with he and

Maris. Rawk collected his package and made his way to the front of the stage. Celeste was packing away her mandolin while her brother talked to the bartender. It was hard to believe they were related. Grint was a dwarf through and through. About forty years old, he looked as strong as an ox and as stubborn. His clothes were plain but well made. The only adornment he wore were the ribbons tied in his long red beard. Celeste looked like a pure blood fermi, with dark skin and dark curls that clung close to her head. She looked much younger than her brother, but Rawk guessed she was only a couple of years between them.

"Hello," Rawk said. He had spoken to Celeste once before and the conversation had started much the same way. He stared nervously at the cloth bag in his hand.

"Hello, again, Rawk. I've seen you here many nights."

Rawk nodded. "I told you last time, you sing beautifully."

She smiled and looked quickly down at the bag as well.

Grint was arguing with the bartender about money again.

"We need our money," the dwarf said.

"We paid you last week."

"And you're still four weeks behind. We are supposed to be paid every week."

"If you don't like it, take it up with the boss."

"I talked to Maloti yesterday. He said we'd get paid today."

"I don't have your money."

Rawk watched as Grint glanced at the cash drawer, as if wondering if he could take the money. But the dwarf gave a grunt and stormed back onto the stage. "I've had enough of this."

"Grint, just..."

"Just what? Just let them keep screwing us over?"

"Let's just hold out a bit longer." She laid a hand on his arm. "It's a lot more money than we were getting before."

"Not if we don't get it." He seemed to notice Rawk for the first time. "What are you looking at?"

"Sorry. I... I brought something for you.'"

Grint grunted again. He was very good at it. They were very expressive grunts. "What is it? No, wait. Why did you bring something for me?"

Rawk shrugged. "I didn't know who else would be interested."

The dwarf took the bag when it was offered and had a look inside. He glanced up for a moment then reached in and pulled out the drum. He looked it over. "This is beautiful. I don't think I've ever seen a bodhran like it."

"Well, now it's yours."

Grint examined the drum some more. "It looks old. It's probably worth quite a bit."

Rawk raised an eyebrow. "How much?"

Grint seemed to calculate in his head. "I don't know. Two hundred ithel. Maybe five hundred."

Rawk glanced at Celeste for a moment. "So, you won't play it?"

"I..." Grint rubbed his hand around the smooth timber of the frame. "Yes, I want to play it. But... I can't take it."

"Why not?"

Grint didn't answer the question. "Are you sure?" he said.

Was he sure? Did he want to give five hundred ithel to a dwarf? Did he trust that he wouldn't sell it? Rawk grunted. "It's yours. Do whatever you want with it." And before anyone could say anything else, he turned and went back to his table.

"Rawk?" Celeste said.

Rawk stopped but didn't turn around.

"Will we see you tomorrow?"

He did turn back then, for a moment, but still didn't say anything. He watched as Celeste and Grint left through the side door. When he turned back, Maris was staring at him. "Did you just give a dwarf a drum worth five hundred ithel?"

"Apparently. Maybe."

"Are you crazy? Go and get it back. The little bugger is probably out in the back alley right now trying to sell it to a... I don't know."

Rawk shrugged. "I doubt it. But it's his; he can do whatever he wants with it."

"I'll go and get it off him." She stood up as if she was going to do just that.

"It's his."

"But I—"

"Come on, let's go and get a sugar stick." He took her hand and led her towards the door.

"I hope that's a euphemism," she said after a moment. "Perhaps we should go straight home."

Rawk looked her up and down. *Again?*

Thersday

THE FRONT DOOR OF THE *HERO'S REST* was still locked so Rawk went around the back to the kitchen. The warmth greeted him as he stepped through the door. Kalesie was mixing a huge pot of stew over the fire. She looked up from her work without slowing.

"What have we got today?" Rawk asked.

"Don't be smiling like that at this time of the morning. It isn't proper."

Rawk hadn't realized he was smiling at all. "What's the stew?"

"Beef."

"Is it ready?"

She gave a sniff. "You didn't like it last time."

"That one with the magamon peppers?" He could smell it, now that he thought about it, sharp and biting. "Then why are you cooking it again?"

"Because it isn't all about you, Rawk. The *Rest* has lots of other customers."

"Get me a bowl anyway, please. Is anyone else around?"

Kalesie looked around accusingly. "Valen is around here somewhere. He's supposed to be mixing this, not me."

"Well, can you get him to put together some food for me? I'm going for a bit of a walk today."

"Get it yourself."

Rawk bit his tongue. There were a lot of advantages to keeping his ownership of the *Hero's Rest* a secret. There were some disadvantages too. Anyway, he knew Kalesie would do as requested.

"Where's Travis?"

Kalesie motioned towards the taproom.

Rawk always felt strange in taproom before opening time. The big empty space looked desolate when he could actually see all of it, tables and chairs set up neatly, waiting for the crowd. Bar stools lined up with unseemly, military precision. And it felt dead, withering without the thing that gave it meaning. The two people in there weren't enough to take that feeling away.

Travis was cleaning tankards. Natan was sitting at the bar. He had a newspaper in his hands but was telling a story. As usual he wasn't the hero of the tale; he was a bystander watching the great deeds being done. He stopped mid-sentence when he noticed Rawk. His stool creaked alarmingly as he shifted his considerable weight.

"Ho, Rawk."

"Natan. You're up early."

"Things to do today, unfortunately."

"You aren't actually going to go and do some work, are you?"

Natan had been living at the *Hero's Rest* for more than six months and, as far as Rawk knew, had never made any mention of money or how he made it. He paid his rent on time, which was all that mattered in the end.

"No, no. Don't say that word to me." He mopped at his brow as if just the thought of work was making him sweat. "I have to meet some people about... I can't tell you too much."

Rawk nodded. "My day is going to be pretty much the same. And I can't tell you too much."

Travis looked suspicious.

"Actually, I'm just going over to Westport to meet with someone."

Travis stopped polishing for a moment. "Who do you know in Westport?"

Rawk tried to think. Travis should know not to ask questions like that when someone was around. "I'm just doing a job for Yardi. Very important stuff. If I don't come back, go and ask Fabi about the dogs— he'll know where to find me."

And he left before anyone could ask any more questions. Upstairs he collected his pack, attached the dwarven staff to the buckles and headed back down to the kitchen where Valen had managed to scrape together a veritable feast of traveling food. Fruit, bread, hard, grainy bisca. Rawk stuffed them all in his pack, plus some dried meat for the pouch on his belt. His water skin was hanging from the hook behind the door. He filled it at the sink and it wasn't until he was jamming the stopper into the mouth that he realized he didn't even give the tap a second thought any more. A couple of weeks ago the thought of using the dwarf–installed contraption had scared him more than battling a wolden wolf. He went out the door and across the ostler's yard before he could think about it too much.

He wondered if he should pretend to head for Westport, but neither Travis nor Natan was likely to leave the taproom to watch, so he headed due west, down the steep side of Two Watch Hill towards the Old Forest.

–O–

Rawk's hand ached on the hilt of his sword. He was tired, and if there were people about he would have been embarrassed that just a couple of hours or walking should have done that to him. He had a scratch on his face from a stray, thorny vine. And he wasn't sure if it was all worth it. He took a deep breath, stepping gingerly from the forest and into the sunshine.

The duen giant's cabin appeared unchanged but no signs of the fight remained in the clearing. The bodies of the duen and the dogs had all been removed. The weapons were gone. The two graves Rawk had helped dig were there though. Weeds and grass were already starting to take over. *Kult* was leaning to the side, about to fall.

Rawk almost turned and went back the way he had come, but steeled his nerves and made his way cautiously around to the far side of the cabin. To the front of the cabin. It faced away from Katamood, and that should have been a clue to the nature of the duen giant, if he had stopped for a moment to think about it. But the first time he'd been here, he hadn't thought. He'd jus come and killed, then left. Having a quick look inside, Rawk decided that not much had changed there, either. It was tidy and dim and a musty smell was taking over.

So he turned and looked out at the forest. It ran for another thousand miles to the northwest, all the way to Freesha. Ancient forest that had remained mostly unexplored, as far as he knew, for the simple reason that people were superstitious idiots. And he was hardly better.

Grunting, Rawk removed the pack from his shoulders and set it on the ground by his side. Then he sat down and laid *Dabaneera* on the grass in front of him, pointing into the forest. He waited. He drank some water. He ate some fruit and dry bread.

And he waited.

It was past noon when he saw movement under the trees. He sat up straighter and resisted the urge to reach for his sword. He resisted the urge to reach for the staff. He had used that to kill one of the duen too. His legs were cramping, but he stayed where he was and watched as the creature took a step into the open. It was ten feet tall, as big as the two that Rawk had killed at the cabin, though it was obviously older. Its hair was longer and almost white. Its leathery face was wrinkled, as was the huge hand that was wrapped around a knotted, twisting staff.

Rawk's hand twitched in his lap and the creature noticed. It stopped where it was.

The back of Rawk's skull itched. He shifted uneasily but kept his hands where they were and kept his eyes forward.

Finally, the duen hobbled forward, leaning heavily on his staff. It went to within a couple of yards of Rawk's spot, then paused, before slowly kneeling on the grass.

"What are you wanting?" the creature asked.

"I am Rawk. I came to talk."

The creature nodded, but said nothing. He looked as if he expected to be attacked at any moment.

"Are you a duen giant?"

"No. Are you be a human midget?"

"No. We are..." Rawk put away his answer and tried to find the point. It took a moment. He was describing the world from a human perspective. He gave s small nod. "I see your point. Are you a duen?"

"That is what we are sometimes calling. My name is being Opok." Opok stared silently for a moment. "Did you be kill my son?"

Rawk cleared his throat.

"And his wife?"

"I believe so."

"And their children?"

A small nod. "The girl attacked me."

"Atine be searching for her pet."

Rawk must have looked embarrassed.

"You be killed Kaj as well?"

"Yes. Atine saw me with the collar and..."

Opok nodded. "And now you have come to be killing me, too?"

"I have come to ask if you like arm wrestling."

The creature looked puzzled. "Apparently knowing the words you be speaking is not necessarily be the same as understanding."

"It's a metaphor about expectations. Anyway, we are sitting here talking, so I believe I already have my answer."

The duen stared for a moment. "So, do I be like wrestling arms?"

Rawk gave a small laugh. "No, I don't think you do." He started to shift to relieve the pressure on his legs, but Opok looked a bit worried so he sighed and stayed where he was. "My friend, Hubb, arm wrestles for money. But now he can't walk into a room without someone taking it as a challenge."

"So if you are not here to kill me, or to wrestle arms, what is it that you are wanting?"

"I want you to stop sending exots into Katamood."

"What be exots?"

"Exotic animals. Creatures from other realms."

Opok's eyes narrowed. "We be seeing many creatures but know naught of which realm they come from. We did not let them through."

"You didn't?"

Opok shook his head. He seemed to give something some thought, then decided to speak. "I be the most powerful shaman for a thousand years and I cannot be open a portal. Even here it be take two dozen shamans to open a portal such as brought us to this world."

"The portals must be natural then," Rawk muttered half to himself.

"They be not. This place has a history of magic, there are lines of power that sing to me and a node is not far away, so perhaps some portals be natural. But not these ones. These ones be made."

"Are you sure? How can you tell?"

"I cannot make them, but I can feel them. I can see them. I can hear their songs."

Rawk wasn't sure that actually answered the question, but he didn't complain because he doubted he understand the next explanation any better. "And you didn't make them?"

"No. No duen be making them. Of this I am certain. They are being made by someone not very far from this place."

"That isn't possible."

"If you be knowing the answers then why have you come to speak with me?"

Why, indeed?

"You be having thoughts?"

"Yes. I'm not used to it, so it may take a while."

Opok nodded and sat quietly, as if prepared to wait all day if that was how long it took.

So, Weaver was right, for once. Someone in Katamood was opening portals. It wasn't certain, of course, but there was nowhere else close. It had to be Katamood. Or Westport at the very least. And he didn't know how to start looking for them.

"I can't make any decisions here, Opok— I can't think— but I would like to visit again, if I can."

Opok looked at him for a moment, and like he did earlier, seemed to reach a decision. "If you come to this place, I will know." The duen rose slowly to his feet.

Rawk nodded and watched the creature hobble out of the clearing. He sighed and climbed to his feet as well. It was a long walk home and he imagined he was going to hobble like Opok the whole way.

Before he went, Rawk stopped by the two graves on the far side of the cabin. Galad and the dwarf. He didn't even know the dwarf's name. He stood for a while, silent and watching, wondering if he should say some type of prayer. But the didn't believe in the Great Path, so it would be hypocritical. And it would be too late as well. Galad and the dwarf were either with Path or not, his prayers would make no difference.

He lingered by the dwarf's small mound. Galad had known what he was getting into; he was a Hero. But the dwarf just wrote stories for the newspaper. He shouldn't have even been in the forest let alone attacking a creature more than twice his size with a dagger.

Rawk sighed. "Sleep well, you two," he said. He straightened *Kult* and moved away into the forest.

–O–

It was getting late by the time Rawk climbed over a low, crumbling section of the wall and stumbled down into the city. He sat down in the alley so he could rub his knee and drink the last of his water. And then he sat there for a while, back against a rough timber wall, because he could. But it wasn't long before the heavy scents of rubbish and dead things urged him to his feet and on towards more hospitable places.

The dim, narrow walk along the alley seemed to last forever. The sky was hardly visible overhead and his fingers were left slick with... something... as he ran them along the plaster between the wooden frame of the wall by his side. The next street was hardly bigger but breathing wasn't offensive and there were other people going about their business. The business probably wasn't legal, but it was reassuring none–the–less.

Rawk limped uphill, small slope though it was at this point, keeping an eye out for a familiar landmark. He was trying to ignore whatever was stuck to the bottom of his shoe, because he wasn't sure that he really wanted to look and wasn't sure if he'd be able to get moving again if he stopped. But, eventually, he *needed* to look or else it was going to annoy him all the way home. So he paused and spent a minute scraping something brown and sticky away on the corner of a building. When he looked up there was an exot watching him.

It was a big thing, as tall as a man, but had four arms of varying sizes and was covered in a rough, leathery hide. It was carrying a flail in the biggest arm, twirling it around as if it weighed no more than a feather duster. The people in the street were, quite sensibly, backing away. Those that were slightly further away thought running was a good idea and did just that.

"It's Rawk!" someone yelled.

The exot started, looking around, though weather it was trying to work out who Rawk was or was looking for whoever had shouted was hard to tell.

"Kill it, Rawk."

The people stopped backing away. They started to cheer. Were they really that stupid?

Rawk swallowed and looked back at the creature. It had a wild look in its eyes. He wondered if his eyes looked the same.

The creature let out a huge roar, and still the people didn't run. They surged back, but were apparently more interested in watching the fun that was about to follow. Rawk looked around again, wondering where all the other Heroes were now? Why hadn't Josey turned up this time, threatening to take his claim? Where were all the other random men and women who thought it was fun to kill creatures for money? He grunted. They were probably in a richer part of town where someone worthwhile was sure to notice their heroics.

Perhaps he could let the creature...

It didn't make a sound as it leaped towards the nearest person. The man stumbled back, but couldn't go too far because of the crowd behind him. He fell, then died when the exot tore open his neck with claws as long as knives. And Rawk had been worried about the flail.

Rawk drew his sword and charged. He let out a battle cry as he went. But his charge wasn't quite the fearsome advance he'd been hoping for. His knee slowed him down. His arm hurt, and reminding himself that it wasn't actually his sword arm didn't help. And the exot stared at him as if he was an ant crawling on its boot. It revised its opinion when Rawk started battering at it. He was too close for the creature to use the flail the way it was intended so it was forced to block three quick attacks with the handle of the weapon instead.

Then it turned, took a few steps and killed a woman who was holding a basket of herbs. It glanced back at Rawk, as if to say, *I could have killed you*. And a moment later it was scrambling up the wall with its spare arms. It disappeared over a roof a moment later. A crow flapped up into the air as it passed, complaining loudly, then settled back down

Rawk stared at the bird for a moment. It was better than the other options. The dead man was bleeding everywhere, eyes staring vacantly. The woman hardly seemed to be hurt at all. But she was staring as well.

The crowd was watching him silently as if he was the enemy. Until one of them said, "Why didn't you kill it? You just let them die?"

Rawk didn't know what to say. "Why did you all just stand there? Nobody would have died if you'd run."

"But you were here."

"I am just a man, you fools. Just one old man." He sighed. "Call the Guard."

But the crowd was still staring at him accusingly. So he turned and left as well, though not with the same speed and agility shown by the exot. That creature was bound to cause havoc somewhere else, very soon. He tried to work out where it might have gone, but he wasn't exactly sure where he was himself, so all he could do was try to head in the direction it had gone. Perhaps, if he was lucky, he would come across some other Heroes on the way.

Three minutes later he came across two dead elves. One was missing an arm. The other had a hole in her chest.

Further down the street, Rawk came across a dwarvish work gang. They had been working on the sewers, digging the deep, sheer sided drain one minute, covering it up the next. Two of them were dead, another four were injured, but the creature was down and bleeding as well, a pick sticking from his leg, a shovel with a broken handle and bloody tip by its side. And as if by magic, a crowd was starting to appear.

Rawk rushed up, pushing through the first of the onlookers and stopped by the side of a big dwarf, almost five and a half feet tall, leaning on a mallet. He was looking at the exot as he wiped blood off his hand.

"What happened?" Rawk asked.

The dwarf glanced over at him. "Came down the wall like a damn spider." And with that, he hefted his mallet and finished the job with one powerful swing.

Rawk winced. "I don't know that—"

The dwarf spat. "I don't like spiders."

"Well, no, but still."

"Well then, you make sure these four good dwarves don't die, and bring back the ones that already have, and I'll see what I can do about getting this thing back as well."

There wasn't much he could say to that. Rawk looked at the dead dwarves for a moment and nodded. "What's your name?"

The dwarf grunted. "Kepler."

"It's 2000 ithel for killing an intelligent exot that's carrying a weapon. You can give the money to their families."

Kepler narrowed his eyes. "The claim for killing an exot? We aren't Heroes."

Dwarves couldn't be heroes. There probably wasn't a rule written anywhere, but everyone knew it was true. Elves could, but not dwarves. "You are today."

"Weaver won't give us any money. If it wasn't for Thacker I doubt we'd get paid for the work he actually hired us to do."

"I'll put in the claim. You'll get the money."

Kepler gave it some thought. "They would appreciate that," he said eventually.

"It isn't much, I know." Nothing seemed like much any more. He could never do enough.

"It's something, which is more than most humans would give."

And it was. But still not enough. Rawk looked around at the crowd and knew that most of them didn't care at all about the dead dwarves. As far as they were concerned all the dwarves could die if it meant they were safe.

"It isn't much," Rawk said. "I'll find you when I have the money."

He looked at the dwarves, then at the exot. He didn't really want to think about either of them, so he turned and walked away. A few blocks further on he came to Meera Square, a place that he actually recognized. In the mornings it was home to a blacksmiths market, but now it was mostly quiet. Except... Rawk narrowed his eyes as the anomaly finally hit him. There were half a dozen children playing on the remains of the Barbarian Gate. The gate had stood in that spot forever, as far as he knew; probably since before Katamood existed, seeing it was nowhere near the walls of the city, but now it was nothing more than a pile of rubble. An impressively tall, rose–red pile of rubble. He considered the symbolism of that for a moment before shaking his head and continuing his slow journey up towards the top of the hill.

When he finally reached the kitchen door, Rawk almost trod on a dead mouse.

"Kalesie, there's a dead mouse here." He poked it with his staff, just to make sure it really was dead. With all the magic creatures around it was better to not assume.

"Another one?" Kalesie scowled without looking up from her cutting.

"Mice are committing suicide on the doorstep?" Or perhaps it was one more local that he couldn't save.

"It's the cat."

"What cat? An exot cat?"

"What? No." The old woman shrugged. "It's just a small, black cat. And if I get a hold of it, I'll wring its neck."

Rawk didn't doubt it. And he wondered if they'd all be eating cat stew the next day.

He pushed the mouse off the step then hung his pack on the back of the door. He almost sat down but decided he would most likely be there for the night if he did, and he didn't want to spend the night with Kalesie. So he made his way towards the far door, contemplating the long slog up the stairs to his room as he went. That seemed beyond him. When Valen came in from the taproom a moment he brought with him a surge of noise. There would be smoke and expectations as well, and Rawk didn't want any of those any more than he wanted a climb.

"Can you bring some tea down stairs for me?"

Rawk made his way down to his new office. He leaned *Dabaneera* and his staff in the corner and lit a lamp with the flint and striker in his pouch. Then, finally, he slumped down in the chair and closed his eyes. A minute later he opened his eyes again and looked accusingly at the light. He would have been better off sitting in the dark. He was exhausted. His legs ached, from the walking and the sitting both, and his mind was numb. He had gone out into the forest hoping to end the threat of the exots but was, literally and figuratively, right back where he had started.

And there were dead dwarves. There always seemed to be dead dwarves. Dwarves and elves and... People. All sorts of people dying in all manner of horrible ways, no matter how hard he tried to save them.

He stayed where he was for a long time. He needed sleep, but when he thought he was about to drift off, Travis entered the room carrying a tall silver pot on a tray. There were also some fruit pies. "So I can call off the search?"

"Who's searching for me?"

"Nobody. We're still searching for Fabi so he can tell us where to look for you."

"Ahhh. Well, yes. I'm here and I'm fine."

He didn't feel fine. Perhaps he didn't look fine either because Travis set the tray on the table hiding the chest of gold and said, "I have tea for you, just in case."

"In that?"

"Yes. I put the leaves in a strainer and poured the water through them. You shouldn't have any leaves in your tea."

Rawk raised an eyebrow. "You might just be a genius."

"I knew that already."

"Of course you did, being a genius and all."

Travis poured a cup of tea. "So, did your mission go well?"

"Not as well as I hoped."

"So..."

"So I think I need to retire."

"You already did that."

"I know. But I really need to do it this time."

"Why is that?"

Rawk sighed and leaned back, rubbing his eyes. "When I got back, there was an exot." He waved away the details. "It got away from me and some innocent people died."

"So now you want to really retire?"

"I don't think I can do it anymore. Before, it was all a game. It was..."

"So, you tried to save the people, and you failed, so they died?"

"Exactly."

"Let's say you really retire and tomorrow you're walking down the street and come across some people being attacked by an exot."

Rawk gave a pained expression. He thought he knew where this was going.

"You wouldn't try to help them, because you are no longer a Hero?"

"Maybe."

"So you would stand and do nothing while they were killed?"

"Perhaps."

"And when they died, you would feel no guilt at all, because it is no longer your job to kill exots?"

"Possibly."

"And nobody would expect you to feel guilty because there are no expectations at all placed on retirees?"

Rawk didn't say anything.

Travis brought the cup of tea over and placed it on the desk. "I think 'conceivably' is the word you're looking for."

"It isn't just about desire any more, Travis. I traipsed around in the forest for a while today then failed to kill an exot, and now I can hardly move anyway. I'm an old man."

"Yes, you are. And you have more chance of working this out than anyone else."

"No, I don't."

Travis shrugged. "Then retire and never leave the *Rest* because life is full of problems and you are not the type of person to stand by and watch. And speaking of retiring and moving on, Maris was here earlier." Travis got a pie and dumped it unceremoniously on the desk as well. "I think she likes the attention she gets because of all the time she spends with you."

"I know." Rawk rolled his eyes. He was happy to change the subject, but Maris would not have been his first choice.

"What does that mean?"

"What does what mean?"

Travis didn't say anything.

"It's just..." Rawk sighed. "At first she was all, like, 'That whole Hero thing doesn't impress me.'"

"And now?"

"Well, she saw me doing my thing yesterday morning and half an hour later we were rutting in the back room of a cafe."

"A cafe?"

"She knows the manager. I put a finger in a tart."

"I wouldn't call her that to her face, if I were you."

"No, a lemon tart."

"I'm not sure that's any better. How was it?"

"I didn't try it. Maris did though."

"Not the tart. How was the sex?"

Rawk shrugged. "The same as usual. I thought it should feel different, after waiting so long."

Travis looked up at him. "That was the first time you had sex with her? It's been weeks, hasn't it?"

"Barely a week. Eight days. Look, the point is, for all her claims when we met, in the end she was just the same as all the others. She's all over me now."

"So, let me get this straight. You are having problems because you're beginning to think that all Maris is interested in is sex?"

"And, she doesn't like music. At all. And she drinks. A lot."

"You're getting too much sex?"

"If I just want sex I can get that lots of places without all the complications."

"So, what are you going to do about it?"

"I don't know."

"It sounds like you need to break up with her."

"What?"

"You need to end the relationship."

"What relationship? We've only seen each other a couple of times."

Travis just looked at him.

"I don't want to do that."

"Because you're a coward? Or because you want to keep seeing her?"

"What was the third option again?"

"The longer you keep seeing her the harder it will be. She could be five minutes away from saying she loves you. You know that, don't you?"

"She doesn't love me."

"Because you're the expert on that subject, right."

"I know what love is," Rawk said. But he regularly encouraged the belief that he wasn't interested in love. And he wasn't, for the most part. Love led to all sorts of complications. Love led to pain. Love died, or was killed by startled thieves, and didn't come back. But some people were crazy. Maybe Maris did love him. Or maybe she thought she did, which was the same thing in the end.

"She said she was coming back later, so you can ask if she loves you then. Between all the unsatisfying sex."

"I'll keep that in mind."

Travis laughed. "I doubt there will be anything much at all in your mind."

"Go away. And don't send her down here when she arrives."

Rawk stayed where he was for a long time after Travis left the room. But it would never last. It couldn't last. He didn't believe that he had more chance of solving the problem than anyone else, but he didn't want to take that chance.

So he pushed himself to his feet and went to examine the row of books on the shelf, running the tips of his fingers along the rough, cracking leather of the covers. There were ten of them now, so Travis had obviously been shopping, but it still wasn't really a library. He read some of the titles, but one was as likely as the next, so he picked something at random and went back to sit down. For a while, he just held the book in his hand and breathed in the scent of it. He'd never noticed the smell of books before; he'd never really spent enough time in their company to get the chance. It smelled old. And of other places. He didn't know exactly which other places, and wondered if the other books would smell different. Did the type of paper make a difference? The type of leather? Or perhaps, in books about magic at least, there may be other factors involved. Sighing, he opened the cover. When his eyes focused he discovered there was a chapter about ohoga portals. "Huh."

He found the page, took a sip of tea, and read slowly, as if he might otherwise miss an important detail. And part way down the first page he found something.

"*Not only are ohoga portals created by sounds—with specific sounds required depending on both the location of sorcerer and the intended target realm— but part of their physical fabric is also sound. Like any sound created by men, the 'voice' of the sorcerer will form an integral part as well. If you know how to listen, you will know who did the work.*"

Opok had mentioned something about songs and hearing, but Rawk probably hadn't been listening to the details at that point. Which was kind of ironic.

But, apparently all he needed was someone who knew how to listen. Easy. He had read the entire chapter about Ohoga portals and moved on to another random book by the time Travis came to tell him that Maris had arrived.

Faraday

RAWK SAT ON THE EDGE OF THE BED cataloging his aches and pains. He hadn't been rubbing Sylvia's cream onto his knee and decided that today was the day he was going to start to regret it. The wound on his forearm, courtesy of the duen's pet wolf, Kaj, was all but healed. The one on his shoulder, from the *other* duen's giant mace, still sent fingers of pain along his nerves if he moved the wrong way. Sylvia wasn't sure if that would ever go away completely. He sighed and closed his eyes.

"Where do you think you're going?"

He turned to look at Maris, curled up under the sheets. "I've got things to do today."

"Really? Like what?"

"I've got to talk business with a couple of people."

"Business? The Hero business?"

Rawk gave her a smile that he didn't feel. "Something like that." He turned back around and started stretching. It was too long since he'd done any exercise at all, apart from being a Hero in busy times.

"If things keep going the way they are going you should be able to move out of here soon enough."

"What's wrong with this place?"

"One small room? A man like you should have more than this."

"A man like me?"

"If you were just a little bit more careful with your money..."

Maybe the tension showed in the muscles of his back. He wasn't looking at her, but she trailed away as if realizing she was saying the wrong thing.

Rawk rubbed his arm and closed his eyes. "I'm going to be busy all day. Maybe we could meet at the Club for dinner then go to the Armory?"

"You want to watch the dwarf again?"

"Grint, yes. And Celeste. And not watching so much as listening."

"Can we do something else?"

"How about we catch up tomorrow then? We can have lunch."

"Very well. I can see my sister, tonight, I suppose."

Rawk turned to watch as Maris stalked naked around the room collecting her clothes. She piled them on the chair and started to dress.

"I think I had to much to drink last night," she said. She combed her hair away from her face with her fingers.

Rawk nodded. "You drank a lot." He'd drowned more than usual as well, which wasn't hard, but hadn't bothered trying to keep up.

Fully clothed, Maris fell back onto the bed. "Do I really need to go to work?"

"I think so, but you know more about it than I do."

"I could stay here." She took Rawk's hand in hers.

"You might get a bit bored on your own."

"I meant you could stay too."

"Like I said, I've got things to do."

"There are Heroes everywhere in Katamood theses days; surely they can handle a few exots for you."

Rawk turned to look at her. He couldn't believe that people honestly thought the only thing he did in his life was chase exots. That was another assumption he encouraged, but he didn't know why anyone believed him. "I'll see you tomorrow," he said.

Maris groaned and she rose to her feet. She kissed him on the lips and hurried out the door.

When she was gone, Rawk carefully stretched his shoulders and his arms, wincing at the pain, and decided it was about time he did some exercise. Too many injuries recently had hampered any efforts to make it into the gymna. He collected his clothes and slipped behind the priceless water–nymph tapestry and through the door it hid. Beyond was a short hall with three doors. The one at the end led to the private stairs that would take him down to the basement. The closest led to the shower room the dwarves had built. He went to the final door and it felt like months since he'd been there. And counting, he realized it had been more than three weeks. Not months, then, but too long.

He pulled on his underwear, then did some serious stretching. Ten minutes later, he lay down on the bench, took up a small weight in each hand and started to lift.

After a couple of repetitions he was wondering if a man's arms could just fall off. He kept going, grunting with the effort and sweating so much he was going to need a shower afterwards. He tried to solve the problem of the exots to keep his mind busy while his body worked through the pain.

When Travis walked in a while later, Rawk was sitting on a stool, hunched over and breathing heavily.

"I saw Maris leaving," Travis said. "I think everyone did. She made sure of it."

"Shut up and go hire me some Heroes."

Travis' brow furrowed as he gave that some thought. "Do you want back up for when you break up with Maris?"

"No. I was just thinking, I can't keep up with the exots; they're everywhere. And all the Heroes are gathered around the docks and a couple of the bigger taverns so it's complete luck if any of them are anywhere near an exot when it arrives. That dwarf work gang had to kill that big mean bugger because there was nobody else to do it."

"So you want to hire some Heroes?"

"Exactly. I knew you'd like the idea. Hire them by the week then pick a spot for them and spread them around the city in the places Heroes don't usual hang out."

"You're serious?"

"So, a thousand ithel a week to stand where we tell them and look out for trouble. And then I get 20 percent off the top of any claim."

"Really?"

"Look, hopefully I can get this all sorted out in a week and it won't matter. Ten thousand ithel won't make any difference."

Travis raised his eyebrows. He almost choked. "You want to hire ten of them? Ten thousand ithel won't make any difference? The *Rest* doesn't make that much money. And the pile of gold down stairs *is* slowly shrinking."

"Very slowly, and these day I can make a fortune killing exots."

"But still... Ten thousand ithel a week? I don't know—"

"I have other streams of income, Travis."

"That sounds like something Yardi would say."

"It is."

"Ten thousand ithel?"

"Yes."

"So... Wait..." Travis' mouth dropped open this time. He had a whole range of 'shocked'. "You own *Keeto Alata,* don't you? One of the biggest trading companies in the world?"

Rawk winced. Yardi was the only other person who knew. "Maybe."

"Holy Path. You've got to be worth... Is there even a number big enough?"

"I'm not worth that much. I *do* have to pay you, after all. And Yardi isn't cheap either."

"I'll take that pay rise."

"I'm sure you will. Organize the Heroes for me first would you? I have some other things to do."

"Oh, that's right's, Weaver—"

"No." Rawk shook his head. "Definitely not."

"What?"

"I'm not having lunch with Weaver again."

Travis shrugged. "I couldn't care less. I'm just passing on the message." He gave the alias and the name of the tavern.

Rawk sighed. "Well, I need breakfast and a cup of tea before I can face the thought of lunch. Maybe a whole pot."

–O–

Rawk crossed over Dragon Bridge. After the fish and garbage smell of the river, the low–grade industrial stench on the southern side was a welcome relief.

"Hello, Mister Rawk." Clinker was sitting with his back against a light post. His short legs were stretched out in the narrow strip of shade.

"Hello, Clinker."

"Are you going to see Sylvia again?" The dwarf boy had his satchel open on his lap, as if he'd just been searching through the contents.

Rawk looked around to see if anyone was paying any attention to him. "I am."

"I can show you the way, if you like." He scratched at his wild, knife–cut red hair.

"I already know the way."

Clinker smiled. "They opened a new tunnel under the canal yesterday. Only for people who is walking though."

"I'm sure I can manage." He was edging towards the cover of the buildings, though it was mainly dwarves around the area and he didn't really care what they thought.

But Clinker jumped to his feet and knotted the string to keep his bag closed. "Come on."

Rawk sighed and followed the boy. He wondered if Sylvia was right. She thought that dwarves and elves were just humans, like any of the races, but had separated further in the past. Sometimes he thought she was crazy. And if dwarves and elves were just distant humans, what of the other humanoid creatures that could breed with humans? What of trolls, zorigami and moai? Were they just humans too? He didn't want them to be. Dwarves looked at life from a completely different angle. And he didn't just mean lower down. And trolls were not much more than animals most of the time. Big, fast, strong, cunning animals who could kill you in a dozen different ways before breakfast.

"Your bag is much quieter than last time," Rawk said to Clinker as they continued to head away from the river.

The boy looked back and smiled. "Thacker's men paid me for cleaning some graffiti off a wall. It was one of those *Words of Wisdom* things. I think it said, 'Time only heals wounds if you remove the infection first'."

Rawk raised an eyebrow.

"Maybe. I might have gotten some of the words wrong."

"You can read?"

"Yes. Sometimes. A bit. Kikum helped." The look on his face suggested he didn't know if that was a good thing or a bad thing.

"And removing the graffiti made your bag quieter?"

"I bought a blanket. Winter will be here soon."

"So it will."

They made their way to a large open area that looked as if it might have once been a park. Now it was hardly more than a churned up mess. There was a small, stone building in one corner that was as clean and shiny as a new sword.

"The tunnel's in there."

Rawk had worked that out for himself. Why did children, of all races, always find it necessary to point out the obvious? The rune carved building certainly wasn't big enough to hold all the people that were coming and going out the two large doorways. It was dwarves mainly, but fermi and elves and normal people as well, moved in slow, noisy clumps and muttering lines.

"There used to be lots of flowers in the park," Clinker said. He wrinkled his nose. "It smelled horrible."

"What happened?"

"This is where they had the riot."

Rawk grunted, wondering exactly what everyone thought Weaver should do. The exots weren't his fault and the City Guard and the Heroes were doing what they could. "Come on."

But he made his way past the building and stopped at the fence beyond. The end of the canal wasn't very far away at all, filled with a swarm of dwarves. Rawk recognized all their tools, and could even name a lot of them, but there were also a handful of large buildings that were the source of a *lot* of noise. Clatter and clank, crash and crack. Maybe, inside, dwarves were scratching a hole in the fabric of the universe to let exots through. Except Opok had said magic was involved and dwarves could not do magic. Rawk sighed. His life would never be that easy.

Smoke poured from the chimneys, so maybe they were just the lunchrooms with cooks working overtime.

"It won't be long now," Clinker said, clinging to the fence. "A couple of weeks is all."

Rawk looked to the left. He could see the other stub of the canal. It seemed nothing more than the width of a road divided them. A road filled with more dwarves working at strange contraptions.

"According to who?"

"That's what Thacker says."

A couple of weeks to go twenty yards through the solid stone. He knew how they felt.

Rawk went back to the tunnel entrance and followed a flow of people down the stairs. A waist high fence kept the two lines of traffic separated. Hissing gas lamps down the middle threw long fuzzy-edged shadows, and made the air taste thick. The hot, heavy space was packed with people going one way or the other, grumbling and talking quietly.

An oak tree dominated the square on the far side, spreading its branches over the ancient cobbles. There were tents and ramshackle buildings that looked like they could fall down at any moment. Some of them already had fallen down and were carefully being rebuilt with makeshift tools and much-used rope. The whole place groaned and creaked in the breeze like the Old Forest.

"What's going on here?" Rawk wasn't sure how the flowers on the other side of the canal had smelt, but it couldn't have been any worse than this. "Are these refugees? Is there a war I don't know about?"

Clinker stopped to look as well. "Refugees? What are refugees? These are people from around here who don't have houses any more?"

"Why don't they?"

The boy looked confused. "Because of the canal. They had to knock down a lot of buildings."

"Oh."

"I'm sure Thacker will work something out. Come on, it's much quicker to get to Sylvia's than it was last time." Clinker wound through the haphazard streets of the campsite, clutching his satchel tightly and keeping a wary eye out. With the tree as a landmark, Rawk now knew where he was and was quite capable of finding the way on his own. But he stayed silent and strode along behind the boy, trying to avoid stepping in the worst of the mess.

There was a mass of people where the square finally let out into High Road. For a moment he wondered if it was the beginnings of another riot but a scream from beyond the wall of people quickly had him thinking otherwise. He drew *Dabaneera* and started to shoulder his way through. Clinker following in his wake, chattering excitedly.

After several minutes of struggle, pushing his way through the surging, stinking crowd, Rawk finally broke into the clear.

The creature was barely a meter tall, most of the time, and seemed to be made of grey smoke. It shifted from two legs to four and back again. Long wispy tendrils escaped from its bounds, flickering in the air, before being drawn back in with a hiss. It was watching an old lady who wore a patchwork dress from Redami, and a girl with pigtails. It had them trapped in a shadowed corner where two tall, time–stained buildings met.

"Great Path," Rawk swore as he flexed his hand on *Dabaneera*. His injured arm tingled.

The crowd was still pushing back, leaving Rawk more and more on his own. He couldn't understand why they were still there at all. What did they think was going to happen after the creature killed the two current targets? Maybe nothing, but who could tell for sure? He swore again.

For a moment, he had time to worry if his sword would have any effect on a smoke monster, then the creature started moving towards its prey and he didn't have time for anything at all.

The smoke flowed forward. It seemed to skate across the cobbles because the legs did not move as fast as necessary. The crowd gasped, the trapped woman screamed and Rawk rushed forward, sore knee throbbing in time to the beating of his heart. He swung his sword as he went past, but the creature noticed him at the last moment. It didn't move out of the way but a hole formed in the smoke, following the blade perfectly. It hissed at him.

The woman wouldn't stop screaming. It had only been a couple of seconds, but it was already getting on Rawk's nerves. He swung again. This time, when *Dabaneera* was half way through the swirling smoke stomach, Rawk changed the direction of his swipe. But the smoke shifted perfectly, staying less than an inch from the steel.

Rawk backed away quickly. He trod on something that let out a terrible stench, like a week old battle. He almost tripped but managed to keep his guard up, as if that would do anything. He backed himself into the corner, coming to a halt against the rough timber wall of a warehouse. The woman, no longer under immediate threat, finally shut up and Rawk heard the crowd scuttling further away. The creature came across the cobbles, its shadow as shifting and grey as it was itself.

Rawk tried to concentrate. He tried to think. He...

There was no time. Rawk readied himself. He crouched for a moment, stepped aside as the creature lunged forward. But a swirling finger touched his arm and Rawk bit back a cry of pain. The slight contact seemed to burn his skin, sending a spasm up his arm. He counter-attacked anyway, barely, gritting his teeth. The sword passed through again, untouched, even when he curved upwards. The blade came into the clear and he reversed his swing immediately, painfully. This time, when his blade was deep in the smoke, his spun it so he was attacking with the flat. The creature couldn't react quickly enough to widen the gap. The steel touched a wisp of stomach and there was a shriek of pain. Or perhaps it was disbelief—could you hurt smoke? And the wail continued, lowering in pitch, going from ear piercing to bone shaking, as the smoke shredded on the breeze.

Rawk took a deep breath in the moment of silence that followed, then gritted his teeth as the crowd started to cheer. He swallowed noisily and tried to raise his sword in salute. That didn't work. It was as if the unseen burn on his arm was sucking the energy from his muscles. He raised his other hand and punched the air. They cheered some more.

Clinker rushed across the gap to him, satchel silent, mouth running overtime. "That was amazing. What was it? Are you hurt?"

Rawk could hardy move his arm. "Yes, it was, I don't know and perhaps a bit," he said quietly, trying to loosen his grip on his sword. It was an effort to move even one finger at a time. He could hardly move anything at all.

Clinker watched, forehead furrowed. He glanced around at the crowd as the cheering settled down to a murmur of excited conversation. Clinker cleared his throat. "Let me take that for you, Mr. Rawk, sir." He reached out and prized Rawk's fingers away from the hilt of *Dabaneera*. When he had the weapon in his hand, the boy held it up as if he had claimed a trophy, or as if he'd beaten the creature himself. The crowd cheered good-naturedly then Clinker started to drag Rawk towards the road that had been their original destination.

The noise of the crowd seemed like a storm around him. Even the smallest sound battered against him. But Clinker clung to his arm and kept him moving. It wasn't going to work.

"I don't think I can make it, Clinker."

"I'll find a goat cab, Mr. Rawk. There's always some just up here."

There was only one, but that was enough. When Clinker had deposited Rawk into the little gig and given directions, the dwarf driver got the two goats moving.

–O–

The door clattered against the bell as it swung shut and Rawk allowed Clinker to maneuver him to his usual chair by the counter. He could at least move on his own now, but it was still an effort. And he was numb all over and it felt as if his thoughts were an old man on a mule, charging at him from the far side of a valley. It was taking forever for him to arrive and it probably wouldn't be worth the wait anyway.

"What have you done this time?" Sylvia came from the back room, drying her hands on a towel.

"I haven't done anything." An idiot wouldn't have believed him. Sylvia wasn't an idiot. Clinker saved him the trouble of having to actually answer.

"There was a monster made of smoke," the boy said excitedly, putting his satchel down on the bench. "It didn't have a weapon or nothing but when it touched Mister Rawk's arm I saw it shudder. Mister Rawk's arm that is, not the monster. And after that his arm kept shaking and quivering. I was up close like, closer than anyone else, and I saw it. Mister Rawk was having a lot of trouble even moving. I would've had to carry him up the hill if I didn't find the cab."

Sylvia threw her towel down beside the satchel. "Is this true?"

"He couldn't have carried me even if he wanted to."

"Kikum would've helped."

"I was coming here anyway."

Sylvia started examining Rawk's arm and shoulder. She prodded at the joints with long, strong fingers and massaged his muscles, pursing her lips as she concentrated. "So it just touched your arm?" She smelled of lemon.

"Yes."

"But you are having trouble moving anything?"

"Yes. Like I got too close to one of your lightening spells. But it's improving. We'd still be down at the bottom of the mountain otherwise." His feet felt as if they'd been stomping around in snow all morning.

"How does your heart feel?"

"My heart? I thought it was going to stop at first, but it was all fine. I must've imagined it."

She went around behind the counter and came back with a hearing trumpet.

Rawk cleared his throat. "I thought it was going to stop," he said, louder than before. "But I must've—"

"What are you doing, Rawk? I heard you the first time."

"Oh. Right. Then what's that for?"

"Take off you shirt."

"What?" He looked at Clinker but looking for a dwarf boy to explain the mind of an elf woman was about as crazy as life got.

"Just take off your shirt, Rawk."

He grunted. "I can't."

Sylvia sighed and proceeded to pull his shirt up over his head. She then held the trumpet against his chest and listened for long seconds. She examined the burn mark on his arm where the creature had touched his skin. She sighed. "You seem fine."

"Thanks for your enthusiasm."

"It's good that you're fine— you visit often enough to keep me in business for the rest of my life— but I can't be sure about anything." She put down her trumpet. "I think you might have been infected with a neurotoxin but if that was the case I don't know how you are still alive at all."

"Tough, I guess."

"You need lots of antioxidants, so eat lots of fruit and grains."

"Now?"

"Yes, as soon as possible." She looked him up and down. "Why are you still here?"

"I was coming to see you, remember?"

The bell above the door clattered as an old lady entered. Sylvia apparently knew what she was after and pulled a small jar down from a shelf.

While the two of them were talking about the price, Rawk gave Clinker five ithel and sent him on his way. The boy smiled like a monkey with a banana and stashed the coin in his satchel. He was out in an instant, shouting something about lunch as he went.

Rawk watched as the old lady left the shop as well, not quite so spritely as the dwarf, then jumped as Sylvia spoke to him. "So, to what do I owe the pleasure then?"

"Well..." It was one thing to ask Sylvia to do some healing, she was an elf after all, but it seemed quite another thing to ask for any other type of help. She was an elf, after all. And a sorcerer.

"Yes?"

"There are exots everywhere. I've been... reliably informed..." Rawk wondered why he was so willing to trust Opok. Even if Sylvia's suggestion that elves were just human was incorrect, he certainly had more in common with her than the duen. And according to the book he'd read the duen were warlike, so they probably wouldn't assist the closest likely enemy. "I've been reliably informed that the portals aren't natural and that whoever is making them is somewhere near here."

"And you think it's me? What about Frixen and..." She waved her hand as if trying to pluck a name from the air. "That beanpole of a man?"

"Valo?"

"Yes, that is him. They are both in Katamood."

"I know. I think Weaver may even know. But those two couldn't make a flagon of wine appear in a tavern, either with magic or a five ithel coin." He tried to hold up his hand but barely succeeded. "But I'm not here to arrest you anyway. I don't think you're responsible."

"Then why are you here?"

"Because I want to find whoever *is* responsible, and I don't know where to start."

"Well, you could start by asking your reliable source for more information."

Rawk nodded slowly. "I could."

"Or not?"

"I think I've gotten all the help I can from him at the moment."

"Your source is a sorcerer?"

"He is."

"And you trust him because..?"

"Because he could've killed me. Because he didn't have to come to talk to me in the first place. Because Hubb doesn't like to arm wrestle."

Sylvia blinked.

"Look, you can sense magic and all that kind of thing so—"

"Wait. You want me to lurk around in the back alleys of Katamood helping you look for rogue sorcerers?"

"I'm Rawk; I don't lurk."

"Well, lurking would be better for me. I'm trying to not draw attention to myself, remember?"

Rawk gave a dramatic sigh. "Oh, all right; I can lurk if you want."

"And what makes you think I would want to turn other sorcerers over to Weaver anyway?"

"People are dying, Sylvia. I thought you might like to stop that sort of thing."

"If I am seen by the wrong person..."

"If an exot turns up in the middle of a... of a child's birthday party..." He'd heard of them, though he wasn't quite sure what they were all about. He didn't understand half the things nobles did.

"I won't do it."

"That's it?"

"That is it."

"I killed a creature made out of smoke on my way here. Just five minutes down the hill."

"There is probably a standard, human cutthroat or two even closer. Do you want me to help catch them as well?"

"Do we have time? I have to go eat some fruit and grains, apparently."

Sylvia threw her towel down on the bench. "I have things to do too. Things that don't involve risking my life on an impossible mission."

"Impossible?" Rawk shook his head. "So you're just going to stand around and watch while people die? I've retired, Sylvia. I'm too old for all this but..."

"Please leave, Rawk."

"Very well." Rawk got to his feet and moved slowly towards the door. "Ummm..."

"What is it?"

"Well, what would happen if someone, accidentally of course, drank some of the hot water with your tea leaves in it."

Sylvia raised an eyebrow.

"And if they continued to drink it?"

"You drank the tea water? You were supposed to breathe the fumes."

"I know, but I was thirsty."

"How do you feel?"

"Great. Well, you know, apart from not being able to move properly and all that. I feel great after I drink the tea."

"I'm not sure. Nobody has every done it, as far as I know."

"Why not?"

"I don't know." She picked up her towel. "I'll look into it. Now get out of my shop." And she turned and went out to the back room. Rawk sighed again and went the other direction. It was going to be along walk down the hill. And a long walk up the next hill.

–O–

Rawk spotted only one guard in the common room, a man with floppy hat and a bored expression, leaning against the wall. Seeing he wasn't allowed to drink he stood out like a Queran beggar at a royal ball, no matter what clothes he was wearing. Weaver was hardly better. He sat at a small table near the back of the room wearing a red shirt with puffy sleeves and a polka dot bow tie. Today's wig was grey and pulled back in a harsh ponytail. He was eating a quail salad, topped with an eye–watering vinegar dressing, like it was going to get up and run away if he wasn't quick, and slurping down red wine. Rawk didn't know much about wine, but he was pretty sure it should have been a white with quail. And the vinegar...

With a nod for the guard, which the man ignored, Rawk crossed the room and sat down at the table. "What's the hurry, Crit?" he asked Weaver over the rumble of noise. The walk down the hill had thawed his feet, but his head felt as if it was stuffed with cotton wool.

Weaver popped the last bit of bird in his mouth and licked his fingers. "I was trying to finish my entree before you arrived."

His whole body still felt slightly off center, as if the smoke monster had sent his consciousness a fraction of an inch to the right. "So, you didn't want to buy me an entree as well? Cheapskate." Witty banter was beyond him. Insults would have to do.

"Do you know how much this place costs?"

"It *is* quite a bit nicer than a lot of the places you've been choosing recently. Though that wouldn't be hard."

"If you don't like my choices you can choose for yourself."

"And pay for myself too, I imagine."

"Of course." Weaver pushed his plate away.

"So what do you do for a living, Crit? I'm sure you can afford to pay for me."

"Didn't Travis tell you?"

"No."

"I'm a cloth merchant from Tharpin."

"Of course. I should have known."

"We have to order at the bar."

Rawk sighed. "What do you want?"

"No, Toman can do it for us." He started to signal to the bored guard.

"And leave you unprotected?"

"I'm sure you can protect me, can't you? You'll do a better job than Toman."

Rawk waved his agreement though he doubted he'd manage to get himself out of his chair before an assassin complete the job, had a dink at the bar and sauntered out the back door. "I need lots of fresh fruit."

"Why?"

"Anti–something–or–others."

A minute later Toman was at the bar giving the orders to a woman who looked as bored as he did.

"You've been busy, I see." Weaver held out a newspaper.

Rawk sighed and took it, unfolding the cheap paper and smoothing it out on the table with numb fingers. The first page was taken up with stuff about all the exots.

"Everyone's been busy," Rawk said. His deeds took up the most room, but there were almost a dozen other Heroes mentioned as well. There were creatures everywhere and Heroes were coming from all around to take their share of the claims. It was just like twenty—five years ago when Katamood was the center of the world when it came to Heroes.

Rawk read the story. "They've exaggerated, as usual."

"Nobody wants to read about taxes and... lamp lighters. Or something."

"Not the regular stuff, but if they are going to make stuff up about me they could just make it up about the taxes as well. I mean, *you* do it often enough."

"Oh, huh. Very funny. I need taxes more than ever now to pay all the claims and for all the damage around here. An elephant thing— it wasn't an elephant but I don't know what it was— knocked down the clock on Hadagast Road the other day. The bloody dwarves charged me nearly four hundred ithel to fix it. And they wanted me to pay to fix the old Barbarian Gate in Meera Square as well. I told them to just leave it."

"I saw that yesterday. I think it looks nice. It was so *ugly* when it was in one piece."

Weaver shrugged. "I haven't seen it; too busy trying to keep the city from falling apart. You wanted the old times back and here they are."

"We have this conversation every day, Crit. *You* wanted the old times back. I was quite happy with the new times, if you remember."

"No, you just thought you were." Weaver leaned forward and gripped Rawk's arm. "I've known you too long, Rawk. We are too close for you to get away with that lie."

Rawk wasn't going to argue with him about it. He didn't have the energy and it wasn't worth it anyway. And it was an argument he probably couldn't win, no matter how right he was. He moved his arm and Weaver withdrew his hand.

"And who's your lady friend?" Weaver turned the paper over to the back page. "She looks nice."

Rawk examined the picture. It showed Maris clinging to him in the market like a damsel he'd just rescued. The picture was stunning; they'd even put in the gaudy earrings. It was almost perfect. Rawk couldn't work out how they did it. A few weeks ago he'd marveled at how the dwarves managed to write out thousands of the newspapers in just a few hours, and in such unbelievably neat writing. But now they were adding pictures as well? It might not have been magic, but it was close, whatever it was.

"What's her name?" Weaver asked.

Rawk glanced up and found the prince staring at him.

The meals arrived at that moment and the woman almost dropped the plates. A splash of bright green sauce hit the table in front of Weaver. He surged to his feet. "Watch it."

The woman was a fermi; the Prince towered over her and she cowered back, plates titling dangerously.

Rawk cleared his throat. "Crit, don't worry yourself about it." The prince kept staring at the woman. Rawk laid a hand on his arm. "*Crit*," he said again, emphasizing the word, reminding Weaver he was still supposed to be under–cover. "Don't concern yourself. I'll have a talk to the manager after we finish our lunch." Rawk motioned to the woman, telling her to leave. She deposited the plates and did just that, darting away through the crowd.

Weaver collected himself. He grunted and sat back down, motioning to the newspaper as if nothing had happened. "She looks nice."

"She is. Her name is Maris. It says it right here. And she works at the Veteran's Club— it says that, too. For once the newspaper got all the information right."

Rawk pulled his stew closer and looked at the plate of fruit suspiciously. After a moment he took out his knife and fork, spent a moment polishing the bone handles, then started on the stew.

Weaver picked at his food. Normally he would have been wolfing it down almost before the plate had hit the table. "You've seen her a few times, haven't you?"

"A couple. Why, is it a problem?"

Weaver laughed. "Of course not. It's just, you would never have done something like that in the old days."

"You're right, I wouldn't. But I keep telling you, the good old days have gone and aren't coming back."

"So you say." The prince produced a scroll case from the floor near his feet and slapped it on the table. "And in related news, you are now the proud owner of an apartment on Terring Road."

"I am?"

"Yes. It was Galad's. You said you'd take it if nobody else turned up to claim it. Remember?"

"Oh, right. Of course."

"Good. And you now owe me twenty thousand ithel."

"Twenty thousand?"

"It's a nice spot; you can see the bay. Or the canal." He waved a hand. "I'm not actually sure what you can see but that was how much Galad owed."

Rawk sighed. "I'm sure you rounded up and added some administration fees. Anyway, how much do you owe me for all the exots I've been killing?"

Weaver shrugged. "I think it's about six thousand."

"Well, just keep everything until I've paid it off."

"Very well." Weaver sat back in his chair, tapping his wooden spoon on the edge of the table. "Are you going to move in?"

Rawk shrugged. "I don't think so. I'm comfortable at the *Rest*."

"See, you aren't ready to grow up yet. You're still yearning for the past."

"I am not."

"And speaking of real estate, do you know who owns the Tapalar mansion?"

Rawk looked up, fork halfway to his mouth. "What? Why would I know that?"

"Well, you were... friends with Lady Tapalar at the end."

"Yes. So? Bree had lots of friends."

"Well, whoever owns *Keeto Alata* owns the mansion. I assumed that was because you introduced Lady Tapalar and Yardi in some way."

"So you already know who owns it then. What's the problem?"

"*Keeto Alata* is a foreign investment company that's drowning in layers of secrets and I'm years away from getting to the bottom of it. Yardi isn't telling me anything."

"She wouldn't be where she is today if she went around giving out secrets. Why do you want to know, anyway?"

"The neighbors are complaining. It's in the best part of the city but it's falling apart. It's bringing down the price of real estate."

"And you want it fixed up?"

"Yes. Or I'll buy it and fix it myself. I might just take it soon. The company pays their taxes and everything but... I'm the prince, I should be able to just make up the rules if I like."

Rawk swallowed and gave a small nod. "You probably don't want to do that, unless you want to scare investors and companies out of Katamood."

"Yes. Unless that."

"Well, just give the message and the threat to Yardi and she can pass it on if she wants."

"Maybe I will." He gave a decisive nod. "I will. I'll write something up as soon as I get back to the palace."

"*You* will?"

"Well, me or a secretary." He waved his hand. "It doesn't matter."

When Weaver left, Rawk sat quietly, crunching on an apple. He picked up the paper and turned the page.

There was news about the canal with quotes from workers and residents living nearby. Twenty yards to go, apparently. Just a couple of weeks. And there were riots south of the river and some gossip about Weaver and visiting ships. There was the news that Edwin Dan Beketh, owner of *Laka Enterprises,* had negotiated the rights to the Melaworth contracts with *Keeto Alata.*

And on the last page was the picture of Rawk and Maris. He'd spent 18 years trying not to think about Bree, and today it was even harder than usual.

Rawk folded the paper and left it on the table. He needed to go and talk to Yardi. But there was a crowd out the front that he had to deal with first. Such gatherings were less frequent these days, he had to admit, probably because there were so many Heroes and so many stories they could tell. It didn't make them any less annoying.

He stopped on the top step. "Hello. It's a bit full in there at the moment," he winced in pain as he motioned back into the common room. "I don't think you'll all fit."

The crowd looked at Rawk for a moment, as if he had gone mad. Then they all started talking at once and a hail of walnuts, each tied with a ribbon, clattered to the floor around his feet.

Eventually, there was a slight pause in the bombardment.

"Have you ever seen an exot like that one this morning, Rawk?"

"How many have you killed this week?"

Rawk rubbed at his eyes. He couldn't think. He went slowly down the stairs and headed for the offices of *Keeto Alata.* Inevitably, the crowd followed.

The keenest of them made it a long way down the hill but by the time he reached the main warehouse and climbed the stairs to the office, he was on his own. Hurno looked like he might have been happier dealing with the crowd.

Rawk looked down at the young receptionist. After the walk he didn't even have the energy for a smile. And he didn't have the energy for any more arguing. "I'm a giant amongst men, Hurno, remember? The last great Hero. You don't keep me waiting."

Hurno looked like he was about to panic. "Yardi did say that, last time you were here, I know. But she also told me that she was not to be disturbed."

Holding back a sigh, Rawk limped around the end of the desk and went to the door of Yardi's office. For a moment it looked like Hurno was going to stop him, but the lad thought better of it. Rawk wasn't sure who would have won that battle. Beyond the door, Yardi was sitting with her feet on the desk and a glass of brandy in her hand.

"Hurno said you were working." Rawk said when the door was closed. "Is this what I pay you for?"

"I was much working. I just this second finished reading a contract and was celebrating." The desk was completely clean. No papers, files or anything that resembled work. Yardi looked around seemed to realize that as well. "Actually, I am still working; this brandy was the subject of the contract."

"Is it any good?"

She held out the glass to him but he waved it away.

"I wouldn't know good brandy from horse piss, you know that."

Yardi shrugged. "More for me."

"As ever." Rawk knew that Yardi didn't look, or sound like a brilliant businesswoman. She looked like someone who worked on the docks and had somehow found some decent clothes. And she sometimes sounded like she couldn't put together a coherent sentence. The former was probably because she had started out on the docks, and the latter was because she knew several languages and sometimes switched grammar and syntax between them. But she had started managing *Keeto Alata* when it was little more than a warehouse and a single contract and had built it into one of the biggest trading companies in the world. Rawk trusted her with everything he had, and if she wanted to buy a boatload of brandy for herself she was welcome to it.

Slumping down into the room's only other chair, Rawk just sat for a moment and looked around. "The plants haven't died yet." The smell of them filled the air, hiding the stench of the city.

"Of course not. I look after them."

"Don't plants need sunlight?" He decided that he actually didn't mind the plants, though having them inside, growing in containers, still seemed a bit strange.

"Forests have ground cover, don't they?"

"Well, yes."

"Right. Different plants need different amounts of light. Some love shade. Like these ones."

"What if you want some that like lots of sun?"

Yardi sighed.

"Do any of them have fruit? My healer says I need to eat lots of fruit."

"No."

"You should get some." His whole body still felt a bit numb, though on the plus side, that meant his knee and shoulder and arm all ached a bit less than usual. He was starting to wonder just how much fruit he was actually supposed to eat.

Yardi sighed again. "You been here twice in a month now, Rawk. I think it's getting to be a bit much."

"I'm retired, you know. I've got lots of spare time on my hands."

"You not retired."

Rawk sighed too. "I have actually. But Weaver and the exots disagreed, so here I am."

"Why are you here?"

"Weaver will be sending a message down later. He wants the Tapalar mansion fixed up." He made a face. "Actually, he wants it for himself for some reason, but isn't brave enough to just take it."

Yardi opened a drawer in the desk and pulled out an envelope. When she threw it down in the table Rawk could see Weaver's red seal on the back.

"Already?"

"It arrived just a minute ago."

"I only spoke to him at lunch time."

"When Weaver wants something, he goes it. You know that."

"Well, he can't have it."

"He can't?"

"No. Fix it up."

"What are you going to do with it?"

"Does it matter?"

"You could live there."

Rawk gave a grunt of laughter. "A lot of things would have to change before that happened."

"How is Maris?"

Rawk looked up at Yardi. For a moment he thought she'd been spying on him, but she'd probably just been reading the newspapers. "She's fine."

"Fine?"

"Are you asking how Maris is or how the relationship is?"

Yardi pursed her lips.

"I've only seen her three times." Rawk looked away. "The relationship is fine too."

The thought that Maris could replace Lady Tapala was ridiculous. He'd once said that Adalee Dan Beketh was a gaudy trinket and Maris was a flower. But compared to them, Bree was a garden with manicured lawns and flowerbeds in one section and wild dark woods in another. She was a whole year of sunlight and snow, thunderstorms and cool breezes compared to their single summer day.

"Fix up the house," Rawk said. "Start tomorrow. Get it back to how it used to be."

"The furniture too?"

"No, leave it empty." Empty seemed suitable. "I'll need to send Travis up there tomorrow to get some stuff."

"I may not be able to get anyone on site until the afternoon. And it won't be actual laborers. Just inspectors and the like."

"No, send a couple of teams to start clearing stuff out as well. I'll send Travis after lunch."

"Very well."

Rawk waved at the bottle. "Give me some of that brandy."

Yardi pulled a second glass from her drawer and poured in a splash. Rawk sniffed it and winced. He took a sip and winced some more. It still tasted horrible. Yardi laughed and downed her own glass.

"So, this brandy is going to make us lots of money?"

"Yes."

"Excellent. Keep the good work then." He put the glass down without finishing the drink. "Now, I've got to go and do something that doesn't involve drinking brandy."

–O–

Rawk paused for a moment to rest and the priest was on him like a stray dog on a chicken bone.

"Do you walk with the Great Path, Rawk? Do you listen when he calls to you?"

He would rather listen to Path than crazy priests but he had never heard anything from the god. He heard something from priests every few days and none of it was very interesting.

"Path is sending exots to challenge our faith. Will you pass the test?"

Rawk shook his head and grunted. "Maybe the exots are coming because Path has forsaken us," he said. "Did you consider that? Is Path really the type of god who would let innocents die?"

The priest looked shocked that anyone, especially Rawk, who was normally an inoffensive target, would ever think such a thing. The man was lost for words and was reduced to doing nothing more than raising his two fingers in the salute of Path as Rawk climbed the stairs of the Veterans' Club, hauling himself up with his hand on the rail.

Inside, Barin waited. He still, somehow, managed to look serious in his ridiculous clothes. He grinned and gave a nod of greeting when he saw Rawk. "Maris has already left for the day."

"I know. I'm coming to see a show." But it wasn't really *a* show, it was *the* show, and Barin would know perfectly well which show that was.

"Grint and Celeste won't be on stage for quite a while yet."

"I know. I thought I'd get some dinner first."

"Well, I think you've beaten the rush."

Rawk nodded and made his way through into the hallway beyond the big man. The mural painted on the wall still unsettled him but he made himself look at it. The mud and fear and death. Those things weren't mentioned when people spoke about 'the good old days.' It was all sunshine and beautiful women in those tales. Some times the beautiful women were even in the sunshine. But the mural was real. It was big and ugly, with moments of beauty. It was wild and it was confusing, even the bits that were beautiful. And it was right there, in your face, and there was nothing you could do about it.

Sighing, Rawk kept moving and turned into the refectory. There was hardly anyone there. A couple of old grizzled soldiers stirred the remains of their stew in one corner. There was a cacophony of Heroes by the big doors out onto the patio. They couldn't help themselves, demanding attention, even though they were just eating dinner. And at another table was... Thok. He should have remembered straight away for the man in question was hard to miss. He was as big as a bear and looked like he'd have trouble putting his shoes on the right feet in the mornings but, as Yardi had already reminded him, looks could be deceiving.

Thok sat alone, book open beside his bowl.

Rawk collected some chicken stew of his own, then an apple— anti oxi–thingies— waved away the cutlery and went to join him.

"Rawk, how are you?"

"I'm numb all over, except for the bits that actually hurt. But most of that will go away. The main problem is, I'm old," Rawk said. "Do you mind if I sit."

"Not at all. You aren't that old."

"I'm way past old." Rawk sat down with a groan, just to prove his point. "I should have retired years ago."

"You're still one of the best."

"Yes. But that doesn't really address the issue, does it?"

Thok smiled. "You could take up debating instead. You seem to have the head for it."

Rawk smiled. "Could you imagine? I'd get frustrated and cut someone's head off." Rawk pulled his spoon from his pouch and started to eat.

"I've been wondering why you carry your own cutlery."

Rawk thought of giving the usual story about poison but his companion would not have fallen for it. "The knives are generally blunt and the idea of a timber spoon in my mouth makes my skin crawl. The feel of it, not to mention the fact that timber is porous; I don't imagine places like this spend too much time washing stuff."

Thok glanced at his own spoon, resting in his empty bowl, as if he had never given it any thought.

"Anyway, how are *you*?" Rawk asked, glad he had gotten the other man thinking.

"I'm living. Though it would be much easier to do if it wasn't for all the exots."

"I'm doing my best."

"You and every other Hero, old and young alike."

"Katamood's the center of the world again, apparently."

"Is that a good thing?"

Rawk shrugged. "How are the wharves going these days?"

"The wharves are going like a bunch of toddlers; noisy, smelly, messy and I can't keep up. Katamood is the center of the world, remember."

"I imagine it will get worse when the canal opens."

Thok shrugged. "Some things change, some things stay the same, even when they change."

Didn't Rawk know *that?* He ate silently for a while. "What are you reading?"

"*Conversations with Gerrum.*"

"That sounds exciting."

"Have you heard of Hacad Gerrum?"

Rawk might have heard the name somewhere but it meant nothing to him. He shook his head.

"He was a philosopher up in Habon during the time of Makas Kent. He dabbled a bit in politics and ended up a part of the group that had Kent kicked out."

"Kicked out? I think that's the euphemism that the word euphemism was invented for."

Thok laughed. "Yes. I imagine Kent would have gone for a bit of a kicking if he'd had the choice."

"You read that kind of thing a lot."

Now Thok laughed. "No." He pulled another book from his pocket and tossed it over to Rawk's side of the table.

Rawk picked up the book and blinked for a moment until he could read the title. "*The Early Sonnets of Jufie.*" He raised an eyebrow. "I'm not sure which is worse, to be honest."

"Have you read Jufie?"

"Path, no."

"Borrow it. Read a few, especially *Fardin Law* and *Green Nights*, then tell me what you think."

Rawk flipped through a few of the pages. He looked at Thok then back at the book, though the words were a blur. He ate a few mouthfuls of stew. "All right. I'll try at least one, but I won't promise any more than that." He ate some more stew, wondering what he had gotten himself in to. "I'm going down to watch Celeste and Grint after this. You want to come?"

"I can't. I've got things to do tonight."

The big man left a short while later, wandering out into the hall with a distracted air and turning towards the entrance. Rawk finished his stew and went the other way.

−O−

Rawk was still in the Armory when the music ended. And he was still there, sitting in the heavy half–light when the rest of the crowd had left.

Before he had even gotten up from his table, Grint nodded in his direction from atop the small stage. "Maris isn't with you tonight?"

Rawk cleared his throat. He looked at the bar tender, but she wasn't looking in his direction. As if that meant she couldn't hear him, the last of the great Heroes, talking to a dwarf. "No. She doesn't like music all that much."

"She doesn't like music?" Celeste said as she packed away her mandolin. "Or she doesn't like *our* music?"

"She doesn't like *any* music, I think."

The fermi sat silently for a moment. "She doesn't like *any* music?"

Apparently the statement had to be repeated before she would believe it. "That's right." Rawk found it difficult to believe himself.

"She does like sword fighting though." As if he thought that was a good thing. There was a moment of awkward silence. "So, how's the drum?"

Grint suddenly looked happy for the first time that Rawk had seen. "It isn't a drum."

"It's not?"

"Well, it *is* a drum. But, more specifically, it's a bodhran. They originate over in..." He saw the look on Rawk's face and cleared his throat. "I said last night that it was probably five hundred years old, but I was wrong." He took the instrument back out of the bag he had just finished packing it into and held it out. "You can have it back if you want." He was still a long way from Rawk, so it wasn't obvious if he actually wanted to give the instrument up.

"It's no good?"

Grint brought the drum down from the stage. "See this symbol here?"

There was a small mark carved into the finely grained timber. It was barely visible. "I think so."

"That's the bodhran's name."

"They have names?"

"Not all of them. Some of them. The important ones. The special ones."

Rawk raised an eyebrow.

"This is Baganoo. Kimbalak made it, and it's quite a bit older than I thought. About a thousand years older."

"And I assume all of that is a good thing."

"Kimbalak is a line of dwarves. The good bodhran makers train just one apprentice in their lives. And the apprentice takes on his name. There were about twelve Kimbalak's until he was killed. So one of them made this bodhran for Prince Medwa of Falangoon in the year 5435. The prince died in the Battle of Two Lakes and the drum was thought to be lost for about four hundred years. Then it turned up in Habon. A collector bought it from a minstrel and gave it to the king of Kenkona as part of a dowry. The king hung it on the wall but one of his ancestors eventually gave it as a gift to some queen who, as far as I can work out, he was boinking in secret. The trouble is, when the queen took it home, her ship was lost during a storm. At least, that's what was assumed."

"Queen Jasmine II of Tharpin?"

"That's her. And that was about two hundred years ago. Baganoo hasn't been seen since."

Rawk scratched his head. "Maybe the ship was attacked by pirates. Katamood was a pirate haven for centuries so this would be a good place for it to turn up."

"I suppose. But, the point is, it's worth more than the five hundred ithel I said last night. It's got to be worth closer to five *thousand* ithel. Maybe more."

Rawk wondered if his mouth had just dropped open. It felt like it should have. "That much?"

Grint looked at the drum and ran his fingers over the taunt skin. "At least." He held it out to Rawk.

"So, you can't accept it because I wouldn't have given it to you if I knew how much it was worth?" Rawk looked at the dwarf. Quite possibly the first honorable dwarf he had known. But no, that wasn't true. Another dwarf had given his life to save him just a couple of weeks earlier. But he didn't know that dwarf, and he didn't really *know* any other dwarves either.

"Something like that. Here, take it." Grint seemed almost desperate now, as if he couldn't be responsible for what happened if he held the drum for another minute."

"What am *I* going to do with it?"

"Sell it?"

Rawk glanced at Celeste and saw she was watching him, head cocked to the side, dark eyes large and round. He cleared his throat as he tried to gather his thoughts. "Then I'd have money but I wouldn't get any enjoyment out of it, would I?"

"*I'd* get enjoyment out of five thousand ithel."

"So you'd sell it?"

Grint ran his fingers over the dark timber. He looked over at the bar tender and sneered. "I don't need money that bad."

Rawk changed the subject before the conversation spiraled off into another round of *Keep it—No, I can't.* "So you've been paid?"

Grint was staring at the drum, running his fingers over the grain. Celeste answered. "No, we haven't. I've convinced Grint to stop fighting it for a while. We still have our other jobs, so we can afford to wait a little bit longer."

"Other jobs?"

Celeste gave a small laugh. "Even if these people gave us our money, do you think they would pay a dwarf and a fermi enough to live on?"

"Go and play back south of the river," Rawk suggested, though he hoped they didn't.

Grint laughed this time as he pack the drum back away. "Have you ever visited a tavern south of the river?"

Rawk nodded. Though he didn't do it often.

"Expensive?" the dwarf asked.

"Very."

"That isn't because the inn keepers are greedy, Rawk. It's because the suppliers charge taverns more down there. About twenty percent more if the buyers are human and about fifty percent more if they are a dwarf."

"Really?"

"Yes. So they can't afford to pay a lot for the entertainment. Not even Harker's Hall comes close to matching what we are getting paid here." He looked at the bartender again. "What we're *supposed* to be getting paid."

"I didn't know that."

"It isn't something that's generally talked about."

"I guess."

"Anyway, speaking of other jobs, I've got to be on the tools at six in the morning so I need to get home to bed." He tapped the drum through the bag and smiled. "Thank you for this, Rawk. Nobody has ever done anything like that for me before." He held out his hand to be shaken.

Rawk didn't know if he'd ever shaken the hand of a dwarf before. He glanced at Celeste and back at Grint. After a moment, Rawk held out his hand too and felt it engulfed by the dwarf's big, rough hand. The grip was strong, but there was no competition there, no attempt to dominate or assert control.

"Well, you're welcome, Grint. Now, all I have to do is see if I can find a thousand year old mandolin."

"This one was my mother's" Celeste said, gently touching the neck of her instrument. "I want no other. Thank you, though." She smiled at him.

Rawk cleared his throat and looked around. "I should go too, really. I don't have to work, obviously, but... Well, there might be exots. There usually are, these days." He nodded and hurried up the stairs as much as he could. It wasn't much.

It was late and the streets were quiet apart from a team of dwarves were working on the sewers; Rawk had seen so many of them over the last few months he thought he would be able to do the job himself. He stopped to watch them work for a minute and changed his mind. He would know how to do the work, which was not the same as being able to do it. The men in the trench never seemed to stop swinging their picks. And the machines lifted dirt up into the trailing wagon in a whirr of dust. And all the while, they wove a song around their work, harmonizing like they practiced every day. A lot of times there were no words, just a strange collection of sounds that held all the meaning they needed. Coming from the other direction, another team was cleaning the street, piling litter and manure into their own wagon. This second group was also singing, and the two songs shifted slightly, merging together. They didn't match perfectly, but twined their threads together like a rug slowly taking shape on a loom, or like a drum and mandolin in the Armory.

It was a quiet melody that wouldn't have carried very far, but filled Rawk's head with distant lands and battles lost.

"Good evening, Rawk." One of the dwarves pulling the cleaning wagon nodded as he approached. He didn't slow his steady pace and was back to singing a moment later.

Rawk nodded eventually, but the reply went unnoticed. He turned and walked up the hill, listening as the cleaners moved on and the sewer team's song drifted away towards a different story.

He was so caught up in the song, listening to the last fragments that could reach him, that he almost didn't see the exot. It was about the size of a large dog, with a scaled hide and long tail. It didn't look all that threatening so, after he recovered from his surprise, Rawk thought of leaving it alone. But then it opened its mouth to hiss at him and in the process displayed a set of long, sharp teeth. Even then, he may have let it go, but it stalked towards him. It didn't look particularly intelligent, but the eyes were as dark and cold as a long northern night.

Dabaneera whispered from the sheath, catching the light. The creature paused, but only for a moment. Either it didn't know what a sword was, or it didn't fear them. Rawk crouched and waited, shifting his grip on the hilt.

"Come on then."

The exot took one more step, then two, and leaped up into the air. Rawk ducked instinctively, spun and slashed. He felt slow, as if he was moving in treacle but his blade met something solid and jarred from his still–numb hand. He turned and the creature was watching him. There was blood on its flank, but not much. Rawk glanced at his sword lying on the cobbles not far away. He couldn't...

The creature snarled once, turned and walked away. It didn't seem to be in a hurry. Rawk was in no hurry to follow. He glanced around again, this time looking for witnesses, then scooped up his sword and left.

When he entered the ostler's yard behind the *Hero's Rest*, Rawk stopped. He leaned against the wall and looked up at the Swarm. The long line of stars was the same as ever. When he was younger, that endlessness of the stars, both of time and space, had been a comfort to him. They had almost been a promise that he could go on forever. Now, the unchanging night sky just reminded him how much other things had changed.

There was a clatter and a crash. He half drew *Dabaneera* then paused. Heart racing, he scanned the yard for danger, but all he saw was the tail end of a cat disappearing over a wall.

"Path, damn it." He slammed his sword back into the sheath and made his painful way inside.

Satyrday

RAWK TOOK HIS FEET DOWN from the desk. It wasn't as comfortable as everyone seemed to suggest. Maybe there was something wrong with his chair. He grunted. He knew he was procrastinating, though he didn't know exactly what he was supposed to be doing. The books were on his desk, beside the remains of his breakfast, but he'd been through those and they didn't really help at all. Or maybe they did and he just didn't know what he was looking for. Now that he thought about it, that was the more likely possibility. He was pleased to distract himself from his procrastination when Travis arrived a few minutes later.

"Only two books?"

Travis put the two new books down beside the others.

"Juskin had both of them. I think he went out this morning and bought them just because he knew I'd be out there looking too."

"Probably. He isn't stupid."

"He probably doubled the price."

"Like I said, he isn't stupid." Rawk waved his hand dismissively. "Apparently the book trade isn't going so well lately, so let him have the money."

"Are you sure?"

"Yes. In fact, tomorrow, ask him outright and if that's what he's doing. If he is, don't bother searching yourself, just go straight to him."

"Very well, then. Did you get bacon?" He examined the plate on the table and grabbed a last tiny piece of rind.

"Yes."

"Kalesie gave you bacon?"

"Yes."

"Is she all right?"

"Not for years. How did you go with the Heroes?"

"I found ten who agreed to the terms. They should be out there, sitting around right now."

"Good, though in other news, Sylvia isn't going to help me find the sorcerers, so I've got to do it myself."

"Sylvia? The healer? Why would she help you? Why would she be any help?"

"So, I would like you to go to the Tapalar mansion this afternoon. You'll need a barrow or something similar because she had a whole collection of books about magic."

"You want me to break in and steal books from the dearly departed Lady Tapalar?"

"There will be workers there."

"So, I don't break in, I just steal?"

"We have permission. But you have to go in disguise."

Travis raised an eyebrow.

"We have permission, but that doesn't mean I want everyone to know. So, you are just one more worker clearing stuff out, all right."

"I suppose."

"Do you have your key ring?"

"It's up stairs."

"Well, you know the mystery key you keep asking about?"

"Obviously."

"You'll need it to get into the library. Upstairs, in the second floor study, you'll find a secret door beside the fireplace. One of the bricks in the fireplace, right near the wall, has a cross carved into it. If you pull the brick out you'll find the lock. There's a whole room behind there."

"Wait. That key has been on that key ring for as long as I can remember."

"Yes."

"So... You've had a key to a secret room in the Tapalar mansion for... How long?"

Rawk shrugged, though he knew very well how long he'd had the key.

"You own the Tapalar mansion, don't you?"

"Yes."

Travis shook his head. "You're full of surprises, aren't you? When did you buy it?"

"I didn't. Bree left to me, via a series of complicated ghost companies and fake identities."

"You said you were friends with her but..."

Rawk saw the knowledge dawning in Travis' eyes. He held up a hand. "Don't go there, Travis."

Travis looked like he was going to say something anyway.

"Really," Rawk said. "Not now. Some other time, perhaps." It felt strange to even hint at the subject. For so long, Yardi had been the only person who knew about his true relationship with Bree. She knew a lot of things.

"Of course. I'll... ummm... I've got to..."

It was almost worth it just to see Travis flustered. Rawk smiled.

"You'll need to find a barrow or something. It may take more than one trip anyway."

"Yes. Of course. Yes."

"Travis?"

"Yes?"

"I'll be having lunch with Maris today. And I've got some other stuff to do. I probably won't be around."

"I'll just leave the books around here somewhere."

Travis could handle the books perfectly well, but he couldn't do much else to help in this situation. Rawk needed someone who could hear the magic, and if it wasn't going to be someone he could trust, it would have to be someone who was too useless to actually do him any harm. Before that, he picked up a book and procrastinated a bit more. But nothing meant anything much to him at all. He also needed someone who could decipher the books for him.

With a sigh, Rawk got to his feet and headed back up towards his room to get some supplies for his new challenge.

"I'll have to bring some stuff down here," he muttered as he started the climb.

–O–

Rawk sat across the street from Valo's house, as if it was a dragon's cave he was about to enter. There might well have been dragons in there, though last he knew, the sorcerer could barely light a candle with sorcery without breaking into a sweat. He'd known where Valo lived for quite some time, longer than he'd known of Sylvia's whereabouts, but had never been concerned enough to do anything about it. So why was he so worried now? He fingered the two amulets under his shirt. Sylvia had assured him that at least one of them was completely useless, but they still made him feel better. He smiled ruefully at the thought that he was clinging old things that didn't work anymore.

"Path, get this done."

Pushing away from the wall, Rawk stepped out into the sunshine. Dodging the clatter and rattle of traffic, he hurried across the street and up onto the porch. A strange smell, cold and heavy like rotting leaves, made him stop, hand raised to knock on the door. But it was just as likely the smell came from outside as in, so he knocked on the warped timber then rubbed at his aching knee while he waited. When the door started to open he straightened up and tried to look as friendly and non–threatening as possible, which was a bit tricky when he had his hand on the hilt of his sword. He tried to relax.

When the door opened, it took a moment for Rawk to recognize Valo. He hadn't aged as well as Sylvia, though to be fair, he must have been almost seventy years old. And he probably didn't have elf blood either. Once, the man had stood nearly six and a half feet tall. He'd had the smooth, hairless skin of a mentaman and hands big enough to crack skulls, thought he'd never used them for such a thing as far as Rawk knew. Now, he was hunched and wizened, the skin was almost hanging off his face. He still had big hands, but the knuckles were swollen to near uselessness. Give him a sickle and he would look like

Death having a bad day. Rawk wondered if the smell was coming from him after all.

"Hello, Valo."

Valo gaped. He took a step back.

Rawk didn't follow. He was trying to look friendly. "I'm not here to arrest you."

Valo backed up some more. "You're here to kill me?" His eyes were wide. Bloodshot whites showed all around.

"No, I just want to talk." Rawk held up a hand but the sorcerer reacted as if he was holding a knife.

Staggering backwards, Valo started to mumble. He raised his own hands.

Rawk finally moved. "I just want to talk, Valo."

The mumbling increased. He started waving his hands.

"Path," Rawk went into the room, shutting the door behind him. He kept his hands away from *Dabaneera*, though in a couple more seconds he'd have no choice but to defend himself. "I just want to talk, Valo."

The sorcerer kept backing away, but it was so slowly that he had barely moved out of sword reach. The mumbling and hand waving continued and Rawk finally decided that he didn't have any choice. He reached for the hilt of his sword. He started to draw...

Valo stopped. His mouth dropped open and his eyes went even wider. A moment later he clutched at his chest, gasping for air. Reaching out with his free hand the sorcerer grabbed for the table and missed. He fell to the floor, writhed for a moment, then lay still.

"Path, no." Rawk forgot his sword and rushed to the old man's side. He crouched painfully and rolled him onto his back. He wasn't breathing. He was dead. "Path, Path, Path. You silly old fool."

A noise disturbed Rawk. He looked up and saw another man standing in the doorway to the next room. Rawk looked at Valo. He looked at the other man. "Frixen?"

Frixen was another sorcerer, quite a bit younger than either Valo or Sylvia. He had a mop of almost–blue hair and a splodge of a nose built for being punched. He was barely more powerful than Valo, but apparently much more healthy. He paused for a moment, mouth open. "You killed him," he said.

"No, I didn't. I just want to talk." Frixen would do. Rawk really didn't care which sorcerer he talked to at this point. He just needed someone who could hear the sound of the ohoga portals.

"You killed him." Frixen was backing towards the door.

Rawk sighed. "I didn't kill him. Look, there's no blood on my sword."

But reaching for his sword was never going to be a good idea. Frixen turned and fled.

Sighing again, Rawk pushed himself to his feet and set off in pursuit. When he burst out through the back door and into a small, trash–strewn alley, the sorcerer had already stopped, choking on the stench as he tried to catch his breath. He was leaning against a rough brick wall about twenty yards away, as if he thought he'd already outrun his pursuer. He set off again after a surprised moment. He might have been younger and healthier, but that hardly made him impressive.

Rawk gave chase, pounding across one main street, dodging people, setting off a chorus of shouts, and into the next alley. He dodged a pile of trash that was almost as tall as he was, the stench urging him on, and vaulted over a wooden crate Frixen had thrown in his path. At the next street, the sorcerer turned. He shoved people aside, leaving a trail of cursing human stepping–stones for Rawk to follow, in case he needed any extra help. Across a square. Rawk bellowed at the crowds, but they were too busy watching Frixen to clear the way fast enough.

Frixen had opened the gap, slightly, but was obviously tiring quickly. "Wait, you idiot. I just want to talk." But the sorcerer kept on with his running, such as it was, and Rawk quickened his pace.

Down another alley, this one with timber buildings looming on either side. There was barely room for Rawk to fit. An old woman stepped into a recessed doorway to let Frixen pass, then squealed in fright as Rawk thundered past as well.

Before the next corner, Rawk lost sight of his prey and, for a moment, he thought the sorcerer had managed to make himself disappear, which would have been impressive for anyone in the circumstances. For someone with Frixen's magical abilities it would have been nothing short of a miracle.

But Rawk came abreast of a large doorway, with doors swung open to reveal a warehouse. Dwarves and humans, presumably working a moment before, had stopped to watch.

"Do you need some help, Rawk?" a dwarf asked. But Frixen had already gone through a door on the far side.

Rawk went through the door as well, barely stopping himself from running headlong into the plaster wall on the far side of the alley. He looked one way. Nothing. And the next. Frixen had stopped again. While he struggled to catch his breath, he was taking the opportunity to upset a tall, narrow shelf of firewood.

The shelf toppled, but only fell as far as the opposite wall. The firewood still tumbled out onto the cracking cobblestones. Frixen found some more energy and moved again but Rawk was not far behind. He climbed through the narrow gap and raced on. The sorcerer was barely moving now.

"I just want to talk." Rawk didn't even have to shout. He was just ten yards behind his prey now. He pushed past an empty crate as Frixen staggered on. He reached out but the other man pushed something in his way and gained a second. Then he upset a pile of trash. Rawk hurdled over the top as he reached out...

His knee gave out as he hit the ground. He shouted in pain as he fell. By the time he looked up a moment later, Frixen was turning the corner with one glance back and a small, relieved smile.

Rawk wanted to lay where he was and die, but it smelled like something had already died there and, also, a small crowd was already starting to gather. So, instead, he pushed himself to his feet and took a deep breath.

"No time for a story today," he said.

The crowd didn't respond. They looked confused. They looked uncomfortable.

"Well..." He patted his belt to make sure he still had everything, checked the ground as well, and brushed a bit of lettuce from his thigh. "Right." And he limped off. At first he didn't care where he was going, as long as it was away from the scene of the embarrassment, but after a couple of minutes turned back towards Valo's house. He went in through the back door and sat down at the table so he could rub his knee and feel sorry for himself. Neither thing helped.

"At least I feel better than you," he said to Valo's corpse. *Though only just.* And he didn't smell better. Either the smell of the dead thing in the alley had followed him, or Valo was gong off much quicker than corpses usually did.

It was a bit embarrassing to be out run by Frixen. Some second–rate wizard had beaten him at a foot race. In fact, two second–rate wizards had beaten him in one day, though Valo might not see it that way. It was like they were conspiring against him... "What *was* Frixen doing here, Valo?" He didn't know why all the sorcerers insisted on coming to Katamood when the influx of Heroes meant any random stranger might kill them on sight. Why would they then take the even bigger risk of getting together? Possibly it was just a social visit, but that seemed unlikely.

A few minutes later Rawk was no more ready to move, but felt he really had to. With a grunt, he rose to his feet and looked around. It wasn't a big place, but he really didn't know where to start looking. Or what to look for, for that matter. What were the chances there would be something helpful just lying around? He searched Valo's body fist, patting down the robes, hoping to find directions to the secret headquarters hidden in a pocket. No such luck. He shuffled through some papers on the table. The light wasn't great and he couldn't get his eyes to focus properly so he scooped all the pages from the table up into a big pile and went out the back door. He tucked his bundle under his arm and made his way onto the main street.

It was a couple of hours before he had to meet Maris for lunch, but the tavern was not far away, so he headed in that direction.

-O-

Papers were spread all over the table. One large pile consisted of things he *knew* were not going to help him. A shopping list, a letter from someone named Beble, in Frenable. A list of pirate ships from eighty years ago. And a lot of other, even stranger things. Another pile, held down by a plate with an apple core and a peach seed, consisted of possible clues. A letter from someone in Katamood dated just a few days earlier. A receipt from a store on the lower slopes of mount grace. Perhaps it was just ingredients from some foreign dish, but that seemed unlikely; vienkak wasn't something Rawk wanted to eat. A list of magic books, though if they were ones that Valo wanted or ones he already had was impossible to tell. That was it. It was a very small pile. A half empty tankard of ale and his bone-handled knife held down the third pile, the largest of all. It was called the 'I have no idea' pile. He didn't even know how to describe some of the things in that pile. Some were in strange languages, and some were just strange.

"Do you want something else, Rawk?"

Rawk looked up and rubbed his eyes. His head ached. His fingers were sticky from the peach, no matter how much he licked. And each second, he was having more and more trouble focusing.

"More fruit?" The waitress picked up the orange peel from the floor and put it on the plate with the other remains. The tang cut through the barley and sweat.

He wondered what the time was. It couldn't be too far off lunch. "No. Thank you though." Rawk wasn't quite sure how much fruit Sylvia considered to be 'lots'. And how long did he have to keep eating it? "I'll be getting lunch later. If your boss is worried about the table I'll pay a few extra ithel to stay here."

"I'm sure he don't mind." She stood there a moment longer. "What're you doing?"

Rawk sighed and sat back, stretching. "I have no idea, really." And he turned back to his task, leafing through pages in a halfhearted manner. 'I don't know. I don't know. I don't know.' And a lot more *I don't knows*. Then he stopped and shuffled through the new additions again. Half way down was a page filled with lines of neat writing. Rawk blinked. He squinted. He knew a couple of languages, at least enough to get by, and unfortunately this wasn't one of them. But at the start of a few of the lines was Valo's name. Underneath it was a similar sheet of paper. There were the same foreign words arranged in the same foreign way and, this time, Frixen's name headed a few of the lines. And on this one, written in thin, spidery script, were five other names as well. Rawk knew some of them. Mistletowe, Balen and Shef were all sorcerers. None of them were up to Sylvia's standard, but they'd all been around a long time. There were two names that Rawk didn't recognize. And then there were another two with question marks as if whoever had done the writing wasn't sure.

So, was this a spell of some kind that they were working on together? And was that spell to open an ohoga portal? Or were they in a secret theatre troupe? A troupe so secret they weren't even sure of all the other members?

Rawk decided he needed a new pile. A 'Hell, yeah' pile. But 'pile' would be stretching it too far, so he folded the two pages and slipped them into a pouch on his belt. He spent the next few minutes looking for something else, anything else, like the missing directions to their secret headquarters.

He was glad when Maris finally arrived. He gathered everything up, trying to keep the piles separate, and pushed them to the end of the table.

"What's all that then?" Maris asked eying the papers suspiciously.

Rawk gave a smile. "Work stuff. Business."

"The Hero business?"

"Yes. It not all just killing things you know."

"Well..."

"So how are you? How was your sister?"

They ordered food and talked about inconsequential things while they waited, though Rawk was beginning to wonder if Maris ever talked about anything else. And when the food arrived Rawk breathed in the spicy aromas of the steak and the thick herb gravy. He cleaned his knife and pulled his fork from the pouch on his belt.

"This is good," Maris said. Soup was dripping down her chin. He didn't even know what her lunch was called, but it smelled almost as good as his own.

"Always is," Rawk agreed. This was one of his usual taverns and he was going to miss it when he finally had to move on.

"Ummm..."

"Yes?"

"Is that..?"

Rawk followed her gaze. He sighed. "How can you tell? His disguise is almost perfect."

Maris almost spat her soup onto the table.

Across the other side of the room, Prince Weaver pretended to notice them, raising his hand to wave then weaving his way through the diners. "I've been looking for you everywhere," he said when he reached their tables.

"You have? And who might you be?"

That seemed to stump him. "I'm... Errr... Tharlis. Yes, Tharlis."

"Nice to meet you Tharlis. What can I do for you?"

"You can buy me lunch, first of all." He pulled out a chair before Rawk could complain. "And then you can introduce me to you friend."

"Weaver—"

"Tharlis."

"Of course, Tharlis. This is Maris. Maris, Tharlis of..."

"Oh, I'm from here," he said, waving his hand towards to city outside. "Just, you know, around."

"I'm not sure I believe you. If you were a local you'd know where I was having lunch today." Rawk smiled when Weaver gave him a 'what are you doing?' look. "What's really going on, Tharlis?"

"I've lived here a few weeks."

"Is that right? And what brings you to Katamood?"

"I'm looking for a life of adventure and was hoping you could be my guide. I can pay you."

"Not enough."

"Look, Rawk..." Weaver looked around to see who was watching. Everyone was making a point of minding their own business, hiding their smiles behind spoons and tankards. "Let's just have lunch. We can discuss business later."

"Sure. Why not? You can buy your own lunch though."

Weaver sighed and signaled to someone in his retinue.

"So, Maris, what do you do?"

She cleared her throat and took a quick drink of wine. "I work at the Veteran's Club."

"Just a waitress?"

"No, in the office. I take care of the accounts and organize the staff. Things like that."

"Must be a bit boring for you, Rawk. All that normality? You must be wishing for the old days."

"I find I'm liking normality, actually. It's nice for a change."

"You'll want all the action soon enough."

"I still get plenty of action, Tharlis. The streets are riddled with action."

Weaver's meal arrived and he started eating without saying another word.

Rawk tried to talk with Maris but she kept glancing at the prince. Every time he looked up she would shift uncomfortably in her seat. As soon as she had finished her meal she pushed back her chair and rose to her feet. "I need to get back to work. We're having trouble with a one of the acts at the moment. They are arguing about money."

Rawk narrowed his eyes. She could only be talking about Celeste and Grint. He didn't say anything about that though. "You can stay a while longer," he said. "I'm sure Tharlis has places he needs to be."

She gave Rawk a quick kiss on the cheek. "No, that's all right. You and Tharlis can catch up. Or whatever."

"I'll see you tonight?"

"No, I'll be working late. Tomorrow."

Rawk watched her go then turned angrily to Weaver.

The prince was still watching the door. "She isn't very friendly. And she's older than I was expecting. I don't know what you see in her."

Rawk put away his knife and fork and grabbed the pile of paper.

"What's all that for? I thought it was Maris'."

"I'm looking for your damn sorcerers." Throwing some money on the table, Rawk headed out the door as well. Weaver called to him, but he didn't look back.

On the porch, someone grabbed his arm. "Where do you think you're going?"

Rawk knew the voice. He shook his arm free without turning around. "Anywhere I damn well please, Ramaner. If you don't like it, you can arrest me."

It looked as if Ramaner would do just that, but he looked around and saw that four people had already stopped to watch. And more were heading in their direction.

"Tell Weaver that if he want's to see me in the future he can make an appointment."

"I am not your messenger, Rawk."

"No, that's right, you're Weaver's messenger. And his servant. You do whatever he tells you to do, don't you."

The general gave a cold smile. He suddenly seemed to feel a whole lot better. "You have no idea."

There was a pop and a flash of light. Rawk looked around but there were just people, from a few different races, crowding in close. "Say hello to your wife for me." That fixed his mood. Ramaner snarled but Rawk was already heading down the stairs and pushing through the watchers. "No stories today."

He could feel the general watching him as he strode down the street. His heart was racing. Turning a corner, Rawk stopped to lean against a wall. His confrontations with the general were usually more subtle than that. He'd certainly never mentioned the other man's wife before. That did seem like sending an army to flush out a band of thieves. But it was done now and Rawk discovered that he didn't feel too bad about it.

He stayed there for a couple of minutes, rubbing his knee and trying to calm his heart. Across the street, some 'Words of Wisdom' were painted on a plaster wall between the exposed timber frame and it was large enough that he didn't have to squint to read it. *The longest battle starts with a single sword stroke, and ends the same way.* It wasn't particularly pithy, but kind of interesting. That didn't mean he knew exactly what it meant. He might have stayed to give it some thought, but the pause was enough time for a woman to start giving him the eye from just down the street. Rawk turned away from her and started to walk again. If only he knew where he was walking *to*. He supposed he should really try to find some of the sorcerers mentioned on Frixen's papers. They had probably already been warned and had either left town or were hiding even better than they had been. He took a deep breath and tried to think. It wasn't something he'd had a lot of practice with.

There was somebody who might be able to help him, slim chance though that was. He turned aside again and limped as quickly as he could towards Juskin's bookshop. He kept to the back streets as much as possible, trying to avoid attracting attention, but it was never going to work.

"Can you tell us a story, Rawk?" A pair of boys rushed down from a porch as he went past, giggling and circling him like terns around a garbage barge.

With a sigh, Rawk slowed down. "And old story or a new story?" he asked. It was a good chance to rest and to check if he was being followed by one of Ramaner's men.

"A new story."

Well, that was something. Nobody ever wanted the new stories. But maybe, with new stories being created almost every day now, people felt that the age of Heroes wasn't winding down to a close at all.

"Let me tell you about... The smoking man."

–O–

Rawk checked both directions along the street, waited for a moment until he thought nobody was watching, then slipped into the bookshop. And all of his efforts were wasted when he realized he wasn't the only customer in there.

"Hello, Rawk."

"Thok. Again. Are you following me?"

"Maybe I write for the newspaper."

"Don't say that. I want to dislike whoever is following me today."

"Did you read some poetry?"

"Not yet."

"Let me know what you think." Thok held up two books. "Anyway, I've got what I was after and some of us have to make an honest living."

Rawk squinted to make out the titles but he wasn't quick enough.

Thok left the shop, leaving Rawk alone with the old, stoop–backed shopkeeper.

"Rawk. I wasn't sure if I would ever see you again, what with Travis coming down here all the time." He looked over the top of his spectacles as if to be sure he was really seeing him.

"Well, Juskin, Travis is working with another source this afternoon."

Juskin raised his eyebrows. "Another source?"

Rawk couldn't help but smile. "That's right, you haven't managed to buy every book on magic in the city."

"Of course I haven't, but..."

"Has anyone else come to you looking for magic stuff?"

He pursed his lips and hauled himself up onto the stool behind the counter. "As a matter of fact, demand for books in that area increased dramatically about two months ago. Maybe six weeks. I didn't make a note of the exact date, you understand."

"Of course. But the point is, people have suddenly been looking for books on magic recently?"

"That's right. They were trying to be a bit secretive at first, as you and Travis are now, but they have become less furtive now. I've actually been scrounging for those books for quite a while now. Though those other have now slowed down again."

"So do you know who these people are? Do you know where they live?"

"Some of them have accounts..." He ducked down behind the counter and came up with a large leather bound ledger and a frosting of dust in his shock of red hair. He started mumbling to himself as he flicked through the pages. "Here's one... Valo Wen."

Rawk winced.

"What?"

"Valo died."

"When?"

"This morning."

"He owes me nearly a hundred and twenty ithel."

"I'll pay that for you."

"No, you don't have to do that. It isn't your responsibility."

"Well, I may have had something to do with his death."

"You killed my customer?"

"I didn't say that. He had a heart attack or something. I just happened to be there at the time."

"You were trying to kill him?"

"No, I was trying to talk to him. He may have believed otherwise."

"Why would he think that?"

Rawk sniffed. "Because any other time I probably would've been trying to kill him."

"Right. Very well then." Juskin turned back to his ledger and started muttering again. "Here. Kassius Mellum."

Rawk had never heard of him. He tried to think of the wizards from Frixen's list who he would be most comfortable facing. "Have you got anyone else? Shef Leeker? Or Mistletowe..." He didn't think he'd ever heard her last name mentioned.

"Mistletowe?" Juskin shook his head. "That is an unforgettable name, but I certainly haven't heard it."

"Right."

The old man tapped the book. "Perhaps if I describe some of the people. They might be using aliases."

"Let's give it a go."

"Right then." He started flicking through pages again.

"You've written their description in our account book?"

"No, but the listings will jog my memory."

"Right."

"Here we go. Darley Pas." He gave a short description but it meant nothing to Rawk. "No? How about Haz Merter?" The description sounded a lot like Frixen. Juskin saw the look on Rawk's face. "You killed him too?"

"No, I did *not*. But last time I saw him he was running very quickly and isn't likely to go anywhere near his usual haunts for quite a while."

"I'm not sure I believe you."

"Well, I'm not sure I care. Who else have you got?"

Juskin stared at Rawk for a moment before turning once more to his ledger. He flipped through some more pages.

"Ah, yes. Of course. How about Fasha Bengoza? She is short of stature but long of nose. Beautiful red hair like my own."

Rawk couldn't help but smile. "Exactly like yours?"

The old man brushed a hand through his hair. "Perhaps not exactly." He smiled as well, and waved away the cloud of dust that he had let loose. "From her accent I believe she might be from Redami." He coughed and waved some more.

"That has to be Mistletowe."

Juskin spun the ledger around and pointed to a line of small, neat text that Rawk was never going to be able to read.

"What does it say?"

The old man spun the book back and read out the address.

"And where is that?"

"South of the river, I think. Around the far side of Mount Grace, maybe."

Rawk sighed. "I think I know someone who can show me the way."

When he crossed the bridge, Rawk stopped and stood in the square, looking around. He knew it was ridiculous, but he was surprised when Clinker didn't suddenly appear by his side and offer to show him the way. After a moment, he realized there were probably a hundred people in the square who do the job just as well.

Not far away was a likely candidate. A street urchin was sitting with his back against the dirty plaster wall of a hardware shop. He was human, which was a bonus.

"What's your name, lad?" Rawk asked as he approached.

"Kikum."

"Kikum? You're Clinker's friend?"

"We aren't really friends; he's a dwarf." He picked at a toenail as he looked up, one eye closed against the afternoon light. "So, whatever he done, I wasn't there."

"He says you're friends."

Kikum shrugged. "Well, he's a lying little bugger."

"Right. Well, anyway, I need to find—"

"He's working." The boy gestured vaguely.

"No, I don't need to find Clinker. I need... Thacker didn't offer you work too? That doesn't seem fair."

"Course he did, but around here they give me plenty of money for doing nothing. Why would I want to do work?"

"To get *more* money," Rawk suggested.

Kikum shrugged. "Clinker got more money than me, he's got a whole stash of it somewhere, and he always shares."

It seemed to Rawk that Kikum would quickly drop all pretense of friendship if he could find the location of Clinker's hoard of money. Rawk looked around, suddenly not sure if he wanted Kikum's help after all. "So, which direction did you say Clinker was?"

"How much is it worth to you? What's he done anyway?"

"How about I don't take you in as well?"

Kikum stared for a moment as if trying to work out if Rawk was serious. "Prince Weaver send you?"

Rawk's lip twitched. He'd been practicing.

Kikum pointed down a street. "Last I knew he was about a hundred yards up that way painting a wall. Could be done by now though."

The directions were accurate, even if the details of the job were not. Two blocks up the street, Clinker was working with an adult dwarf to clean writing off the side off a statue's pedestal. Rawk stood back and watched them work for a moment. All that was left of the writing was 'Never' on the left and 'life' on the right. There was no clue as to what might have been between them.

"More *Words of Wisdom*?" Rawk asked.

Clinker and his workmate both turned to look at him. Clinker smiled and his companion said, "Indeed they were, sir." He gave a nod.

"Never give up on life," said Clinker, screwing up his face as he tried to remember. "Is that right, Bung?"

"Yes it was, lad. Well done." Bung turned back to continue his scrubbing. "You'll be reading Gagar in no time."

Rawk grunted. "It isn't particularly wise."

"It comes from an old moai saying, I believe, sir. Can't rightly say for sure though."

"Are moai wise?"

"Can't say that for sure either, sir. I've never met a moai that I know of."

Rawk had. She'd been as quiet as a feather in a stream. "So, how long will you two be? I need a guide."

"I've got too much work to do, I'm afraid, sir," Bung said.

"I was actually thinking..." It took a moment for Rawk to realize the dwarf was joking. He gave a small smile. He didn't know that he'd ever heard a dwarf tell a joke.

Bung broke out into a huge grin that split his beard in two. "Off you go, Clinker. I can finish this."

"But Thacker—"

"Don't you worry about Thacker. I'm your supervisor, so I decide if you've earned your pay." He took the scrubbing brush from the boy's hand. "Now, off you go and help Mister Rawk."

Clinker dusted himself off, collected his satchel from the ground at the base of the statue and slung it over his shoulder. He set himself with a deep breath. "Where do you want to go today?"

"I'm looking for the corner of Friar Street and Halcum Way."

Clinked cocked his head as he thought.

"You don't know the streets?"

"Of course I know the streets, Mister Rawk. I know all the streets. I'm just trying to think of the best way."

"Oh. Right."

A moment later he gave a nod and set off up the hill.

"Not so fast. I'm still numb from the smoke man."

Rawk followed as the boy walked and talked. There wasn't room for him to interject most of the time, so he didn't bother. He just listened to the news from south of the river and let it wash over him and around him like the crowds in the street.

"The canal will be done ahead of schedule, I reckon," Clinker said eventually. "Did you see how close the ends were now?"

Rawk had seen. He'd been watching the end canal crawl across the city for months. Twenty yards at most until it touched the short stub that stuck out from the Bay of Kata. "What's with the big cleared area over near Wizer Road? It looks like it's acres."

Clinker shrugged. "Something to do with the construction. There's a couple of other areas left empty as well but Thacker ain't giving anything away. At least not to me."

"I'm sure you'll be the first person he tells."

Clinker smiled.

When the surface of the road was broken by the first step, Rawk stopped to rest. The road didn't go very much further here. It stopped at the place where Mount Grace suddenly became too steep, even for stairs.

"We seem to be running out of road, Clinker."

"We go around to the far side now." He pointed to a side street.

"Oh."

"Come on."

"So you're still friends with Kikum, right?"

"Yeah."

"Maybe you should rethink that."

"What? Why?"

"I saw him before I found you. I think he's just using you, letting you do the work so you can pay for his stuff."

"He's my friend."

"Do you have a stash of money somewhere?"

"No." He wasn't very good at lying.

"Why don't you give it to Sylvia to look after? Ask her to give it only to you."

"Kikum wouldn't steal my money."

Rawk shrugged. "I'm just telling you what I think."

"He wouldn't. Come on."

Rawk could tell the lad was at least giving the matter some thought. "So, how much money do you have?"

Clinker looked back over his shoulder as he walked.

"I'm not going to steal your money."

"I've got nearly two hundred ithel."

Rawk almost tripped. "Two hundred ithel? Great Path, lad, that's astounding. You really should give it to Sylvia to look after for you."

Clinker wrinkled his nose and kept walking.

"Are you sure this is the right place?" Rawk asked when they the young dwarf finally stopped. He looked around for a street sign but apparently the dwarves hadn't gotten around to erecting them in this part of town.

Clinker nodded.

"Very well then." Rawk pulled a five–ithel coin from the pouch on his belt. "Don't give it to Kikum."

Clinker smiled and hurried away, leaving Rawk on his own in the gathering darkness. He suddenly wondered why he hadn't delayed his visit until morning. If it wasn't an hour's walk back to the *Hero's Rest*, he might have gone home anyway. But it *was* a long way, and he was sore and tired, and he was here now. With a sigh, Rawk looked around. He was standing in front of a bakery, the strong smell of yeast accosting him, even at the late hour, and that left houses on the other three corners. He bought something to eat, then stood in the doorway as he decided which house to try first. A small girl peeked out through a window across the road, so he crossed that one house of the list. He couldn't see any people in the other two but one of them had bright floral curtains that were pulled back to admit the last of the day's light. The last house looked rougher and curtains were pulled closed.

He licked his fingers and dusted pastry flakes from his shirt. "We have a winner..."

Loosening *Dabaneera* in the sheath, Rawk headed for the winning house. He cursed when a horse nearly knocked him over. Taking a deep breath, he decided the house wouldn't disappear, sorceress or not, so he looked to see if there was anything else that could kill him. He crossed the street safely and stopped in front of the dirty, white timber door. He touched the amulets under his shirt and knocked. It may not have been the best plan, but

Misltetowe wouldn't expect such a quiet, dignified entrance.

Rawk waited. Nothing happened. For a long while, it continued to happen.

"I don't think she's home."

An old man, bits of dinner clinging to his long beard, was hanging half out the window of the house next door.

"Oh, well do you..." But if the old man wasn't even sure about the one piece of information he had, he probably wouldn't know where she actually was. "Maybe I'll come back later, then."

"Suit yourself. I can tell her you dropped by, if you like. If I see her, of course."

"Of course. But I want to surprise her, so I'd prefer you didn't say anything at all."

"Suit yourself."

"I will. Thanks."

Rawk looked up at the second floor window. He looked down the street. He looked up the street. The old man was still there, watching him. Rawk gave a nod and walked slowly away. At the corner he turned and went down beside the house. There was a narrow lane at the back. He stood in the shadows and the stench for a while, remembering the bakery fondly, as he watched the back door. If Mistletowe wasn't home when he'd knocked earlier, he wondered if she would come home while he was waiting around the back. He sighed, checked the lane, and made his way quickly to the door.

The door was locked, of course, but it wasn't all that solid. One kick near the middle hinge and it collapsed inwards with a crash. It fell across a table and Rawk stepped over it into a small kitchen. After a moment he picked the door back up and set it back in place as best he could. There was a serious, solid lock of dwarvish design but it wasn't much use when the other side of the door was held to the frame by a couple of screws in the hinges. The dwarves would think of a solution to that problem soon enough, too, if they hadn't already. He righted a chair that had been knocked over, picked up a couple of run—away apples and put them back in the bowl on the table.

The kitchen was spotless. There was a neat pile of dishes on the bench and a vase with yellow flowers under the window. The pot—bellied stove in the corner was flanked by a row of precise, shining tools— a poker, shovel, scraper and broom. It hardly looked like anyone even lived in the house.

The next room was a sitting room with a couch near the fire and a shelf half—full of books. The books were all innocent things— tales of romance and some historical volumes. The interesting ones were probably hidden somewhere. The front door had another of the impressive locks. Mistletowe obviously didn't trust her friends *that* much.

Upstairs was as nondescript as down. A neatly made bed with plain brown covers. There was a chest of drawers and some clothes, mostly darker shades, hanging from a rod in the corner, lined up like a queue of women waiting at a cistern. There were two boxes under the bed. There was nothing interesting in the first but the second held the stash of magic books. There were a couple of amulets as well that were probably magic in some way or other but he had no way of knowing for sure. He was just sliding the box back into position when he heard the door opening downstairs.

Rawk swore under his breath. He was stuck upstairs when he should be down there hiding behind the door or something.

There were voices. Two people. A woman and a man. He assumed the woman was Mistletowe. It was a long time since he'd heard her talk, and even that had been in less than optimal circumstances, but this woman definitely had the right accent. The man? He had no idea, but he sounded young.

"I'm going to get changed," Mistletowe said. "I'll be back in a moment."

Yes, hiding. Rawk looked around, though he knew perfectly well where every hiding place was. There weren't any. He couldn't fit under the bed. He could wiggle in behind the hanging clothes but then it would just look like he was standing there wearing a dress. They weren't his color.

Footsteps on the stairs.

"Path." Rawk went to stand in the corner that would be behind the door, if there actually was a door. It wasn't much, but better than nothing.

Thankfully, when Mistletowe came into the room she was still talking to the man below, looking back over her shoulder and not really paying attention. She was halfway across the room when Rawk grabbed her. He had his dagger to her throat and a hand over her mouth. She smelled of too much cheap perfume.

"If you even twitch you hands," Rawk said in her ear, "I'll cut your throat. If you say anything— just one single word under your breath— I'll cut your throat."

The sorceress froze. It seemed to be a long time before she even breathed.

Rawk kept the blade poised, the razor sharp edge touching the flesh, and slowly moved his hand away from her mouth.

"I have no money," she said quietly, barely a whisper. "Does it look like I have money?"

"I don't want your money, Mistletowe."

The woman finally moved, half turning to look over her shoulder before thinking better of it. "Rawk? Is that you?" She made it sound as if he was a long lost friend, not someone who'd tried to kill her several times over the last ten years, not someone who was holding a dagger to her throat.

He didn't answer. "Who's your friend?"

There was a hesitation, just a moment that may have been nothing. "His name is Harris. You don't need to worry about him; he's barely more than a boy."

"A play thing?" Rawk wondered if he was the type of man who should be judging someone for something like that. "Tell him he'll have to go."

"He'll want to know why."

"Then give him a reason."

"He won't believe me."

"Make him believe." Rawk pressed the cold edge of the dagger against her neck and she swallowed noisily.

"Is everything all right up there?"

Rawk looked over his shoulder. It sounded like Harris was at the bottom of the stairs.

"*Make him believe, Mistletowe.*"

"Harris, I..." Mistletowe cleared her throat. "Something's come up."

"Between the bottom of the stairs and when you reached the top?" He sounded confused, and rightly so.

"I know. I'm sorry. It sounds crazy but..." She rubbed at her pointed nose as she thought.

"Are you sure you're all right?"

"I'm fine, but I think you should go. It's... It's a woman thing. You know how we are."

"Well..."

In other circumstances, Rawk might have smiled. Poor Harris obviously had no idea what Mistletowe was alluding to. Rawk wasn't sure that he did.

"I know where to find you, Harris. I'll come and see you tomorrow."

"Did I do something wrong?"

"I'll see you tomorrow."

"Very well, but..."

Apparently he didn't know what else to say. A moment later, Rawk heard the sound of the door closing. He pushed Mistletowe onto the bed and drew *Dabaneera*. He stayed close enough to reach her quickly if needed. "What are you doing?" he asked.

"What am *I* doing?" She pushed her long red hair away from her face.

Rawk realized the question was a bit vague. "You and Frixen and Valo? What are you all doing?"

"Nothing," she said, examining her fingers. "I don't know who you are talking about."

"You know very well. Why would you come here, of all places? If Weaver finds out what's going on— if he finds out that *anything* is going on— he'll string you up."

Mistletowe looked up. "You aren't going to?"

Rawk sighed. "I just want to stop all these damn exots. I want to get through an entire day without having to kill some wild animal roaming the streets of Katamood."

"Even if I could tell you, Rawk, I would not. Magic is a part of me; would you walk around blindfolded just because Weaver decided he didn't like people with blue eyes?"

"What?" Rawk shook his head. "Look, why in Path's name are you even in Katamood? Travel a week in any direction and you can do all the magic you like."

Mistletowe looked around, as if the answer was written on the wall somewhere, then shrugged. "Katamood is the center of the world, Rawk. I am drawn to this place, just as you are. It is just that before now, it was too dangerous for me to come."

"It's still too dangerous."

Mistletowe laughed. "Magic is dying everywhere, Rawk. All the lines of power point to Katamood, but they are not what they once were. They are... blocked from lack of use."

"Magic is dangerous thing, in the wrong hands."

"So are swords. I don't see Weaver trying to ban them."

"Yes, well..."

"You have no idea what you are getting yourself into. The Cabal is only just getting started. None of us is very powerful on our own, but together..."

"What is the Cabal getting started at? What are you doing?"

"We are bringing magic back to the world. We are returning the world to the way it should be."

Rawk was watching the sorceress closely and saw when her eyes darted over his shoulder. He tried to roll away but the man behind him still struck him a glancing blow across the side of the head. It wasn't a particularly solid blow, but still left Rawk reeling. His attacker was a young man with heavy brows and a terrified look in his eyes. His weapon of choice was a poker from the kitchen. Rawk tried to get his sword up but another blow got through and he collapsed, head ringing.

Rawk was pretty sure that Harris had used up his yearly supply of courage and wouldn't be a threat against an armed man, even one who was stunned. Mistletowe, on the other hand...

The sorceress was on her feet in an instant. She strode to Rawk, standing over him as much as her short stature would allow, and started to chant softly.

Harris stood close by. He was still holding the poker but looked as stunned as Rawk felt. But as Mistletowe continued with her spell, the lad seemed to gather himself.

"Quickly, Missy," he said. He grabbed her by the hand and drew her towards the stairs. Mistletowe struggled, but Harris was stronger. He didn't seem to realize what was going on.

As she was going out the door, the sorceress finished her spell and threw it back over her shoulder. Rawk tensed as he felt the ripple of magic wash over him. But it was weak, soft at the edges like a fraying carpet.

Was that the best she could do?

Rawk got his feet on the floor and pushed himself upright. He set off in pursuit but he could hardly keep his feet under him. His vision was blurred. He reached up and decided that the blood running from the gash on his forehead probably had as much to do with that as his rattled head. He was halfway down the stairs when the front door slammed behind his quarry.

"Path, damn it."

He caught his heel on the edge of the last step. The floor rose up to greet him. It was the kind of greeting you expected in an alley down by the docks. He slammed into the tiles and *Dabaneera* clattered away across the room. He tried to stand though he knew it was useless. His shoulder hurt as he pushed himself up, but he ignored it. He wished he hadn't because as soon as he put some weight on his leg, his knee sent a flare of pain all the way up to his back. He bit back a scream of pain and consoled himself with the fact that it had only been a little scream.

−O−

Sylvia wasn't home. Of course she wasn't. Why would she be home when he needed her most? Rawk considered going to find Janas but chances are it would be a wasted walk. Even if the old woman was home, she was unlikely to help when he had told her recently that he had found a new healer.

He sat on Sylvia's doorstep for a while, hoping she might return, but he'd been hit on the head a lot during his life, often by jealous men, more often by jealous women, so he knew quite a bit about the recovery process. The pain in his head was receding, so he figured it wasn't too serious but he still didn't want to fall asleep, just in case.

With a sigh, Rawk pushed himself to his feet and started the long, painful walk down the hill. It wouldn't have been quite so painful without all the stairs, but he definitely didn't want to go around the long way.

It was barely past sunset, so there were still plenty of people around. A dwarf on stilts was moving up the street lighting lamps with a glowing taper. The hiss of the lamps sang counterpoint to the dwarf's soft song. An old woman was carrying an over−full washing basket, possibly taking the clothes home to get them ready to return to customers in the morning. She was walking slower than Rawk. A pack of feral kids stampeded past, shouting and poking each other with sticks. A morose looking horse, rider half asleep, clopped across in front of him.

Nobody seemed to notice Rawk, which was a good thing. Maybe they didn't recognize the beaten old man limping down the street. Maybe they just didn't believe it was him, south of the river at this time of the day. Whatever the reason, it was a good thing. Only a crow, perched on a window sill overhead, paused in its preening to watch him pass.

By the time he made it to the river his knee was just a dull ache and his head not much more, though there was a lump the size of half a peach on his crown.

"Stupid idiot, Harris." But he had to respect the lad. He had obviously been scared out of his wits, but came back to help anyway. He either really like Mistletowe or really wanted to get laid with anyone at all. Probably the latter.

Rawk's knee started to hurt again as he started to trudged over Dragon Bridge and up the spine of Two Watch Hill. Then his knee almost collapsed under him for no apparent reason and he stopped in the middle of the street, hoping the feeling would pass. He wondered if he should take *Dabaneera* from its sheath and use the sword as a walking stick. But there were still people around and the ones in this area were more likely to realize who he was. And his arm was hurting a bit too, now that he thought about it. Or it was going numb. More numb. So numb he wasn't sure if he could feel it at all. Or something. He gritted his teeth and kept walking. The next time his knee went funny he had to stay where he was for several minutes, carefully massaging the offending joint so he didn't hurt his arm too. People swirled past on either side.

"Are you all right, Rawk?"

He looked around. He didn't know the woman who had spoken to him. She was young and attractive, with a floral apron and pristine white bonnet.

"Yes, thank you. Just got a knock on the knee earlier. It's a bit sore."

"It looks like you got a knock on the head, too."

He felt at the bump. There was a line of dry blood as well. "I'm sure a pretty girl like you knows how jealous paramours can be."

She smoothed her apron. "Oh, I don't have a paramour."

"You don't?"

"Do you need some help getting home?" She took a step closer and Rawk could smell a hint of jasmine. "It is still quite a way up the hill."

Rawk looked around, taking a moment to work out exactly where he was. Then he looked her up and down. "No, I don't think so." The Veteran's Club was just a block away; Maris might still be working.

"Oh."

"The knee really isn't that bad. I'm sure there are lots of injured men who would love for you to help them home."

The woman nodded, though it looked as if she doubted there were any injured men anywhere in the world.

"Thank you," Rawk said, as she walked away.

When he decided he could move again, Rawk made his way towards the Club. He scaled the lofty height of the stairs, hand on the rail the whole way, and limped into the foyer. The door that led from there to the offices was closed, which meant Maris probably wasn't there. The Armory would be open though. Rawk dreaded the thought of all those stairs down to the basement room, but headed that direction anyway. The battle–mural in the hallway made his head ache even more. The life sized pictures crowded close. The mess hall and the taproom were full and the noise flowed out the door and washed over him like the clamor and hubbub of war. A man walking towards him seemed almost to be warrior charging at him through the slop of mud and blood. Rawk felt his hand hovering near the hilt of his sword and noticed that the stranger was reacting the same way. If he was here then he was probably a veteran and would know how it felt to be in battle.

Rawk flexed his hand and moved it away from *Dabaneera*. He nodded to the other man but felt his back twitching as he continued on.

The Armory was quieter than usual, but Rawk's usual front row table was taken. He started to turn away but noticed who was sitting there. Travis was wearing his best shirt and had made an attempt to comb his hair. There was a vacant seat beside him but before Rawk could think to take it someone set two tankards of ale down on the table and sat down. Natan was wearing his customary black though he too seemed to be dressed up for the occasion. As the big man took up his drink he reached out and laid his other hand on Travis' arm. The two of them leaned in close and said something, laughed, touched hands for a moment.

Rawk turned away and headed slowly in the other direction. He lowered himself into a seat near the back of the room with a grateful sigh and waved to the woman behind the bar. A mug was thumped onto the table a minute later and Rawk didn't care that it was ale. He downed it in one go and waved for another. When the waiter came he also ordered a meal. He would pay twice as much down here as he would in the mess hall above, but he really didn't care about that either.

Over the next hour, the music soothed his aching head and sore muscles as much as any of Sylvia's potions would have. Rawk grunted at the thought. He knew it wasn't true, but he *was* soothed, none–the–less.

He watched Travis and Natan through the crowd. They held hands, touched legs under the table. Travis had said he was seeing someone but hadn't mentioned a name. Natan seemed like the most unlikely choice in the world.

He was... Rawk shook his head. He lived a few yards from the man but didn't really know anything at all about him. He stayed quite and listened to the music.

A couple of hours later, the music wound down and Rawk was still nursing his second mug of ale. He was feeling much better. The crowd started to disperse, leaving swirls in the tobacco smoke, and Rawk watched Travis leave hand in hand with Natan, moving along with the flow. It still didn't seem right to Rawk, but if Travis was happy it was none of his business.

When everyone else had gone Rawk started to push himself to his feet. It should have been a simple enough task, he'd done it countless times before, but he discovered that he wasn't quite as soothed as he thought. His knee and head started to throb in unison while the rest of his body felt like a sack full of wet sand.

On the stage, Celeste and Grint were packing away their instruments. It seemed the dwarf was muttering under his breath. He was certainly looking at the barkeeper as if he wanted to go over and give her a piece of his mind. It appeared he was about to do just that, but his sister laid a gentle hand on his arm and he turned to look at her. Neither said anything but, after a moment, Grint sighed. His shoulders slumped and he picked up his drum case. He seemed to notice Rawk for the first time and nodded a silent greeting. Rawk raised his chin in reply. It was about the only movement he was capable of.

When they were ready to leave, Celeste and Grint looked over again. They spoke for a moment. Celeste shook her head and Grint started to walk towards Rawk. Celeste reached out, as if to pull him back, but the dwarf was already weaving through the flotilla of tables.

"We were just going to..." Grint leaned in close to Rawk, squinting in the dim light. "Are you all right? You look a bit green. And I assume you know you've got a big bloody lump on your head? And when I say 'bloody', I'm not swearing."

Rawk managed to look down at his hand. It didn't look green to him, but he wasn't about to argue with the dwarf. Then he was going to say he was fine. What else was he supposed to say? *I can't move. I seem to be stuck.* It all seemed a bit ridiculous. And telling his problems to a dwarf seemed ridiculous as well. But he thought that he really did need some help. Perhaps Mistletowe's spell hadn't failed. Perhaps it had just taken its time.

"I think I need some help," he croaked.

"What's the matter?"

"I think a sorceress cast a spell on me."

"Oh, very funny..." Grint's eyes narrowed. "You're serious?"

"Yes."

"But you aren't sure?"

Rawk gave it a moment's thought. "I am sure." He explained the situation.

"Right then." Grint waved Celeste over then started to work on the problem like a dwarf— logically and out loud. "I suppose you don't want every man and his dragon knowing about this? Being a Hero and all. Being Rawk and all."

"That would be good."

Rawk watched Celeste cross the room. She carried her mandolin carefully, like she was cradling a baby, but walked with a smooth grace that suggested she'd never tripped over or bumped into anything in her life. Celeste arrived at her brother's side and gave a small smile. "Are you going to come?"

Rawk looked at her. "Come where?"

She looked at Grint. "What? I thought..."

Rawk looked at Celeste. "You were going to ask me to go somewhere?"

"I didn't ask. He's been ensorcelled."

"Really?" Celeste looked around as if the villain might be hiding in the corner.

"It was a while ago. It just took a while for the spell to take hold. Apparently."

"Do you need our help? What do you want us to do?"

Grint grunted. "I was working on that."

"Well?"

Grint gave her a look that must have passed between a million brothers and their younger sisters millions of times all over the world. "Give me a chance."

"Well, sorry."

The dwarf turned back to Rawk. "Can you move at all?"

"I don't know."

"If we support you?"

"I don't know."

"Well, let's have a look."

Rawk winced in anticipation as Grint grabbed him by the arm and helped him up onto his feet. His knee didn't agree with the treatment, but he was able to stay upright with assistance.

"I think it will take me all night to get home."

"Well, we can't really do anything here anyway. Let's at least get you up stairs and we'll go from there." Grint handed his drum bag to Celeste and moved to stand by Rawk's side. "Here, wait." He took off his cloak and threw it around Rawk's shoulders. He reached up and fastened the clasp at the neck and pulled up the hood.

"I look ridiculous," Rawk said. "The cloak isn't even close to fitting." It was fine around his shoulders but ended about three feet from the floor.

"Do you want to be disguised or not? It's the best we can do. Anyway, they'll be looking at the cloak and not at you, so all the better. Come on."

The two of them made their way slowly to the door. Rawk didn't know if he'd manage the stairs but the dwarf was stronger than he looked and almost carried him up to ground level.

"Let's go out the back door," Celeste suggested. She raced ahead when Grint nodded.

The back door was only ten yards away but the journey seemed to take forever. They exited into a narrow alley with a loading dock nearby. There was a wagon parked in the silver moonlight. A pair of draft horses were stamping and nickering in the traces.

"This man says he can give us a ride," Celeste said.

The driver took a pipe from between his teeth and spat onto the cobbles. "I'm not *giving* you anything, missy. Pay up or you can walk." He held out a dark, hairy hand. "And if I'd known a dwarf was coming I'd have doubled the price."

"You are already asking a king's ransom." Celeste sighed then went through a pocket on her mandolin bag and handed over what seemed like an awful lot of money for a five–minute trip. When she was done, she rushed to help Rawk up onto the back of the wagon.

Rawk settled down onto the boards and wondered if they would have to just roll him out when they reached the *Hero's Rest*. He managed to turn slightly and look at Celeste. "Do you know the healer called Sylvia?"

"Of course."

"Go and get her for me."

She stared at him, lips pursed.

He sighed. "Please."

"Surely there are closer healers."

"I'm sure there are, but I need Sylvia. I'll pay whatever she wants."

"Very well."

"Tell her Mistletowe did something to me and it's getting worse."

"Mistletowe?"

"Just tell her. And be quick about it."

Celeste put her mandolin and Grint's drum into the wagon then dashed out of the alley. She looked like she could run forever, and Rawk hoped that she could.

The driver grunted. "Don't know why he can't sleep it off in the corner like the rest of us." He started the wagon before Grint was settled and the dwarf almost tumbled back out onto the ground.

"Steady on."

"Everyone seems to be in a hurry so I ain't going to waste any time." He turned back to look and grinned a wicked looking grin. "If you fall out, you little bastard, I won't be stopping."

At the *Rest* Rawk mumbled for Grint to go inside and get help.

"I'm not waiting here all night."

Rawk grunted. He couldn't have climbed off the wagon, even if he had wanted to. He doubted the driver wanted to take him back down the hill.

"If Rawk sees him in the tap room there'll be hell to pay."

Rawk's lip twitched but he didn't try to say anything. Grint's presence was probably disguising him as much as the silly cloak— why would the great Rawk go anywhere with a stinking dwarf?— but with the dwarf gone the distraction was gone as well. If he managed to start a conversation, the driver might pay more attention and would likely take two away from two and come up with Hero.

Grint returned a minute later with Travis and Valen in tow. The three of them managed to get Rawk down to the ground without dropping him then half dragged, half carried him inside.

"I can't move at all," Rawk said, though they had probably worked that out for themselves. His head hung limply. His boots scraped across the floorboards.

Kalesie was already gone for the night and a helper had just wiped down the huge bench in the center of the room so they hauled him up and dumped him on the damp boards. Rawk laid where they put him, looking up at the vegetables hanging in bunches from the ceiling. The smell seemed like a weight pressing down on him, as if a whole wagonload of the vegetables had been dumped on top of him. He managed to move his head.

"You can't put him there," the kitchen girl said. "Kalesie will have a fit." The thought seemed to make her smile.

"I think it would be best if Kalesie didn't find out," Travis said to her. He eyed Grint as if the dwarf would've been even more of an issue.

They all stood looking at Rawk.

"What should we do now?" Grint asked.

"Your drum," Rawk said. He could hear the sound of horses' hooves leaving the ostler's yard.

Grint swore and ran outside. When he returned, nobody had moved. Valen looked like he wanted to be somewhere else. The boy was chewing on his thumbnail and glancing at the door. Rawk noticed, for the first time, that Natan was standing there as well. The big man was watching silently, dark eyes intent.

Travis burst into action. "Boiling water, Valen. Quickly." And he started going through the pouches on Rawk's belt. Money, bone−handled cutlery, dried meat all came out onto the bench before Travis finally found the tealeaves. It wasn't long before Rawk was trying to sit up, with Grint's help, and Travis was pouring hot water down his throat. It was no good. Rawk coughed and choked though he did get down a mouthful.

"A towel," Travis shouted to nobody in particular.

Valen went to look, apparently happy to be doing something again instead of standing watching.

Rawk watched as Travis poured the boiling tea into a big bowl then set it carefully on Rawk's lap. Rawk stared at the bowl but Valen was searching through a cupboard in the corner and each sound seemed to assault his eyes. The smell of tomorrow's boiling meat was like thunderclap.

Natan came over from the doorway, stopping in front of Rawk and looking into his eyes. "I know something of healing," he said to nobody in particular.

Rawk wanted to look away but couldn't. Not even his eyes were responding to his orders. After a moment of uncomfortable staring, Natan reached up and took hold of his face, one hand on each side. His big, fleshy hands were warm and soft, but surprisingly strong.

Rawk blinked as the warmth seemed to spread down his neck and up over the top of his skull. A slow wave of cool followed and Rawk was shivering all over.

After a moment, Natan turned away. "A healer is coming?" He removed his hands but the waves continued. He breathed a storm out into the still air.

"Yes," Travis replied.

"He is skilled?"

"The best."

"Then I shall refrain for I fear anything I do would confuse the situation for him." He sniffed the tea. "That should help. But now, I will leave you to your ministration, Travis."

"Sorry, Natan..."

"Don't be silly, my dear." He gave Travis a quick kiss on the cheek. "I suddenly remember that there are things I need to be doing anyway."

"I will see you tomorrow?"

"Of course. You will be serving me breakfast, I assume." And Natan turned and left the room with a dramatic swirl of his black cape.

Rawk might have slept after that.

He was roused by a sound at the door to the taproom. Mykle had opened it a crack and was looking through. A lightening flash of noise came with him. He looked nervous. But then again, he normally did. "There's some elf and a fermi at the front door wanting to get in," he said, looking over his shoulder as if to make sure they weren't attacking the place, or scaring away all the real customers.

Before anyone had a chance to say anything, Sylvia pushed Mykle aside and came into the room. Celeste came at her heals. The elf looked furious. The fermi looked even more nervous than Mykle and Valen combined. An avalanche of sound came with the two women and it was all Rawk could do to stop himself from screaming before Mykle finally shut the door and went back to the bar.

"What happened, Rawk?" Sylvia put a satchel down on the floor then stood in front of him and grasped his head between her hands as Natan had done.

"Mistletowe..." was all Rawk could manage in reply. The elf's hands were soft and cool but the grip was vice-like. Or perhaps he was just so weak he wouldn't have been able to fight his way out of a knitting circle.

Sylvia mumbled to herself. Her face was very close. Her eyes were very green and intense. Rawk had never really noticed before. Just like he hadn't known she was an elf until a couple of weeks ago. And she was beautiful, though most elves were, he supposed, in an elfish type way.

"Either Mistletowe has weakened considerably, or you were only struck a glancing blow. I can't believe you let her get the better of you. I told you you're getting old; you need to be more careful."

"Companion," Rawk said around a wet-blanket-tongue. And then, "Warrior." She didn't need to know the whole truth.

Sylvia looked around the kitchen. "What have you given him, Travis?"

"He had a little bit of tea but choked on it. Other than that, he's just been breathing the stuff."

Sylvia nodded. "That is about the best you could have done, really. I think Mistletowe used a *farnaris* spell. It turns the target to stone though it usually happens very quickly if done properly."

"Can you stop it?"

"Perhaps. The tea will help him relax, which is important." She turned to someone. Rawk couldn't see who it was. "I need salt and bicarbonate powder. Do you have them?"

Rawk couldn't move his head to look, but he heard the kitchen girl sniff.

"Tess," Travis shouted. Rawk blinked at the explosion of sound. "Do as she says or you will be looking for a new job."

Rawk decided to draw in a breath. He felt the fumes from the tea entering his mouth. They tickled his tongue and sang all the way down to his lungs. He breathed again. It seemed like the right thing to do.

"I'll need some other things, too. Celeste, bring my bag."

Sylvia's piercing green eyes disappeared again and Rawk found himself looking at her ear. Yes, her pointy ear. He should have noticed years ago. Then that was gone too and he was looking at someone else. Celeste. She was a fermi–dwarf bastard. He didn't like fermi or dwarves any more than he liked elves. But he supposed he did like Sylvia, now that she wasn't trying to kill him. Though she said she'd never been trying to kill him. Not really. She'd just been trying to stop him. Was that true?

Rawk was surprised, and a bit disappointed, when Sylvia's eyes reappeared, surrounded by her pale face. "I've given him some larmin which should slow things down," she said, "but we need to get him to drink some of this."

Rawk doubted very much that he could drink anything. He would have told her that, but he couldn't move his mouth properly now. Not even a little bit. He breathed again. He really liked tea.

"I'm going to put this tube down his throat so we can basically pour the liquid straight into his stomach."

Rawk couldn't see the tube but he decided that having it shoved all the way down to his stomach didn't sound like a lot of fun. But he couldn't say anything about that either. So he sat there while the elf put the tube into his mouth and pushed it further and further down inside. He felt that he should be choking but couldn't feel a thing. Sylvia pushed his chin up so he was looking at the ceiling. There were lots of cobwebs there.

Then they were pouring something in the end of the tube. It was thick and yellow like some horrible slime he'd once seen in... He didn't know where. It was a swamp. And when the liquid hit his stomach, Rawk spasmed. His whole body seemed to shift a few inches upwards without passing through the intervening space.

And when he hit the bench again he could feel his body. He could feel fire racing along his nerves. He could feel blood that was too thick pumping through his veins. His skin felt as if it was covered with a thousand stinging ants.

Sylvia put her hands on the side of his face again and stared into his eyes, concentrating. "I think it is working," she said after a moment.

He was asleep before they finished pulling the tube from his mouth.

−O−

Rawk didn't know how long he slept, but it couldn't have been that long. He'd been taken from the bench and placed on a rug along the wall. Valen and Tess had gone, but everyone else was still there. They were sitting on stools and on the floor not far away, talking quietly and listening as Celeste played a soft, gentle tune and sang in her clear voice. Rawk lay still for a long time and listened as well.

When he started to drift off again Rawk rolled over. It was a slow, painful process, but the fact that he could move at all was a big improvement. Everyone turned to look at him.

"Don't stop, Celeste," he said, but she had already stopped and simply sat on her stool looking nervous. "Would you like a job? You and Grint?"

She looked confused. "Doing what?"

"Singing, of course."

"Where?"

"Here. At the *Hero's Rest.*"

Celeste and Grint looked at each other, then at Travis.

Rawk gave a small smile. It hurt his teeth. "I own the *Rest.* Nobody really knows that, and I'd like to keep it that way. So, anyway, Travis will do whatever I tell him to do."

Everyone looked a bit surprised.

"You own the tavern?" Sylvia asked.

Rawk smiled some more. "A bit more grown up than you though?"

"Perhaps."

"We can't," Grint said. "We have a contract with the *Veteran's Club.*"

"When was the last time you got paid?"

Grint shrugged. "We got some money not long ago."

"All of it?"

"No."

"Then they broke the contract."

"I'm not singing in the taproom," Grint said.

Rawk grunted. "I want to be able to hear the music. We had Lika Olend in the tap room the other day but I still don't know what he's really like."

"Then where?" Celeste asked.

That was a good question. Then he smiled. "There's a storage room that Travis would love to clean out."

"No, Travis wouldn't."

"Well then, Travis should delegate."

Celeste and Grint looked at each other again.

"Well, do you want the job or not?"

"How much are you paying?"

"More than the *Club.*"

"You don't know how much they pay."

"Not much, apparently."

Grint sneered.

Celeste looked at her hands. "Maris said they might be moving us into the main theatre."

Rawk laughed. "So they can make more money and still not pay you? Look, the store room is a nice big room and you can help Travis work out where you want stuff to go." What else could he offer? "And... And I'm going to charge people three ithel just to come in, so you two can have one ithel."

"We'll have to talk about it," Grint said.

"You're worried about breaking the contract?"

"If we get a reputation for doing stuff like that..."

"Dwarves might get a reputation for a lot of things, but breaking contracts will never be one of them."

"We'll do it," Celeste said.

"Celeste!"

"Let us not be careful, just this once." Celeste was talking to Grint but continued to look at her hands. She looked quickly up at Rawk for a moment. "Now, we really should go. We have work tomorrow."

"We don't even know how much he's going to pay."

"I trust him."

Rawk drifted away towards sleep as they continued to argue. The last thing he saw was a small black cat, sitting in the doorway out to the yard, dead mouse at its feet.

Sunday

RAWK'S WHOLE BODY ACHED. He felt like he'd wrestled a greivus and been used as a seat after he'd lost. Sylvia would probably tell him that was better than the alternative. His back ached as well, but in a completely different way. He was pretty sure that was just from sleeping on the floor; he'd given up on that type of thing for a reason.

Kalesie was bustling around the room like she did every morning, but Valen and the other helpers were at least pretending to be quiet as they attempted to keep up with the shouted orders. Life continued without him. Rawk wondered if they would really notice if he wasn't there at all. Then he wondered if it mattered. Did the world really need an aging Hero any more? Did the world need any Heroes at all? The dwarves could probably come up with a more efficient solution to the exot problem if they were given the chance. Plus every other problem.

Rawk groaned and sat up. The ache that gripped him was definitely an improvement on the feelings of the previous night. He kept reminding himself that, in case he forgot. And his numbness from the smoking man seemed to have backed off as well, as if Mistletowe's spell had cleaned it from his system.

When he opened his eyes again he noticed Valen racing from the room, heading towards the front of the tavern. He returned a minute later, following Travis.

"You're awake."

Rawk closed his eyes and took a deep breath. "It would appear so. And I suppose that's a good thing, really."

Travis sat on a stool and took a carrot from a pile Kalesie was working on. "How do you feel?"

"Terrible. Surprisingly good. What I think I need is some food."

"Sylvia said you might be hungry."

"Then how come you're eating and I'm not?"

"Oh. Sorry." Travis got another carrot and threw it to Rawk.

Rawk managed to raise his arm, but he wasn't nearly quick enough. The carrot thumped into his chest and he spent a moment scrabbling around to pick it up with clumsy fingers. When he finally took a bite he almost spat it back out again.

Travis smiled. "Yeah, she also said that stuff might taste a bit funny. That should wear off after you've eaten a bit."

Rawk grunted and took another bite. By the time he was done with that, Travis had organized a bowl of stew. He took Rawk's spoon from the pouch on his belt, which was hanging from the side of the bench, and passed them both across. Rawk started eating, hardly pausing for breath. He spilled it down his shirt, dripped it on the floor, and he felt better by the moment.

"What else did Sylvia say?"

"She said you were lucky. If she'd been a few minutes later— or if we hadn't given you the tea— then it would've been too late."

"It already did feel like it was too late at the time. Can I have some more of this?"

"You want me to ask Kalesie?"

Rawk glanced at the woman. She didn't look happy, but then she never did. "How about you just get some?"

"Of course." He took the bowl and brought it back a minute later after withstanding the cook's stern gaze. "The tea was my idea, you know."

"Yes, well done," Rawk said around another mouthful of stew. "Thank you."

"I think you owe me one." He used the remains of his carrot as a pointer. "And that, friend Rawk, is worth quite a bit more than the time I let you hide behind the bar to get away from Halipturn."

Rawk smiled. "Yes. That wouldn't have been the end of the world. How many are we up to now?"

Travis shrugged. "I'm not sure. I think it's gotten to the point where the exact number doesn't really matter."

"That's what I thought."

"Sylvia's final words before she left were something to the effect that if you don't rest then she will not be responsible for what happens."

"She's said that kind of thing before."

"And I'm guessing you didn't listen."

"Oh, I listened."

"But you didn't rest?"

"Of course not."

"So what are you doing then?"

"Nothing strenuous. I'll be going to see Maris, I think."

"I thought she was all over you."

"Yes but..."

"But what?"

"I think I'm going to tell her I won't be seeing her any more."

Travis raised his eyebrows.

"When she finds out that I've poached Celeste and Grint I don't think she'll be talking to me anyway."

"Really?"

"They have to be making a fortune for the Veteran's Club. She won't be very popular with her bosses and it will be all my fault."

"You may be right," Travis agreed.

"If she'd just paid them they wouldn't have even considered coming here. And I probably wouldn't have thought to ask."

"And we're going to pay them more than the Club? Even though we could have gotten away with paying them less as long as we actually paid them?"

"Are they worth it?"

There was no hesitation. "I don't know what they are being paid, but yes."

Rawk nodded. "I'll need to work out when they can come."

"Tonight is going to be their last night at the club."

"Oh."

"We talked a bit last night. It might be a week or so before we can have the room ready, but I thought we might be able to spread the word beforehand."

Rawk nodded. "Hire some extra people to help with the cleaning if you like. Just sell all the regular stuff but let me know of anything unusual. That drum I found is worth a fortune. It's got its own story and everything."

"Where is it now?"

"I gave it to Grint."

"You gave a fortune to a dwarf?"

"You've heard him play. Is it worth it?"

Travis didn't have an argument for that either.

Rawk was feeling a lot better though he didn't know if he'd be able to fight a mushon. "Now, I have to go and visit Maris." That task was going to be just as scary as facing a mushon, but not nearly as physical.

He climbed slowly to his feet and managed it with a bit of help from Travis. He knew what the other man was going to say, but didn't give him the chance.

"I have to tell her some time today, before Grint has a chat with her, so I'd rather get it over with."

"If you're sure."

Rawk stood wavering for a moment, physically and emotionally. Then he sat down again. "I think I would like some more breakfast first."

"Good idea." Travis looked around. "Like what?"

"I want some bread and honey. And some tea."

"Right."

"And some fruit." He didn't want to eat fruit for breakfast but anti–oxi–majigs.

–O–

Rawk felt as if he was walking into battle. His heart was racing, his hands were sweating and his limbs felt weak. He liked to think it was the residue of Mistletowe's spell but the symptoms increased with every step towards Maris' home.

He'd gone through the conversation a dozen different times, in a dozen different ways, as he rode the cab down the hill but none of them seemed right. And now he was just a block away, having sent the cab and the pair of grumpy goats on their way, and he still didn't know what he was going to say. He liked Maris. She was fun, even when she wasn't in bed, but... He'd never had to end a *relationship* before. He'd kicked out women who'd outstayed their welcome, but that was totally different.

He tried to keep his thoughts on the task at hand. If he gave himself any excuse he would not go through with it. He grunted. "People end relationships every day," he said. "Normal people. Boring people. Stupid people. Some even do it by accident. If they can do it, I can do it."

Rawk stopped at the last corner. He needed to rest after the exertion of his ride and took the opportunity to think some more. He had the feeling he was going to say, 'Hello,' then eat lunch and have sex. Maybe it wouldn't be in that order. It would be fun, one way or the other— if the remains of Mistletowe's spell and the smoking man didn't embarrass him— but would only make the problem worse.

He pulled a strip of meat from his belt and chewed on it while he leaned against the building.

His thoughts, scattered and wandering as they were, were interrupted by a shout from down the street. Rawk looked up in time to see what looked like a pony exit a building in a hurry. It would've looked a lot *more* like a pony, he realized, if it didn't have grey scales, a bristling green mane and a single spiral of horn on its head. *A unicorn?* The creature turned back the way it had come. Hooves clattered against the cobbles, sending out sparks as it tried to gain traction, and it charged back inside. When it disappeared there was a growl and a scream of pain that sounded horribly human. Swearing, Rawk found some energy. He drew *Dabaneera* and rushed forward. Tried to rush forward. It felt like he was hobbling at nothing more than a fast walk. Still, he almost stopped completely when he realized that it was Maris's house. He followed the exot into the building.

Inside was chaos. There were three of the creatures. They had different colored manes, but each was as fierce and wild eyed as the others. They had a Hero bailed up in the corner of the room.

"Josey!"

She was covered in blood from a dozen wounds and it was amazing she was still alive at all. The unicorns worked as a team, using their horns as swords, jabbing and slashing. They had huge teeth and obviously knew how to use them as well.

Josey slashed wildly at one of the creatures. It was the act of a tired, injured woman.

Rawk shouted as he charged in. He wasn't quite sure why he did it. Sneaking up behind them when they weren't ready might have been a better idea. Still, he got to one before it could turn in the cramped space, sliding his sword in between two of the thick, hard scales. It came back out with a very satisfying sucking sound. But another rounded on him before he got the blade all the way clear and he backed away in a hurry. He almost tripped on the chair where he'd hung his cloak a few nights ago. His foot came down on one of the books that had been on the shelf above the door. And he wasn't just distracted by the *presence* of the book and the chair. He was distracted by the fact that he knew them. They were part of his life. They were Maris's. The room smelt of her.

He swung instinctively at the unicorn's horn as it lunged forward. The blade took away a chip but that didn't seem to mean much at all. The creature kept coming. Pushing him back towards the door. Rawk didn't know how Josey had survived against three of them. *Am I really that old?* But he was sick too, not allowed to do anything strenuous. He got a prick on his wrist that stung like a giant benzo wasp. He got a slash across his chest. Sweat ran down his face. His hand ached on the hilt of his sword. And he was tired. It felt like he was fighting in water.

At last he saw his chance. But he was too slow and the chance was gone. But he was already lunging and had to twist aside to avoid being skewered. His knee screamed at the sudden change of plan. He stumbled as the exot came in hard again. Somehow, he managed to slash it across the cheek. It reared back, roaring with pain, and Rawk stepped in to finish the job. Except this time his knee *did* give way beneath him and he fell, crashing into the last intact chair. He looked up at the clatter of hooves. He was barely holding onto *Dabaneera*. He couldn't do anything with it. Not in time. He watched as the unicorn came at him, head low. And he watched as it stopped suddenly. It turned around. There was a sword wedged between two of its scales, letting a stream of dark, thin blood down onto the floor. Josey was close behind, barely standing, trying to hold a dozen wounds all at once.

"I knew I recognized her," she said. "I'm sorry."

"Are you all right?" Rawk asked.

"No." And she collapsed, landing on the corpse of the final unicorn with a dull thud.

Rawk crawled to her side. He listened for a heartbeat and, when he found one, dragged her down to lay flat on the floor. She was bleeding everywhere so he hauled himself to his feet and started looking for something to use as bandages. There was the curtain, but it was too thick. The tablecloth.

He moved across the small room. Before he had reached the table he could see an arm poking out from beneath. He wanted to rush forward, to throw the table aside and pull Maris free. But he didn't move. He couldn't. She might yet live. It was possible. But Josey's apology suggested otherwise. She knew about that type of thing.

He'd had dinner at that table. He'd had sex on that table.

Eventually, Rawk did cross the last of the space and flipped the table over. There was no doubt that Maris was dead. She had a vacant, staring hole where her left eye used to be. Her hand was clutching uselessly at a wound in her stomach. Her legs were twisted and trampled. There was small sea of blood beneath her. It was slowly turning into a large sea of blood. Maris wasn't moving. She looked peaceful, but Rawk doubted that that had been the case in the last few moments of her life.

Rawk jumped when somebody clattered into the room behind him.

"What's going on here?"

That was a stupid question. Rawk turned and saw Waydin standing in he door. The soldier was looking around the room and soon came up with an answer for himself.

"Exots. Path, this is the worst yet. They... Is that you, Rawk?"

"Yes, it's me."

"What are you doing here?"

"I'm a Hero, Waydin. I fight exots." Rawk looked back at Maris. He decided that he should be sad. He should be feeling grief. But he didn't. He felt nothing, as if his emotions had been plucked out, leaving him vacant and staring as well. He wiped at his face. "We need a healer."

"She's beyond—"

"Not Maris. Her." He pointed to Josey, lying on the floor and still bleeding.

"You know her?"

"She needs help, Waydin. She's alive, but won't be for long."

"Prince Weaver will want a report."

"Damn you, Waydin..."

Rawk heard the sound of a bell out in the street. He pushed past the guard and flung the door open as he went out. There was a crowd gathering. They were slowly edging closer as it became apparent the danger was over.

And at the back, crowding onto a wagon with a water—tank on the back, were a group of dwarves.

"There's no fire," Rawk shouted to them.

"So we see," the leader replied. "That was a waste of time."

"Do you know Sylvia? The healer?"

"Of course."

"Come here then. Help me."

Half a dozen dwarves jumped down and pushed through the crowd. They followed him as he limped back inside and summed up the situation in an instant. They grabbed Josey as gently as they could. One hurried to Maris, but backed away, shaking his head to his companions. Rawk followed them silently, gritting his teeth against the pain. And he took a hand when it was offered, allowing himself to be pulled up onto the water wagon. He sat by the Josey's side on the very top of the tank, holding her steady as the driver got the horses moving. The bell rang and a path cleared, though if the one was related to the other was impossible to tell.

—O—

Sylvia sighed and stepped back. "There is nothing I can do, Rawk. She is gone."

Rawk nodded, barely an acknowledgement at all. He felt empty. Drained. "Thank you for trying."

"What happened?"

Rawk explained. It wasn't easy.

"The woman from the newspaper picture?"

He nodded.

"You've been seeing her for a while?"

"Yes. Does it matter?"

"Should it?"

"I was going to stop seeing her." He felt guilty for his intentions now. He felt guilty for speaking those intentions out loud.

It looked as if Sylvia was going to ask why, but she remained silent.

"There were a lot of reasons." *She drank too much. She didn't like music.*

"I'm sorry, anyway. She seemed a good person."

Rawk wondered about that. Did good people honor their commitments, even if those commitments were with some dwarves? Even if? If it had been any dwarves other than Celeste and Grint would it have bothered him? Did his emotional investment in their music make a difference? If she hadn't been paying the dwarf cleaner, would Rawk have held it against her? Would he have cared? And those thoughts made him feel guilty as well.

"Josey was a good woman, too," Rawk said. "An honorable woman. She didn't deserve..." He looked over at the woman, at the body, and didn't say anything else for a long time.

Eventually, he went through the pouches on his belt and pulled out the sheets of paper he'd found at Valo's house. "What's this? Do you know what it means?"

Sylvia took the crumpled sheet, smoothing it out on the bed near Josey's feet. She read for a moment, then looked up. "Where did you get this?"

"Valo and Frixen had them. One each."

"It's a spell. A very powerful spell."

"What does it do?"

"I'm not sure. I would have to study it a bit more."

"Do you think it opens a portal?"

The silence was answer enough.

"Do you know any of the other names?"

"No."

Rawk nodded. "Some of them might be fake names. Mistletowe was using a fake name."

"Mistletowe Oc?"

"Yes. Frixen, Valo and Mistletowe are hardly powerful on their own, but how about together?"

"If these people can complete this spell successfully as often as they seem to be, then together they are powerful indeed." She turned the page and read on the back. "This seems to suggest that they would be able to control both ends with complete accuracy."

"So they deliberately put a portal in Maris's kitchen?"

Sylvia looked down at the paper and didn't say anything.

"You need to help me, Sylvia. Can't you see that? It's one thing for a sorcerer to open a portal and let some exots through. But to target someone like that?" To target someone that Rawk knew.

"Why would they attack Maris and not you, if that was indeed what they did?"

"I don't know. Maybe they thought it was easier to get me that way than to actually kill me."

Sylvia raised an eyebrow. And she was right; three unicorns in his room in the middle of the night would have killed him quick enough.

He almost surged to his feet but managed to control himself. He wouldn't have *surged* very impressively anyway. He relaxed his grip on the hilt of his *Dabaneera*. "Will you help me?"

"You shouldn't be doing anything, Rawk. You should be at home resting."

"But we both know that isn't going to happen. Katamood is my city and I won't lie around in bed while innocent people are dying." He wasn't sure he could save them, even on his feet, but he was going to try. He shouldn't have left Maris where she was. Waydin was an idiot and... But Josey had been alive at the time. And those who were living were more important than those who had already died.

"There are plenty of Heroes around."

"Yes, but they will just keep killing the exots as they turn up. They won't go looking for the source."

"I don't think it's a good idea, Rawk."

"Did you use magic to cure me last night?"

Sylvia looked down at the paper in her hands.

"Thank you. I know that was a risk for you. But I guess that's just the type of person you are."

"You won't make me feel guilty."

"How about scared?" Rawk said coldly. "Weaver is going to start sending the Guard door to door soon, searching for sorcerers. I told him I'd try first, but he won't wait long."

"I am safer hiding from a couple of soldiers than drawing attention to myself by helping you."

Rawk sighed. "Maris had a hole where her eye used to be, Sylvia. Her stomach was ripped open."

"Oh, *all right.* I'll help. Just shut up, would you."

Rawk smiled. "Thank you." But then he looked at Josey. "What happens now?"

"Someone needs to send a form in to Weaver's secretary."

"Weaver cares that much?"

Sylvia almost laughed. "He just wants to know if he is owed money. But seeing I don't want to draw attention to myself, I normally get Thacker to organize for another healer to do the form."

"And what happens if nobody knows what actually happened?" Rawk thought of the dwarf out in the forest. The little man had died saving him from the duen and now he was buried in a shallow grave next to Galad.

Sylvia shrugged. "Nothing happens."

Rawk rubbed at his eyes.

"You should be resting," Sylvia said.

"I need to talk to Thacker too; can you take me?"

"Did you hear me?"

"Yes. People have died. More will die. There are more exots turning up every day, Sylvia. I don't have time to rest." He needed to rest. He felt tired down to his bones. "Look, taking me to see Thacker will be a lot less strenuous than anything other crazy adventures I might get myself involved in."

Sylvia shook her head. "I will look at your wounds first, then I will take you. But we need to be quick for I have appointments later."

She considered stitches for the wound on Rawk's chest, but in the end just bound it tightly like she did the rest. "I suspect you will just pop the stitches anyway."

"Thank you."

When she was done Sylvia tied up her hair. She then took a green scarf from under the counter and wrapped it around her head and face in an elaborate, intricate design. "You draw attention everywhere you go," she said in answer to his unasked question. "It is attention I would prefer to avoid."

Rawk stayed on his stool as Sylvia locked the front door. He finally heaved himself to his feet when she led the way out to the back room. Collecting a cloak from a hook on the wall she continued out into the alley behind the shop as she dressed.

"Not too fast." Rawk struggled to keep up as the elf headed up the hill. His legs were aching by the time they reached the main street and he stopped to rest for a moment, rubbing his knee and looking around.

"Are you applying the cream?"

Rawk stopped rubbing. "Of course."

"It is cumulative, Rawk. Using it every now and then is useless."

"It isn't that bad, anyway," he said. "And I've been busy." The last bit was true. Too true. He tried not to think about all the things he'd been doing. Or, at least, he tried not to think about the things he hadn't managed to do in the last hour.

"Come. It is not far."

Rawk got himself vertical and followed again. At the next intersection they turned towards the top of the hill. At first there were steps every ten yards but soon they were on a flight of stairs that led up the side of the mountain. And at the very top, where the stairs met the cliff, was a passage.

Rawk stopped to look. The opening was about two yards wide and a frame of twisting vines was carved around the edge in startling detail.

Sylvia was looking at him. "Are you coming?"

"Thacker lives in a cave?"

Sylvia started to walk. "No."

Lamps lined the wall, hissing quietly and creating multiple shadows on the smooth, patterned walls. There was a bend ten yards beyond the opening, sharp to the left then back the other way.

"Who is he keeping out?"

"Pardon?"

"Bends in the passage like that are there to stymie the charge of attacking forces."

"Oh. Yes, I knew that, I suppose." She was looking at the passage as if seeing it for the first time.

At the far end was daylight and Rawk stepped out into a deep, steep sided valley that was filled to overflowing with a town the like of which he had never seen before. He looked back the way he had come, as if he might see the ohoga portal that had taken him away from Katamood. But there was nothing, just the mouth of the tunnel with a new carving decorating the rock around it.

"What is this place?"

Sylvia gave an exasperated sigh. "It is Katamood, Rawk. The suburb is called Caldera." She started unwrapping her scarf.

"I've heard of Caldera. I just thought it was around the far side of the mountain or something."

"No, that is still Mount Grace." She pushed a lock of loose hair behind her ear.

"But..." Rawk looked around. The town seemed to have been carved from the red stone of the mountain itself. The buildings blended into each other, flowing along the edges of curving, circuitous streets. "How come nobody knows about this?"

"How come nobody knows about the town where lots of people live? Perhaps you mean how come you do not know about this?"

Rawk shrugged. "Maybe."

"It isn't a secret, Rawk. But the people who know about it don't feel the need to talk about something that is just a part of their lives. And the people who do not know generally do not want to know. It's just dwarves and elves living up here, after all."

"It's not a secret?"

"How could this be a secret? I told you once before, you— and most humans— walk through life seeing what you want to see."

"I'm sure Weaver doesn't know about it."

"Possibly he doesn't know the details. Thacker pretty much runs everything south of the river. It is only when there is a problem that Weaver lowers himself to take an interest."

"Like when taxes aren't being paid."

"Exactly. But Thacker makes sure things like that don't happen because he really doesn't want Weaver taking an interest in anything down here."

Rawk followed as Sylvia started to walk again.

The town was a thing of beauty. The red stone— polished and shot through with patterns of quartz and another, yellow stone— was decorated with brightly colored panels of silk and timber. Colorful curtains flapped in the windows, gardens overflowed from rooftops, spilling down walls, merging with dooryards and parks. Smoke billowed from dozens of chimneys and the sound of industry could be heard above the general clamor of city life.

At the next intersection, Sylvia stepped up onto a raised platform, like a dock beside the road. Rawk stopped beside her.

"What are we waiting for?" He sat down on the top of a post.

"A tram."

"A what?"

"A tram. It is similar to a train, though I am not actually sure of the differences."

"I've heard of a train..." But he still had no idea of what one was. Comparing it to a tram didn't help at all.

A whistle blew. Rawk turned and watched as something swung around a bend just down the road. The contraption clanked and rattled up the slight slope, sending out billows of smoke as it came closer. Rawk rose to his feet and stepped back. He almost fell. His hand strayed to the hilt of his sword.

"Do not be afraid, Rawk. That is the tram."

Rawk cleared his throat. "I'm not scared." It was obvious that the thing was a common sight in Caldera. Nobody else paid it any mind, apart from making sure they weren't in the way. They parted before it as if it was second nature. So Rawk set his shoulders and watched; if a bunch of dwarves weren't scared, he wouldn't be either. There were people inside, dwarves and elves, some humans and others, looking out the open windows, and standing on the steps that ran along both sides.

When the contraption finally came to a noisy, smoke filled stop, a lot of the people piled out, and Rawk nervously stepped in. He considered staying on his feet, but an opportunity to surreptitiously take the weight off his knee and to rest again was too good to pass up. So he drew *Dabaneera* to keep it out of the way and sat next to an old dwarf who had his head buried in a newspaper.

There was one of the all–too–accurate pictures of Rawk on the front. He was arguing with Ramaner, looking old and tired. He gave a grunt and shook his head.

"Where are we going?"

"Thacker's office is around the far side of the valley; it is about two miles, but won't take long on the tram."

And once the contraption got up to speed Rawk could well believe it. It stopped fairly regularly but was still much quicker than walking. And much better on his aching body. Bitter smoke drifted around the cabin. It dried his mouth and made his nose itch.

He watched the buildings trundling by. Some were as much as three stories high with grand, broad windows letting in the light and the breeze. There was a blacksmiths shop. A dwarf, hairy, muscled back bathed in sunshine, worked at an anvil with the calm steady precision of a man who knew exactly what he wanted to do and exactly how he was going to do it. Not far away, two boys turned a handle to power a lathe for a dwarf.

"Surely if the dwarves are smart enough to have a machine like this tram they could work out a machine to turn a lathe."

Sylvia nodded. "They could, but the noise and the expense would be horrendous for a small business."

"Oh." Rawk admitted the tram was very noisy, but hadn't really considered the cost. "So, who pays for the trams?"

"Thacker organizes it. We're getting off here."

The tram stopped across the street for a building that backed up against the wall of the valley. It was tall and wide, but only went a couple of yards back from the footpath, so Rawk guessed it also went back into the mountain.

The front doors were swung wide and inside was a small foyer with various paintings of Katamood on all four walls. Talented artists had done the pictures, but there was nothing to suggest that the place was of any importance at all. They went through another door at the rear of the room then up carpet lined stairs to the second floor.

There, finally, two dwarf guards flanked a door. They looked like boys standing there, both with axes almost as big as they were, but Rawk didn't doubt they would be able to handle themselves. Dwarves weren't a warlike people, but when they set their mind to do something, they usually did it properly. He wondered how much that trait added to humans' distrust of them. A large number of humans were willing to get through life with the least effort possible and perhaps they felt threatened by that commitment to perfection.

Sylvia nodded to one of the dwarves. "Rake, is Thacker in?"

"Of course." The little man hardly moved.

Sylvia went through the door without slowing and Rawk had no choice but to follow.

Inside was... An office. It was much more impressive than Rawk's office. Wide, glazed windows looked out over the red and green patchwork of the valley. An ancient map of Katamood dominated one wall and the others were lined with shelves. And each shelf was full to overflowing with books and scrolls. And so was a table in the corner. And a couch near the windows. Rawk didn't know what he had expected, but it certainly wasn't this. Apart from the books, it was clean and tidy and smelled of mint.

The dwarf behind the desk wasn't what he had expected either. Thacker was barely forty. His beard was neatly combed and tied with a dozen ribbons that signified guild affiliations and qualifications, as far as Rawk knew. He'd never seen so many before. In fact, most dwarves didn't bother, seeing a dwarf making a barrel was obviously a qualified cooper, otherwise he wouldn't be doing the job.

"Sylvia, good to see you. It's been a while."

"I have been busy."

"It seems to be like that for healers these days. And Rawk! I didn't think to ever see you here. What can I do for you?"

Now that he was here, Rawk was wondering if it was really a good idea.

"Come on, out with it then. You're here now."

Rawk grunted. He chewed his bottom lip. He cleared his throat. "I was being followed someone from the newspaper a while ago, when the exots first started coming."

For a moment, Thacker said nothing. Then he nodded. "Jargo. He hasn't been seen for quite a while."

Rawk looked at his hands. "He's dead."

Thacker straightened some papers on his desk. He nodded slowly. "How do you know this?"

"I saw him die."

Thacker didn't say anything.

"I was fighting a duen." Rawk looked at Sylvia. "I slipped and Jargo saved me. He attacked the duen with a dagger. He gave me time to get on my feet again."

"He saved you?"

Rawk nodded. "I slipped."

"I will need to tell his wife."

"He was married?"

"Has a young daughter, too. She's barely two years old, I think."

"Why would he risk his life? The duen was twice his size. More. It was crazy." Rawk's hand was gripping the hilt of *Dabaneera* so tightly it hurt. He wanted to go back and change what had happened, but it was the sword that had caused all the problems in the first place. If he hadn't gone out into the forest looking for the duen...

"Do you want to see Biki?"

"What?"

"Do you want to talk to Jargo's wife?"

"No." He shook his head. "Path, no."

"Very well. So, is there anything else I can do for you?" He divided his glance between Rawk and Sylvia. "I have to say, I never thought I'd see you two in the same room."

Rawk didn't really want to talk about it. "You know who she is?"

"Of course. I know who everyone is. And I would've thought after the last couple of days that Sylvia would be keeping a low profile."

"Why? What's happened?"

"Sorcerers dying everywhere."

Rawk shared a glance with Sylvia. The elf shrugged. "Who?"

"Well, there was Valo yesterday morning."

"That was a heart attack," Rawk said. "That hardly counts."

"I'll let him know next time I see him. And last night, Mistletowe Oc died in slightly more unusual circumstances."

"Mistletowe died?"

"Died. Was killed. It's a fine line in the end, but a very distinct line none—the—less." Thacker checked a sheet of paper on his desk. "She was found in an alley down near the harbor with her heart in her hand and no injuries."

Rawk grunted. "Apart from the hole in her chest, you mean."

"No. There were *no* injuries."

"Then how do you know it was *her* heart?"

"I had a surgeon cut her open, obviously."

"And she had no heart?"

"Apart from the one in her hand."

"So..."

Thacker shrugged. "Magic is the only explanation I can think of." He glanced at Sylvia.

Sylvia was looking pale. "It is possible," she said, "but it would take tremendous power. And precision."

Rawk sighed. "Either way, we've lost that lead."

"We cannot..." Sylvia was getting paler by the moment.

"There's someone with a lot of power against us so we quit? Surely that's the reason why we have to continue."

"Continue what?" Thacker said. "What lead?"

Sylvia nodded. "Rawk has convinced me to assist him in finding out who is opening portals to let the exots through."

"Who says someone is doing that?"

"A sorcerer that Rawk knows."

Thacker grunted. "How can I help? A Path-knows—what appeared out west the other day and ran riot for a while. Of course there were no Heroes anywhere about so five good dwarves died."

"Some dwarves working on the sewers died Tewsday as well. A work gang killed the exot and I told the boss I'd get the claim to him."

"I heard that. I know the men who died, so if you get the money to me I'll see that their families get it."

"Thank you. I'll organize it." Rawk cleared his throat and pulled out the sheet of paper from Valo's house. "Well, if you know who everyone is..." He blinked for a moment until his eyes adjusted, then started reading out the names.

Thacker nodded his way through the whole list. "Masten Mad is the name being used by someone called Layla Pro. Up until couple of days ago she was staying in at the *Hen Peck*."

"Was?"

"Yes. She moves fairly regularly and it sometimes takes a few days to find her again. And Shef Leeker is calling himself Hagen something, or something Hagen, and living on the *Deep Green Harpy*. I think he and the captain have got something going on."

"The *Harpy* still has a captain?"

"It's got to have a captain if it's registered and it's got to be registered to be berthed."

"But why?" Rawk hated ships. He couldn't imagine choosing to live on one.

"Berthing for a ship is cheaper than rent for a house. And the *Harpy* is quite a bit larger than a lot of houses." Thacker pointed at Rawk's sheet of paper. "Of the others, I know Balen is over in the west of the city somewhere but he's careful. I don't know any of the others."

Sylvia shook her head. "I would much rather talk to Shef than Balen anyway."

Rawk shrugged.

Thacker straightened some more papers. "So, is there anything else I can help you with?"

"No. Well..."

"What?"

"I need some stairs built at the *Hero's Rest.* And the quicker the better."

"*You* need them built?"

Rawk looked at Sylvia. "Yes. I do. I own the *Rest.*"

Thacker gave a grunt and pulled on his beard. "Well, I didn't know *that.*"

"Only a handful of people do, and I'd like to keep it that way."

"Of course. Where do these stair need to go? Won't be easy if you want them to match the rest of the building."

"To the basement, direct from the outside."

"Oh. Right. That might not be *too* bad."

"Good. Can you send someone around to talk to Travis?"

"I can't send anyone; I don't own any businesses, I just try to keep everything running smoothly. I'll talk to few masons and see if they'll go and give you a quote."

"Don't worry about that. Just send the best around and if they rip me off they'll never work in Katamood again. Not north of the river, anyway."

"All right then. I'll see if Gabbo's available."

"Thank you."

"There is one more thing," Sylvia said.

"Yes?"

"I have read the stories about Rawk in the newspapers. And I have seen the pictures."

"Are you checking up on me?" Rawk said with a smile.

Sylvia ignored him. "I would like to make sure that I am not mentioned. I am taking a risk as it is, just being near Rawk, but wearing a scarf will not help if my name is mentioned. And the scarf may not help if there is a picture and Weaver is paying attention."

Thacker nodded. "I think we can manage something." He glanced at Rawk and cleared his throat. "I'm heading down to the newspaper offices now. You can come and talk to them with me as well, if you want. It's just a couple of buildings down."

Sylvia nodded. "Thank you."

"I'd like it if they didn't have those pictures of me, too. They make me very uncomfortable."

"I think I can get them to stop with Sylvia, but it isn't going to happen for you."

"Why not?"

"You sell advertising, Rawk."

"No, I don't. I'm not a salesman." He wasn't sure if he even knew what advertising was, in this instance.

"No... If they have a picture of you they can put an advertisement next to it and charge twice as much as usual."

Rawk had no idea what the dwarf was talking about.

They walked to the newspaper office and Rawk could hear it before they made it inside. He stopped in the doorway and stared. The room was huge, almost the size of the main hall at the Veteran's Club, and it was buzzing with activity. There were about two dozen people— dwarves and elves, mainly, but a couple of other races as well— and they all seemed to be involved in what must be the most important activities in the world. Everyone seemed to be having three conversations at once but it was doubtful if any of them could be heard over the rattle and clank of machinery.

"It's done with machines?"

"Of course. Did you think they wrote them out?"

Rawk quickly looked back at the machine. "Of course not."

Thacker pointed and gave a quick explanation of the printing press. Raw was rather pleased that he managed to understand most of it.

"And the pictures?"

"Photographs? Well, I'm afraid I don't know much at all about them. There's a bright light and chemicals..."

"A bright light? And a popping sound?"

"Yeah, that's right."

"I've been wandering what that was. I thought it was magic."

Thacker laughed. "Well, now you know. You'll have to make sure you do your hair every morning."

Rawk grunted and ran his hand over his bald head. "How do you pay for it all?"

"Taxes."

"Weaver pays for it?"

Thacker pursed his lips. "He's your friend, isn't he?"

"Yes."

"Then yes, I guess he does. Very nice of him. They are trying to make it self sufficient though."

"So Weaver doesn't know he's paying?"

"Not exactly. We haven't yet worked out a way to convince him that it was his idea."

"Pardon?"

"Weaver won't listen to anyone else's ideas, so you have to make him think everything is his idea. It took us about two years of hints and nudging before Weaver came to us with the idea for the sewers."

"That was your idea?"

"Of course."

"What about the canal? He never stops telling me how he had to convince you the idea would work."

Thacker laughed. "I'm pretty sure he still doesn't understand the details. Now if we can just get him to come up with the idea for public housing we'll end these riots."

"I thought the riots were about the exots."

"What? No. That would be like rioting to stop the wind from blowing; it's just nature." He paused for a moment. "Well, we thought it was. Either way, we can do something about the exots, even if Weaver doesn't help.

But we had to knock down a few hundred houses to make the canal; the owners were supposed to be compensated but they are only the lesser races, after all."

"Why didn't you just go around the city?"

Thacker shrugged. "We wanted to but the ground south of the mountain is basically sand. We could do it, but there is no way Weaver would want to pay for it. Even with special accounting practices."

Rawk raised an eyebrow.

"We over budgeted the canal by a few hundred thousand ithel so we have the money waiting for the housing, we just need to get some land. And to do that, we need Weaver's approval. Biki is one of those who is currently homeless."

"The reporter's wife?"

"Yes. She and her daughter are staying with the newspaper's editor at the moment, but I'm not sure how long that will last."

Rawk had no idea what an editor was, but he smiled. "I have a place on Terring Road she can have." He saw the look on the dwarf's face and held up a hand. "It isn't charity; she can just pay what she can for now and we'll work it out later."

"I'm not sure."

"Well, ask her, and if she wants she can go up and talk to Travis and he can organize for her to have a look."

"You can ask her yourself. That's her over there."

Rawk turned so quickly he stumbled and hurt his leg. There was a young dwife sweeping the floor between two huge, noisy machines. While she worked, she was keeping an eye on a small girl who was playing in the corner. "That's her? She works here?"

"She didn't use to. She's normally a cook, but the tavern she worked in got knocked down as well."

Rawk nodded and swallowed. He almost stayed where he was but Sylvia and Thacker had suddenly wandered away so he was on his own and looking sillier by the moment. With a quick look around, Rawk hurried across the room. Then he was standing behind Biki and still didn't know what to say. He would have stood there until he looked silly again, but Biki saved him the wait by poking him in stomach with the end of her broom as she continued to sweep.

Rawk grunted in pain and surprise and Biki spun around.

"I'm sorry. I didn't see you there."

Rawk held up his hand as he hunched over and tried to get in a decent breath. "That's all right."

"Perhaps you should sit down."

He did the opposite and stood up straighter with a deep breath. "No. Don't worry."

"Rawk?" she said, finally recognizing him.

"Yes."

"What are you doing here?"

Rawk looked around. What was he doing here? "I..." He cleared his throat and looked down at his hands. "I knew your husband."

She looked down as well, then across at where her daughter played with a ball. "You knew Jargo?"

"Yes."

There was a moment of awkward silence. It was obviously the time when Rawk was supposed to say *how* he knew Jargo. He cleared his throat. "He... I was being attacked, out in the Old Forest. He saved me. He came out of nowhere and distracted the exot."

There was silence again. When Rawk looked up, Biki was crying. The little girl came across and wrapped her arms around her mother's legs, understanding that something was wrong, though she didn't know what, exactly. Biki held her daughter. "Where is he?"

"Nobody else knows any of this. I told Weaver there were no exots out there..."

Biki nodded. "I understand."

"We buried Jargo in the forest. Galad is there too. We— Fabi and I— were injured. We had no way of getting them back."

She swallowed. Nodded. "Can you take me?"

"I..." He was going to say no, but he should never have looked at her face. "Not now. It takes a while to get there."

"Tomorrow?"

Rawk looked across at Sylvia. He wanted to find who was opening the portals, but after losing Maris, even if he was about to end the relationship, he didn't think he could deny Biki. "Yes, I'll take you tomorrow. Come to the *Hero's Rest* early in the morning."

"What is happening?" Sylvia asked.

Rawk jumped. "Don't sneak up on me."

"I surprised the great warrior?"

"Biki and I were talking."

"Rawk is going to take me to where Jargo is buried."

Sylvia raised an eyebrow. "He is?"

Biki nodded and Rawk sighed. "You might like to come too, Sylvia."

"I do not think..."

Rawk was looking at her. "Yes, I think I will." Rawk nodded to Biki then headed for the door. "But first, we have to visit Shef."

"We are not really going to find Shef now, are we?" Sylvia said once they extracted themselves from the newspaper offices.

"Of course we are. Should we wait until someone else dies?"

"We should take a moment to make a plan."

The *Deep Green Harpy* was legend in Katamood. It was a ship that had been tied to a dock on the Bay of Kata, just south of the river, for just about as long as anyone could remember. It was probably joined to the dock by several colonies of limpets by now. It probably wouldn't take long to walk if there was a tunnel out that side of the mountain. He asked Sylvia if they needed to catch a tram but she didn't answer.

"Did you not hear me? We need a plan."

"What are you worried about? Shef is better than Valo, but he's no match for you."

"And Mistletowe is no match for you. All it takes is one warrior lurking around the corner."

"Well, if you're handling the magic side of things I can take care of any lurkers."

Seeing Sylvia wouldn't tell him, Rawk came to a decision on his own and started walking east. He dodged a tram and a wagon, tried to ignore the dwarves. They seemed much more relaxed here and, he had to admit, they didn't smell nearly as much as the ones he was used to.

The tunnel out of the valley wasn't hard to find. It was narrower than the last one and wove a lazy course through the stone. There were dwarves there, but they all stepped aside to let him pass.

At the far end, Rawk found himself in a small park with flowering trees and paths that wove much like the tunnel had. He tried to get his bearings but that was difficult seeing he'd only once been further south than Sylvia's shop, and that was just the previous day. And before he'd started going to the shop he'd barely been away from the edge of the river. But it couldn't be *that* hard. All the had to do was head down hill until he could see the bay. Easy.

He started walking.

Sylvia reluctantly followed as she rewrapped her scarf. "I am the one who will probably die, you know."

"Yes, but I promise to avenge you swiftly. I'll tell stories about you. Kids love a tragic death to get the Hero all emotional."

"You would get emotional if I died?"

"Of course not." He smiled. "But most of the stories I tell are half made up anyway, otherwise they be so boring nobody would want to listed. 'How did you kill the makajeet, Rawk?' 'Well, I snuck into its cave when it was sleeping and stabbed it.' Nobody wants to hear that."

"The makajeet? I have heard that story. Is there not something about a mountain of skulls and a pit lined with spikes?"

"And there *were* skulls. About five of them. I think they were from rabbits. Or squirrels. Three or four of them might have been mice. They were damn big mice though." He held his fingers a couple of inches apart.

"Well, that is practically a rat."

"I know." Rawk laughed. "I didn't know you had a sense of humor, Sylvia."

Sylvia shook her head. "Perhaps I only acquired it after you stopped trying to kill me."

"You know I was joking with the whole stabby sword thing, right?"

"I must have missed that bit."

"See, if you'd had a sense of humor back then you would've know."

His view of the bay didn't arrive until he was halfway down the hill, but Rawk was pleased to see that he was heading in the right direction. He could see a ship entering the mouth of the river, doing some of the strange, arcane things that ships did when sailing into the wind. He could also see some of the docks and what could only be a small corner of Fek Bazaar, which was as good a landmark as any.

—O—

Some people claimed the bazaar was the largest market anywhere in the world and Rawk had never seen anything to make him disagree. It was a sprawling, twisting maze of a place that seemed to be never ending. Daza Parade ran more than a mile down the middle and the entire length of it was filled with four rows of canvas stalls and pavilions that, as far as Rawk could tell, had been there as long as the buildings along the sides. There were dozens of side streets filled to overflowing with goods from around the world. He heard a dozen languages in the first five minutes. The scent of spices striped the air as he walked; sweet, bitter, sharp; hiding the stench of people.

Rawk picked his way through the crowd. He avoided eye contact, but still seemed to shake every second hand and wave to everyone else. There were some children trailing along not far behind and it was only a matter of time until...

"Rawk," a girl tugged on his arm, "tell us a story."

"I can't right now, sorry."

"Oh." The look on her face made Rawk feel as if he snapped her pet stick and thrown it on the fire.

"Sorry." He shoved a coin in her had and kept going, past Thif's Well and up the gentle slope to a run down tavern called *Happy John's*. A fight spilled out onto the street, two men rolling, arms wrapped about each other, too drunk to do anything that required coordination. Rawk danced around the commotion and slipped through the gathering crowd. Sylvia complained about humans as they started down the far side. But a moment later she came to a sudden stop and fell silent mid–sentence. She had her hand on his arm and he could feel the tension in her grip.

"What is it?"

"A portal just opened."

"Where is it?"

"Close." She looked around and a moment later a dozen creatures, like two–foot high, feathered monkeys dashed from an alley in pursuit of a terrified dog. The dog continued down the street, ears back, tail low, but the creatures stopped. They looked around, chattering amongst themselves. The crowd backed away, clearing a space around them. Then, as one, the monkeys seemed to pick the weakest target. The young elf boy, basket of fruit in his hand, didn't stand a chance.

Rawk swore. He drew *Dabaneera* and charged forward, cursing his knee and the fleeing people, but had barely halved the distance when the boy was torn to shreds.

Sylvia could have done something, Rawk thought as he let out a battle cry.

Dabaneera cut through the rear-most monkey and it fell without a sound. Or maybe it just couldn't be heard above the boy's agonized screams. Rawk laid about him, sending arcs of blood. His shoulder ached from his wound. His knee throbbed but he barely noticed until he had dispatched four of the creatures.

After that the others finally noticed they were under attack and turned their attention to him. The biggest one stooped down to collect an apple from the basket the boy had dropped. It took a bite and Rawk thought he could hear the crunch, even through the noise of the panicked crowd. It was then that he realized the exots were all wearing belts. They were armed. Rawk took a step back as each drew a short, curved dagger and stalked towards him. Apple smiled a wicked smile and tossed the fruit aside dismissively.

"Path." Rawk looked around. "A little help, Sylvia." He didn't care who helped, really.

Sylvia looked like she didn't want to help at all.

The boy still screamed. At least he was still alive, and that was probably a good thing. The noise was annoying though, like a mosquito in the dark, gnawing at the edges of Rawk's consciousness. He shifted his grip on the hilt of his sword. The remaining creatures were encircling him but he kept his eyes on Apple. That one seemed the most theatrical so it might well be the leader. It was also on the opposite side to Sylvia, and hopefully she was working on some magic that would protect his back.

A monkey on his left attacked. Rawk swung *Dabaneera* in the general direction, but knew he was just being tested. He didn't turn away from the leader.

Then there was a clatter behind him. Rawk almost turned to look, but a monkey started to scream a horrible, soul—tearing scream, then another joined it. So he managed to keep his eyes forward and attacked the closest monkey. He swatted away one riposte, and killed the monkey with a back handed flick of his sword. Then he stabbed another and barely avoided a wild slash from Apple. The exot screeched at him, showing long, yellow teeth. Rawk turned aside for a moment to cut down an opponent on his flank then was facing Apple again.

"Come on, you little bastard."

If the creature understood him, it gave no indication. So Rawk stepped in and to the left. He simultaneously swung his sword wide to attack from the right. And Apple died with a gurgle and a hiss of disbelief.

The crowd cheered, emerging from cover, closing in again.

Rawk took that as a sign that the danger had passed. He spun slowly but still managed to hurt his knee and discovered that all the monkeys were dead. The four he had not accounted for were not much more than piles of blackened, smoldering feathers that weren't going to be attacking anyone. He drew in a shuddering breath and noticed the stench for the first time.

"Thank you, Sylvia. Your magic is as effective as ever."

But the sorceress didn't pay any attention. She rushed to the elf boy to see if she could help. He had fallen silent, so Rawk didn't like the chances. Watching, he sheathed *Dabaneera* and rubbed his knee. Neither made him feel better. He glanced around but could see no danger. Apart from the crowd. They were closing in. Those at the front were trying to hold their ground, but they were being pushed ever closer.

"I cannot help him," Sylvia said. She rested the boy's head gently on the ancient cobbles. "It is amazing he lived as long as he did."

"Path, damn it." He seemed to be failing a lot recently, even when he won.

"Indeed."

The best way to help was to stop the exots from coming. "Come on then. We have things to do."

"We are going to just leave him?"

"Are you going to fill in Weaver's forms?"

Sylvia followed as he pushed his way though the crowd. He limped down the hill towards the bay.

"Is your knee all right?"

"I twisted it a bit."

"You seem to do that a lot."

"You seem to ask questions a lot."

"It is how I find things out."

Rawk grunted and quickened the pace, just to prove he could. It hurt.

–O–

The *Harpy* was berthed close to the point where river and bay met, almost in the shadow of the southern river fort. It would have been a prime position if not for the unpredictable, tumultuous nature of the water there. The pewter and whitecaps of the bay met the muddy churn of the river and anything could happen.

The suburb around there was about the same. The locals clashed with those who came off the ships and East Corner was the place where trouble was likely to start. It was where the first seed of Katamood had been sewn thousands of years ago and it showed. The buildings that were in one piece looked like they wouldn't be for much longer. There was hardly a patch of white plaster to be seen between the dark wooden frames.

"We are just going to walk in there?" Sylvia asked.

"No. We're going to knock."

"We are going to knock?"

"The doors on those ships are a lot tougher than they look, you know— they have to be to stand a life at sea— and it isn't really worth the effort of breaking them down when somebody will normally open up if you just knock."

Sylvia leaned to look out through the door of the bakery where they'd been lingering for the past five minutes. "Perhaps nobody is home."

"There's only one way to find out."

"Actually, there are several ways."

"There are?"

"We can wait for dark and see if a light comes on."

Rawk raised an eyebrow though it was obvious that Sylvia realized the suggestion was ridiculous.

"We can send someone else to knock." But that wasn't much better.

"And if someone answers the door, what then? We fire a flaming arrow at the ship so they all come to us?"

"If we are going to do that we can just skip the knocking bit all together." Sylvia winced. "Do you even have a bow?"

"Come on." Rawk paid for an apple–and–cream pastry and ate as he crossed the busy street to the wharves.

And the wharves were even busier. There was hardly room to move. Dwarves were everywhere. They strained under the weight of goods from a dozen countries. Boxes, rolls, sacks and packages went from wagons to ships or back the other way. Gangplanks rattled and flexed as workers came and went. Cranes creaked as they swung bulging nets out over the decks and lowered cargo directly into holds. Everything was covered by the scent of fish and salt and rotting seaweed. It was a riot of noise and smells and other worlds but it all seemed to work like clockwork. Seeing dwarves were involved Rawk imagine that they got together each morning to choreograph each move for the day so that nothing would go wrong.

Then he walked in and the first thing he did was bump into someone. The dwarf dropped the barrel he was carrying on his shoulder. It thudded onto the ancient timber but stayed intact.

The dwarf looked up. "Watch it there..." He suddenly bowed and tipped his hat. "Sorry, sir. Didn't see you there. You're all right, are you? Didn't drop it on your foot?"

The barrel had gone nowhere near his foot and it had most definitely been Rawk's fault. Before he had a chance to say as much the dwarf had hauled the barrel back onto his shoulder and been whisked away by the press of people. After a moment he was lost amidst a confusion of dwarves and humans, all lugging barrels and boxes and sacks as quickly as they could.

Pushing on through the crowd as well, Rawk angled towards the *Deep Green Harpy*. The ship looked worse close up. It appeared to be more tar than timber. The main mast was gone, replaced by a sad looking tree that might once have bourn some type of fruit. And a clothesline dominated the forecastle. The gangplank looked like it would break at any moment.

Rawk hurried up then paused to look around. Most of the deck was covered with raised gardens. Vegetables grew in neat rows. A puddle of water was spreading away from a bucket like blood away from a corpse. He checked to make sure Sylvia was still with him and hadn't been the straw that broke the gangplank's back.

"Are you ready."

"Last I knew, Shef was quite a capable sorcerer, Rawk. We cannot just walk into something like this with no preparation."

"Well what have you been doing? It's taken a while to walk here."

"Rawk."

"People could be dying right now, because of this bastard. Do you really want to go and have some wine while we give it some thought? Anyone would think you were scared." He made his way to the forecastle, took a deep breath and knocked. If Sylvia wasn't ready then there was going to be trouble.

A woman answered the door. She was bigger than Rawk, with a tussock of black hair on her head and a bleary look in her eyes.

"Sorry," Rawk said, smiling. "Did I wake you?"

The woman rubbed at her face with a big, meaty hand. "No, I was just..." She motioned vaguely over her shoulder.

"Of course. Are you the Captain?"

"Yes. What do you want?"

"Well, Captain, I was wondering if Hagen was home?"

"Do I know you?"

Rawk was stunned for a moment. Everyone knew him. He thought quickly. "Maybe. I used to collect taxes for Thacker. But I... we—" He motioned to Sylvia— "actually do a bit of work with Hagen now."

The woman looked over Rawk's shoulder and gave Sylvia a nod of greeting. "What's your name?"

Rawk thought of some of the names on the list. He ruled out those that had been regulars in Katamood before Weaver changed the rules. "Trog." He winced.

"You don't look like a Habonese."

"Only on my mother's side. My father was a horse."

"A horse?"

"No, a pig. That's it. That's what my mother said." He smiled. "I knew it was some type of farm animal. And this is Freanna."

Another nod. "I suppose you'd better come in then. I'll get Hagen."

Inside was a huge kitchen and dining room. A pot simmered on the stove as thin fingers of smoke searched for the chimney. The table was laden with a mountain of chopped vegetables that Kalesie would have been proud of. It smelled much better inside than it did out.

The port wall was lined with a long bookcase. It curved to follow the wall and each shelf bowed as well as they struggled to hold the weight of the books. An ornate, carved handrail protected a set of stairs that gave access to the deck below.

The Captain went down quickly, ducking her head to avoid being knocked out.

Rawk looked at Sylvia. "Are you ready?" he whispered.

"Ready for what?"

"I don't know."

"That is the point, is it not? We do not know what we have to be ready for. You barge in here without a plan and expect me to save you."

"Yes, but..."

"I cannot just cast a spell in a second if..." Sylvia said, a bit too loudly. She tried to calm herself down, taking a deep breath and smoothing the front of her dress. "It takes time. And first I have to work out what he is doing."

"Just get to him first."

"Rawk, you really have no idea, do you?"

Rawk realized he didn't know any details about how magic worked. It just did, and that was normally a bad thing for him. His thoughts were interrupted by the sound of footsteps on the stairs. Magic might be a bad thing again very soon. He took a deep breath and moved closer to be bookshelves, hoping to stay out of sight, for a moment at least.

Shef came up the stairs. He paused for a moment when he saw Sylvia, then kept coming.

Rawk was an idiot. He knew he didn't have any control at all over the situation and wished he had listened to Sylvia. It was too late now though. He moved quickly along the side of the stairs. Shef was still looking at Sylvia.

"Silver Lark," he said. "I'm not sure who I expected, but it certainly wasn't you."

Sylvia swallowed. "Can I not drop in on old friend?"

"Of course. Give me some names and I'll see if I can point you in their direction."

Rawk drew *Dabaneera* as he crossed the last few paces. Shef heard and turned to look, but was too late. Rawk rounded the end of the stairs a moment later and had the point of his sword pricking the flesh just below the other man's rib cage. Then he saw the Captain coming up the stairs as well. He was too late to do anything more than shrug his shoulder into the cudgel blow and go back the way he'd come.

Shef smiled. "Ah, yes. That's more like who I was expecting." He was already weaving his hands. He started to mumble under his breath.

Rawk cursed and tried to shake some feeling back into his arm. The Captain followed, closing the gap while Rawk was still caught between the books and the railing. The shelves were going to hamper his sword arm more than the blow. He paused to meet the first attack and *Dabaneera* got stuck in the soft timber of the cudgel. He disarmed the woman when she ripped the sword from his hand and threw the cudgel away with it. And she came in harder.

But some of her advantage had been lost. The closeness of the books restricted her as much as him, now that the weapons were gone.

He blocked a punch. Didn't see a kick and wondered if his shin was broken. But he backed away a step without incident. He took another kick on his shin, deliberately this time, and pressed forward. Three punches, all to no avail, as expected, then he slipped a blow past the Captain's guard, rocked her back. And he kept at it, keeping her busy while he looked for an opening. She backed away this time, blood trickling from her nose, eye already blackening. An opening came, then was gone while Rawk still considered it. She got in a kick that normally wouldn't have worried him, but it was his bad knee and he almost fell at the unexpected pain.

To top it all off, Rawk stepped on the discarded cudgel. He almost sliced the end off his boot on his own sword, still stuck in the timber. He stumbled and the Captain was on him in an instant. A kick that winded him. A blow that left his ears ringing. Another that knocked him sideways. He fell against the shelf, eye to eye with a big, leather bound volume. Rawk pulled the book from the shelf and use it to slap aside a punch that would have knocked him out into the bay. He swung again and heard bones break. And again. He hit the Captain across the side of the head and she fell to the floor. Rawk almost hit her again, but her eyes were rolled back and her mouth was hanging open. He looked at the book. He blinked and it was even harder than usual to get his eyes to focus. *Seven Matters of Land and Claim.*

He grunted. "That would put me to sleep, too."

Then he remembered Sylvia battling against Shef and turned to see what was happening. There wasn't much at all happening, as far as Rawk could tell. There was no lightning or thunder. There were no fireballs, which was probably a good thing seeing they were on a ship that had been liberally covered with tar. The two of them were staring at each other, hands raised, whole bodies tense.

"You wouldn't do it," Shef said softly. Rawk could see a bead of sweat slowly trickling down across the other man's forehead. "I don't think you can cast a *kincarch*."

"Well, continue chanting your *zaniel* and we will both see if I can still do it," Sylvia said. "Or let your spell go and sense for yourself."

Shef mumbled something and moved his hands a fraction.

Sylvia raised an eyebrow. That was the only part of her that moved.

Shef faltered.

Sylvia looked cool and calm. He hands were as still as stone. "Do not try me, Shef. I am *really* not in the mood."

Rawk wasn't sure if he should intervene, but was worried that Sylvia might have to kill the other sorcerer.

And if anyone did that, he wanted to be the one. So he carefully pulled a dagger from his belt. He walked slowly forward, but the room was constantly moving and creaking anyway, and Shef was concentrating so hard that it was unlikely he would have heard a stampede of uliphants.

"What if I do stop? I may trust your word, but not—"

He started to turn and Rawk dashed across the remaining space. He threw the sorcerer onto the deck, thumping him onto the carpet hard enough to rattle cups on the table, and pressed the razor–sharp edge of the dagger down into his throat. "You don't trust me, Shef? You've hurt my feelings." Rawk held onto his rage. He wanted to kill the man, then and there, but information was more important than revenge.

Shef swallowed noisily. "I didn't mean to." He could barely do more than whisper as he tried to see the blade against his throat. "It's just that last time..."

"Yes, I know. Last time we met I tried to kill you." He grabbed Shef by the collar and hauled him to his feet. Then he found a chair and put him in it none to gently. "But look at Silver Lark. She's proof that I can be in the same room as a sorcerer and not kill them." Shef's back was to her, so looking wasn't an easy thing.

"You killed Valo."

Rawk sighed. "I did not. I was there, but he died all by himself."

"I don't believe you. And what about Mistletowe?"

"Well, *that* obviously wasn't me, was it? Do you think I can remove someone's heart without leaving a wound in one of the usual spots? You'll have to talk to Sylvia if you want to know about Mistletowe." Rawk smiled as the other man glanced over his shoulder at Sylvia and completely failed to hide the look of awe that crossed his face.

"*Fiddernich?*" Shef said.

"You've never told me what the *kincarch* actually does, Silver Lark? Is it worse than what you did to Mistletowe?"

"That depends on how you like your steak, Rawk."

Rawk had no idea what that meant, but Shef obviously did. The awe quickly disappeared to be replaced by terror. "I don't really know anything."

"You don't know anything?"

He shook his head. "I get a note with an address and a time on it. I go there and cast a spell, then leave. It's a different address every time." He looked from Rawk to Sylvia and back again. "That's all I know."

"There are others there?" asked Sylvia.

"No. Yes. Of course, yes. Frixen, Valo and Mistletowe."

"That's all?"

"There are others, but everyone stays hidden."

"Then how do you know about the other three?"

"They're locals, too. We've known each other for years. So I went and found them after I recognized their signatures at the first casting."

"And you don't know any of the others?"

"No. Frixen did though. He knew some."

Rawk pulled the spell paper from the pouch on his belt and held it out.

Shef took it nervously and started to read. He was sweating again. "Where did you get this?"

"Frixen gave it to me."

"No, he didn't."

Rawk shrugged. "Then I just found it lying around in the street. Now, which do you think is more likely? And why do you think Frixen's alive when Valo isn't?"

Shef put the paper on the table and pushed it away, as if he didn't even want to be near it. "Well, if you have Frixen then you don't need me. I can't tell you anything."

Rawk cursed himself silently. That hadn't gone to plan. "Frixen might have passed on some information, but that doesn't mean I trust him. And you might want to consider the fact that Valo *didn't* help at all."

Shef shook his head.

"Do we have any more use for him then, Silver Lark? Do you want to just *kincard* him now?"

"*Kincarch*, Rawk. How many time do I have to use the spell before you get the name right?"

Rawk shrugged and looked at Shef. "At least once more I'd say. What do you think, Shef?"

Weaver's freshly starched white sheets had nothing on Shef; he looked like he was about to pass out. "Look, there's a woman, her magic sounds like an elf, and she was missing an arm, I think."

"Did Frixen name her on the list?"

A shake of the head, but Rawk wasn't interested. He could see Sylvia's face and it was obvious she knew he who he was talking about. And she wasn't very happy about it.

"Did you get a note today?" Rawk asked. "An address and time?"

"No. Not today."

"Right."

"Thank you, Shef. That will be all." Sylvia started to leave.

"That's it?"

"Yes."

"You aren't going to... Wait, if you were holding an *kincarch*, how did you know I was holding a *zaniel*?"

"Do you really think I would cast a *kincarch* or a *fiddernich*? I am not that type of person, Shef."

"Then I will kill you."

"So you want me to kill him?" Rawk smiled. "He killed Maris, so he probably deserves to be turned into an overdone steak, but I will gladly run him through." He'd never really killed anyone in cold blood before, but he found that he was looking forward to it.

Sylvia laughed. "No, Rawk. Just leave him."

Rawk looked from Sylvia to Shef and back again. He was pretty sure Shef wasn't just going to forget the whole thing had happened. "It's all right for you; you can protect yourself with magic. He needs to die, to protect us, but I think I would like to do it slowly. We don't have any other business today, do we?"

"Don't worry, Rawk. Shef won't bother us."

"He won't?"

"I won't?"

"That's right, because in a minute or two, Shef is going to start thinking."

"Right."

"And he is going to quickly start to wonder who *did* cast a *fiddernich* on Mistletowe, if it wasn't me."

Rawk smiled a cold smile. This explanation was sounding good so far.

"And then he's going to wonder if Mistletowe deserved such a fate. He's going to wonder what she did. Or who she talked to."

Rawk wasn't sure he understood the finer points of the discussion, but he trusted Sylvia. "I can save you the wondering, Shef; Mistletowe talked to me. She was dead just a couple of hours later."

Shef swallowed as if he had an entire apple stuck in his throat.

Rawk clapped him on the knee. "I'm glad we cleared that up for you." He gave a satisfied grunt, as if everything was sorted, and rose to his feet. "I'm hungry, Silver Lark. Let's go get something to eat."

"What do you want?"

"Steak?"

Out on the deck, Rawk checked over his shoulder to make sure nobody was listening. "What was that all about?" he muttered. Sylvia might have been sure they were safe, but Rawk picked up the pace to try to get as far away as possible without looking like he was running.

"That many sorcerers working in unison probably need a *Hadir*, a heart. Someone at the center controlling everything. It will normally be the most powerful of them all. That is who Shef is now worried about. He will probably be trying to work out if The *Deep Green Harpy* is still sea worthy in about two minutes."

"It isn't. Even I can tell that."

Sylvia gave him a look, which was impressive with the pace they were going through the still thick crowd. The day was drawing to a close, fingers of darkness reaching out from the buildings, but that didn't seem to slow the pace of the docks. One of lamp−lighting dwarves was teetering down the street on his stilts like a stick insect.

"So, you aren't scared of this *Hadir*?"

"Petrified, Rawk."

"You don't look it."

"I am an elf."

"Right. And what about this one−armed elf?"

"Falling Leaves."

"Really? Falling Leaves?"

"You know her?"

"Of course not. I just can't believe the names you lot come up with."

Sylvia gave an exasperated sigh.

"Do you know where we'll find her?"

"Well, I can narrow it down to one of the several dozen brothels in the city."

"You don't even know if it will be a high class brothel or a dive?"

"No. It completely depends on her mood. And it could well be several in one night."

"Wouldn't it be easier to follow Shef?"

"Perhaps, if we had done that before barging in and threatening him. But now he will either be especially careful about being followed, or he will be dead. Either way, the chances of success are greatly reduced." He'd better get started then."

"Well..." If he had stopped to think for a moment, or even just to listen to someone else who was thinking things might have been different. "I guess we'd start looking for Falling Leaves then."

Sylvia gave him another look. "I told you before, I have appointments."

"Then I'll find her myself. Or I'll go find Balen." Though finding a one-armed elf woman probably wouldn't be any harder, even if he didn't know what she actually looked like.

"Balen is stronger than both Shef and Falling Leaves. Surprising him will not be easy."

"So?"

"So, tomorrow we find Leaves, skulk in the shadows and follow where she leads."

"We can't. We're going into the forest tomorrow."

"All the more reason for you to rest now."

"I don't need to rest." It was the last thing he needed. If he wasn't going to go around killing sorcerers or exots, then he wanted to have sex. Sex with someone he didn't know. Sex with someone who wouldn't be there in the morning. Sex with someone who wouldn't talk to him and wouldn't ask questions. He wanted to empty his mind.

Sylvia laid a hand on his arm. "Go home and sleep. I'll come to the *Rest* in the morning so we can visit Jargo's grave."

Rawk considered doing as Sylvia suggested. For a moment. Then, after she had hurried away into the Bazaar, he went to find something to kill. But, of course, there were exots appearing in the city everywhere, except when he wanted one.

He roamed the city for two hours, stalking down alleys and s low, limping manner, looking in the dark corners, as if that was where the creatures were more likely to appear when there was no information to suggest that was the case.

And as the evening wore on, his travels took him to the Veteran's Club. It was still too early for Celeste and Grint to be playing, so he went to the refectory and lined up to collect some stew, though he really didn't know if he wanted to eat. He ignored the cutlery that was available and looked around, trying to find a vacant table. There weren't any, of course, but a Hero at a table waved him over.

"Hello, Frew," Rawk said as he approached. "I didn't know you were in town."

Frew was a little man with big lips and even bigger hair. "Everyone is in town," he said. He gestured to the four others at the table. "Do you know anyone else?"

Rawk looked around as he sat down and pulled his bone handled knife and fork from the pouch on his belt. He shook his head.

"Han, Otho, Milk and Kreer. And I believe we all have you to thank for our current employment," Frew said after taking a long drink of ale.

"Pardon?"

"We are all getting paid to stand on corners waiting for exots instead of sitting in taverns waiting for exots."

As usual, Travis hadn't wasted any time. "Yes, that's me. I'm not guaranteeing how long it will last, so get the claims while you can."

"Two today for me," said Milk, a big, contrarily dark man with one ear said. "Nice and easy, too."

"Are there more of you?"

Frew nodded. "Another six or seven, I think." He started to rattle off some names, but Rawk only knew one of them.

"Good. Well, I want you six to go south of the river tomorrow."

"What? Why? Let them worry about themselves," Han said.

"Think of it this way, if you all spread out a bit more, there is more chance of making some extra money."

Han sniffed. "I'm not sure if I want to protect a bunch of dwarves."

Rawk looked at the man. "Then you can stand wherever you want, but I won't be paying you." He looked around at the others. "Anyone else? Good. I'll try to organize some more Heroes to replace that one." Rawk stabbed at a potato. "Just because they're dwarves or fermi or... or bloody elves, that doesn't mean they deserve to be killed by some bloody unicorn. Nobody deserves that."

"Dwarf–lover."

Suddenly hungry, Rawk concentrated on his food and wondered how long before anything would be happening in the Armory. He was vaguely aware of Frew and the other Heroes quickly and quietly sending Han away from the table.

–O–

The music drifted away into the corners and the crowd sat silently for a moment, catching a collective breath. But Rawk stayed where he was as they rose from the depths of the magic and slowly started to make their way towards the more mundane world above.

There was one man who obviously wasn't going anywhere. He was standing near the door and kept adjusting his expensive doublet as if all the passing people were crumpling the material. When everyone else had left, the man stood for a long time, watching Rawk, before finally moving towards the front of the room. He stopped a yard from the stage and straightened his doublet again. Grint and Celeste were studiously packing away their instruments.

The man cleared his throat and Grint was finally forced to look up. "Hello, Maloti."

"Chritsa has informed me that you will not be back tomorrow night."

"Right. So, what's the question?"

"We have a contract."

"There were rumors of that, but I haven't really seen any evidence so far."

"You signed it."

"I signed something I *thought* was a contract."

"I can show you if you like." He started to pull a leather scroll–tube from his shirt.

"No thanks."

"Do you think you can just walk away? I will make sure you never work in Katamood again."

"You're going to stop me from being a cooper?"

Maloti was confused and suddenly flustered. "What?" He tried to gather his thoughts. "Look, the managers of all the big venues know each other. We talk. You'll be back to playing in taverns by the end of the week."

"Firstly, I don't think Gerwhen, the manager of Harker's Hall, sits around chatting with you and your friends. And secondly..." He glanced at Rawk, as if unsure if he should be saying anything at this stage.

Rawk cleared his throat and Maloti spun around. "What do you want?" And then he seemed to realize who he was talking to. "Rawk? I didn't see you there."

"You didn't see me? You spent five minutes staring at me when everyone else was leaving."

"Well, yes, but..."

"Anyway, can I give some advice to this dwarf for you?"

"Of course. If you could make him see sense it would be best for everyone, especially him and his sister."

"Well, Grint, I suggest you stop talking and just leave. Maloti and the Veteran's Club have broken the contract and this isn't an argument worth having."

Malotie's jaw flapped a couple of times. "We have not broken the contract."

"You were supposed to be paid every week, Grint?"

Grint nodded.

"I have the money here," Maloti said. He pulled a purse full of clinking coins from his pocket.

Rawk snatched it off him before he could react. "Is that all of it?"

There was a slight hesitation, enough of an opening for a swordsman of Rawk's skill to land a blow. "So, even now you can't bring yourself to pay all the money owed." He snatched the leather case off him as well and started to slip the scrolls from inside. Maloti started to protest but was silenced with a cold look. Rawk unrolled the paper and read. "Twenty ithel a night?"

"That is a decent wage for a dwarf and a fermi for a couple of hours work."

"I dare say it is, if they actually get it." Rawk opened the purse as well and counted the money. "How often do they play?"

Maloti stayed silent but Celeste quietly said, "Five nights a week."

"So there is less than two weeks pay in here. Is that all they are owed?"

"Yes." Maloti was quick to speak this time. He'd had a chance to ready himself.

"You have paperwork?"

Another hesitation.

"Can we do up some paperwork for this payment?"

"Of course." He thought he was out of trouble now. "If you'll just follow me up to the office."

A few minutes later, standing in the office where Maris used to work, Rawk stopped Maloti from doing up the paperwork. "Is this all they are owed?" he asked again.

Maloti cleared his throat.

Grint calculated in his head. "We are owed four hundred and forty ithel all up."

Rawk looked at the manger.

"That could be about right." He sighed and went through a door at the back of the room.

Rawk leaned against the timber desk as he waited, remembering the first time he had seen Maris. It seemed a lifetime ago but it was measured in weeks.

"What are you doing?" Grint asked quietly. "If he pays us everything—"

Maloti came back with a strong box and opened it with a huge black key. He counted out the extra money, making neat piles with a flourish of his hand. "Four hundred and forty ithel," he said eventually.

Rawk smiled as if it was all sorted. "Right. Do up the paperwork then."

Grint tried to communicate with looks and silently mouthed words while Maloti scribbled but Rawk waved away his concerns. Then the manager signed two pieces of paper and spun them around on the desk for Grint and Celeste to sign as well. The dwarf looked unsure as he handed one copy back to Maloti.

Rawk took Grint's copy. "Right," he said, "now it would be in your best interests if you didn't bother them again."

"What? But I have paid? If they break the contract—"

"I have a piece of paper that says you paid these artists four hundred and forty ithel for a total of twenty-two days' work."

"That's right. It is all that they are owed."

"The contract clearly states that they are to be paid weekly. I read it. So the fact that you had to pay them four hundred and forty ithel in a lump sum is a clear indication that you broke the contract, isn't it?"

"Well..."

Rawk raised his eyebrows. He was sure Sylvia did it much more convincingly but it seemed to have the desired effect.

"Yes, but..."

"If you talk about Celeste and Grint, if they get robbed, if someone starts spreading a rumor, if anything unusual happens at all, I will be contacting my lawyers. And, also, I'll let Weaver know and he'll have so many auditors down here you'll wish you had a job cleaning fish on the wharves." Rawk smiled. "Are we clear?"

He didn't wait for an answer. He turned on his heel, a bit more gingerly than he would have liked, and left the room with Celeste and Grint hurrying to keep up. He hadn't gotten to kill anything, and he hadn't gotten sex, but he felt a whole heap better than he had a few hours ago.

Out on the street Rawk paused and grunted in surprise when Celeste threw her arms around him.

Rawk wasn't quite sure how he was supposed to respond. Before he could decide, she pulled back smiled at him. "That was amazing. I think I would have given in to him. I've never..." She started to laugh, covering he face with her hands and ducking her head as if embarrassed.

Grint gave a bark of laughter. "I've never seen anything like it either. Talking a man like him into a twist is quite a feat."

Rawk smiled. "It did feel good. The look on his face..."

"I don't think he expected that from you at all," Grint said.

Celeste was trying to get herself under control. "He under estimated you, Rawk. I think you have a new tale to tell when somebody stops you in the street."

"Huh. It isn't the type of tale the children are after, really."

"Tell it nonetheless." Celeste gripped her mandolin tightly. "I am..." She looked at Grint. "We were going to get something to eat. Would you like to come too?"

"I'm not sure—"

"We're celebrating a new job," Grint said.

After a moment, Rawk nodded. "Very well. Where are we going? It has to be somewhere close by, I'm afraid."

Munday

RAWK WOKE WITH A START and saw Travis sitting in his cane chair watching.

"That is *very* creepy, you know?" Rawk said.

"And it's not a lot of fun sitting here watching you, either. You know you talk in your sleep?"

Rawk grunted. "What did I say?"

Travis suddenly looked uncomfortable. "Nothing. I couldn't understand."

Rawk guessed he'd said something about Maris. He couldn't remember what he'd been dreaming, but it wasn't too hard to guess. He closed his eyes for a moment and took a deep breath. "So what do you want, exactly?"

"Sylvia is here. And a dwife."

"So why didn't you wake me? Get out of here. I'll be down in a minute."

"Very well."

"Wait. We need to hire some more Heroes."

"They won't bring her back, you know."

Rawk ignored the comment as best he could as he started to search for some clothes. He concentrated on the task for a moment as he gathered his thoughts. "I fired somebody yesterday— ask Frew who it was before you go paying anyone— and sent four others to patrol south of the river."

"What? Why?"

"You don't think I should?"

"Not really. They can sort it out themselves."

"And what if an exot appears on Celeste's doorstep?"

"Celeste's?"

Rawk waved a hand. "Or Grint's. We're making a big investment with those two; we don't want them dead."

"Whatever. It's your money."

"That's right."

"Speaking of money, a dwarf turned up yesterday afternoon and started talking about stairs down to the cellar. I assumed you had something to do with that?"

"Was it Gabbo? What did he say?"

"He didn't shut up, bloody dwarf. But the main thing was, apparently, that he can build some stairs in the ostler's yard, near the street, for about five thousand ithel. It will take a couple of days and he can start straight away."

"What did you say?"

"I said we'd need another quote."

"What did he say?"

"He said he'd be back today to start because he'd already been told he had the job. You trust him to give you a fair price?"

Rawk thought of mentioning the threat he'd made about not getting any more work. "I trust him," was all he said in the end.

"You're crazy."

"Thacker said he was going to send around the best mason."

"Who's Thacker?"

"A few weeks ago you told me that dwarves know how to do things properly."

"I also said I don't like them."

"Do you know a mason who you think is better than the best dwarf mason in Katamood?"

Travis looked around the room. "No."

"He's here to work, not drink ale. So, just leave him alone and let him get on with it."

"I'll tell Sylvia you'll be down in a minute."

"Thank you. See if they want some breakfast."

Rawk was still buckling on his belt when he hurried own the stairs a few minutes later. His crooked dwarf staff was tucked under his arm, making things difficult. *Dabaneera* clattered against he wall and nearly tripped him up as he reached the bottom and pushed through the door into the common room. The breakfast crowd turned to look at him for a moment and he gave a small nod of greeting then he looked at his usual table. It was empty. From behind the bar, Travis motioned out into the kitchen.

Neither Sylvia nor Biki were there either.

"Where are they?" Rawk asked Kalesie.

"Where are who?"

"Sylvia and Biki."

"The elf and the dwarf? Where do you think they are?"

Rawk looked over at the back door. "Next time they can sit where ever they like."

"Ain't no stinking dwarves going to eat in my kitchen."

"It isn't your kitchen, Kalesie. It belongs to *Keeto Alata*."

She glared up at him. "You get away with a lot because you're friends with the owner, but if dwarves and elves aren't in here to work, then they aren't in here at all, and even that would be stretching my good graces. The day someone says different is the day I leave."

"They were in here a couple of nights ago."

"What?"

Rawk headed out the door, leaving her standing and glaring.

Sylvia, scarf half–unwrapped, was sitting with a bowl of stew on the small table just outside. Biki was scraping up the last dregs of hers. In the corner of the yard a bunch of dwarves were already hard at work, digging up pavers and unloading stone blocks from a waiting wagon. A couple of them were also standing around looking at the wall that divided the yard from the street.

"Good morning, Sylvia, Biki," Rawk said.

"Rawk. Good morning. You're late."

"*Early* is such a fluid concept."

Sylvia shook her head, but Biki gave a small smile.

"How's breakfast?"

"Good," Biki offered. There were a bunch of flowers on the table beside her.

Sylvia grunted. "If Kalesie did not spit in it, it is only because she did not think of it."

"I wonder if she realizes that the wind is coming from this direction. Soon your smell will be wafting around the kitchen."

"My smell?"

"Of course. You smell like elf. It's terrible."

"What do elves smell like?"

"Trees. And fresh air. It's horrible for someone who grew up in the city. Give me a minute."

Rawk went back inside and grabbed his pack and water skin from behind the door. He found some ham and an apple then filched bread and cheese as Kalesie watched suspiciously. He smiled at her, mainly because he knew it would annoy her, then headed back outside.

"They did not waste any time," Sylva said, motioning to the workers as she rose to her feet and fixed her scarf.

Rawk felt like saying, 'They're dwarves,' as if that would explain everything, but Sylvia already knew that, so he grunted instead and headed for the street. The two women were a few steps behind him when he passed through the gate. There was only a small crowd waiting but they started to call out questions and a sizable, rumbling tangle of easily amused people rushed around from the front of the tavern as well.

Rawk held up a hand and waited a moment for the noise to die down. "Thank you." A walnut tied with a ribbon hit him in the head. It hurt a bit. He blinked and looked around for who had thrown it, but a moment later walnuts started raining down. Normally they just threw the stuff near his feet, but the combined crowd was larger than usual, so many had to lob their missile over the heads of those closer in. He was hit again and again. Drawing in a deep breath, Rawk tried to stay calm, but it wasn't easy. "Thank you," he said again. And again, it didn't do any good. He looked behind him. Sylvia and Biki were hiding inside the ostler's yard.

"Rawk, were you scared?"

"How big was the exot?"

"Have you ever fought a unicorn before?"

And the walnuts kept coming.

Rawk held up his other hand. After one especially painful blow he'd had enough. "Stop with the damned walnuts," he shouted.

The questions faltered. The rain of nuts slowed to a drizzle, then stopped completely.

"Just stop, for Path's sake. Don't you all have something better to do? Don't you all have jobs to go to? How do you pay for all the nuts?"

There was silence for a moment.

"My brother said you fought a sorcerer yesterday."

And the questions and the walnuts started again. Rawk drew *Dabaneera*, roared a battle cry and stuck out into the crowd. They parted before him, shocked, frightened, but many still trailed behind as he made his way westwards. He looked back once and saw Sylvia and Biki slinking along behind, trying to remain out of sight. They didn't want to be seen, and that was fine with him.

Rawk wished he could slink as well. But all he could do was keep up the pace and hope the crowd tired of the game soon. The most enthusiastic of them lasted almost a mile before turning aside. Rawk kept going, striding through the streets. After a while, he turned and saw Biki walking beside him, almost running to keep up. He slowed slightly.

"They mustn't like you very much."

Rawk stopped. "What? They love me."

"Then why do they throw walnuts?"

"Well... I have no idea at all." He looked at her. "Why? Do you know?"

"There was a dwarf king, Garen of Turrin Gorge who was loved by all the dwarves, as was his eldest son. But Yarrow, the second son, was not happy with his place in life. When the king was on his deathbed, Yarrow met with his brother in the palace gardens. They argued and

Yarrow drew a dagger. The crown prince died beneath a walnut tree.

"Yarrow was able to hide the crime and ruled for many years, using fear and corruption to become even more powerful. When the dwarves eventually learned what had happened they could not confront him outright for people who did *that* usually died quickly. So they started to throw walnuts tied with ribbons. They acted as if they were honoring him and he could say nothing without admitting he knew what they were suggesting."

"And what happened? Did he repent?"

Biki shook her head. "No. Yarrow decided he was not going to let the people get the better of him, so one day he had his cook make some walnuts into a pie."

"That's how your story ends? You need some practice telling stories."

"Yarrow died, Rawk, because it turned out he was allergic to walnuts."

Rawk smiled and gave a small nod. "That's much better. What's allergic?"

Sylvia answered. "Some foods can make people sick. Very sick in some cases."

"Jargo was allergic to milk," Biki said.

Rawk looked away from the dwife and didn't say anything. He wondered if Jargo would ever have a story. But that was probably up to him.

Rawk knew where he was going now, and this time he was not afraid of who he might meet, so the journey was quite a bit quicker than the last time he had made it. The two women kept pace, and nobody talked more than was necessary.

The ruins of the city grew up out of the forest, crumbling, jagged edges blurred by greenery. A house with, somehow, teeth of glass still in a window gaped at them. A chimney, standing on its own in a pool of green, loomed over them like the bare trunk of a stone tree. And wherever they went, a hush followed them. Rawk saw an exot, a red leathery thing with six legs and crested head, but it disappeared into the undergrowth before he could even think of what to do.

When they arrived at the huge log cabin, Rawk paused just under the trees again. There was just the cabin and the graves.

After several minutes, Rawk noticed Sylvia looking at him. He shrugged and the elf walked out into the open. He really had no choice but to follow. Galad's sword was still upright in the ground, but the Y—shaped stick he had used as a marker for Jargo was tilting to the side. He resisted the urge to fix it now, instead moving out of the way as Biki slowly approached.

Eventually the dwife knelt by her husband's grave. It was obviously which one is was, seeing it was quite a bit smaller than the other, and Rawk wondered if he should have made the graves the same size. Would a smaller grave be some type of subconscious indication to others that the man buried there was somehow less? Or was it an indication that he was a dwarf, and therefore a good thing? Biki didn't say anything, merely stayed where she was and quietly cried for a long time. The flowers she carried were looking bedraggled after the long walk and the stems had been crushed and twisted in her hands, but after a while she set them down and tried to neaten them as best she could.

"You buried him right next to your friend?" she said with a small smile.

"Of course." But it hadn't been a natural thing at the time. It had taken thought. It had felt like he was doing Jargo a favor. "He saved my life," Rawk said. "And I still don't know why."

"Because he was Jargo."

"Yes. I suppose so." He pointed to the lopsided Y at the head of the grave. "Did he believe in Path?"

"No."

Rawk nodded. After a moment, he went and removed the stick. He drew *Dabaneera,* examining the blade. It was a good blade. Not as good as *Kult* but good none–the–less. "He didn't die a warrior," he said, "because that indicates a decision to go out looking for battles, even if it is a reluctant decision. But he died bravely. He died fighting for what he believed in, and that is an even greater thing." He was only just coming to understand how much greater. "I would like to leave this…" He held up *Dabaneera*.

"But that is *your* sword."

He shrugged. "I can get another." He didn't want another. He didn't want any sword. But Jargo had died because of the stupidity of warriors and people in Katamood were dying because of the stupidity of sorcerers. Somebody had to stop it. "I can get another." He set the tip on the ground and pushed it down, sliding it deep into the earth so it would not move. After a moment, he took his dwarvish staff and pushed it down beside the sword.

"Thank you. You do him much honor."

"No, thank you, Biki. Thank you for your forgiveness."

She looked surprised by that, as if the thought of blaming Rawk had never crossed her mind. "He was Jargo."

"Rawk. You may want to reconsider the placement of your sword."

Rawk spun to look at Sylvia. And he followed her gaze to the corner of the cabin. Opok was standing there, leaning on his staff, watching Biki.

"You have come to honor the fallen?" the duen said, bowing his head for a moment.

Biki rose to her feet and backed away a step.

Rawk went the other direction. "Hello, Opok." He stopped a few steps away, realizing he was actually unaware how the duen traditionally greeted each other. Besides, he had the feeling that if he tried to shake hands he would end up with a couple of broken bones. "You arrived much quicker this time."

"Greetings, Rawk. I could have be quicker last time, but was reluctant."

"So was I."

The duen smiled and turned to Sylvia. He gave a small nod. "Mother."

Sylvia recovered quickly. "Opok. It is a pleasure to meet you. You are a sorcerer?"

"A shaman, yes, but your power be a great river to my trickle." He squinted and looked more closely. "Though your power be dammed for a long time."

Sylvia cleared her throat and glanced at Rawk for a moment. "Magic is not allowed where I live."

Opok nodded. "I see." He turned and bowed to Biki. "Your distress be great. Can I be of assistance?"

"You are one of the creatures that killed my husband?" It was hardly a question at all.

Opok looked at Rawk.

Rawk sighed. He didn't know what to say. He wasn't given more time to consider as Biki drew a small dagger from beneath her cloak. Rawk quickly moved to stand in front of her, though he doubted Opok was in danger.

"Opok harmed nobody, Biki. I killed his two grand–children in the forest, then came here looking for more."

The dwife looked up at him for a moment.

"Opok's family did nothing more than defend themselves."

"They killed Jargo."

Opok knelt slowly on the grass. "Will my death be enough?" he asked. "Or will you be requiring more after that?"

Biki shifted the dagger in her hand. She moved forward to stand just in front of the duen. She was still shorter than he was. "I do not know."

"Will ten duen deaths be enough? Twenty?"

"I do not know." She was looking down now, examining the weapon in her hand as if wondering how it had come to be there.

"I don't think there would ever be enough deaths for you. You cannot be filling an emptiness by digging another hole. All you do be doing is move the emptiness to another place. There have already been too many deaths."

"I want him back." Biki said. She fell to her knees as well, letting the dagger fall on the grass by her side.

Opok nodded. "I be understand." And he said no more for a long time, merely sitting with Biki as she cried. The duen seemed to have the patience of a mountain. Finally, the dwife rose to her feet and returned to Jargo's grave.

"Are you be coming only to visit the fallen, or do you be having more questions about wrestling arms?"

Rawk looked at Sylvia. "Mainly the fallen, I think."

Apparently Sylvia had other ideas. "You told Rawk you can feel the portals from here. Can you tell me anything else about them?"

Opok stared into the trees. "Many strange things are happening," he said after a moment. "It is as if the magic be holding its breath."

"Pardon?"

"There be great surgings of power, like a drawing of breath, but then the breath is held and released later. Sometimes three of four breaths are being held at once."

Rawk watched Sylvia's brow furrow as she tried to think. If she was confused, he wasn't even going to try to work out what was going on.

"So they are binding the spells, but then not engaging them?"

Opok shrugged. "I do not be completely knowing the terms you use, but it seems you understand."

"So what does that mean?" Rawk asked.

Sylvia stared blankly for a moment, then shook her head as she collected her thoughts. "A spell is like... Magic is in the air all around us all the time. Spells are merely a means of forming the magic into useful shapes."

"I'm with you so far." At least he thought he was. It wouldn't take much to lose him though.

"Well, imagine the magic is a fire that's always burning. The spell is a fry pan and the result is cooked bacon."

Rawk nodded. "I like that spell."

Sylvia sighed. "Shef and his friends are putting the fry pan on the fire and it is heating up, but the bacon isn't cooking."

"It isn't?"

"No. They are taking the cold bacon out of the fry pan and putting it back in the cupboard."

"But..."

"That is correct; it should not be possible. But even worse, the bacon is then apparently cooking later on, without the repetition of the spell."

"So there is cold, self−heating bacon somewhere in Katamood?"

Sylvia's eyes narrowed. "Please tell me you know what a metaphor is."

"Does it still get crispy edges?" he said, just to annoy her.

"You are impossible, Rawk."

Rawk took a deep breath and closed his eyes. "All right, but tell me, seriously, I assume you need something to hold all this restrained magic bacon."

"I suppose so."

"So are we talking an item or a person? Is it something we can break to release the magic?"

Sylvia looked at Opok. The duen shrugged. "There is much power. I be knowing of no talisman that could hold enough for even one portal, though the magic practiced here be much greater than what I have known."

"What about a person, then?"

Opok looked Rawk in the eye for long seconds. "I be hoping not."

Rawk listened as Sylvia and Opok debated bacon and magic around in circles. He could follow almost not of it and in the end he didn't even bother trying. He just waited until they were done, so he could lead the way back to Katamood.

–O–

"Where are we going, Rawk?"

Rawk stopped at the corner, clutched in the creeping fingers of darkness that stretched out from the buildings, and looked back. "You don't have to come, Sylvia. I want to show Biki."

"No, I will come."

"Then be quiet and wait. It isn't far now anyway."

He found the address that Weaver had given him and pulled a small collection of keys from his pocket. He searched through them for a moment before finding the right one. The door opened easily, letting into a small, narrow hallway. Up one flight of creaking, narrow stairs with flaking plaster on the walls on both sides. There was another short hallway at the top with doors off either side. Rawk found the next key and let himself into room 12. It wasn't very large, but it was tidy. There was a small, pot-bellied stove in the corner with a couple of cupboards nearby and a large copper dish for washing. There was a scarred timber table in the middle of the room and the bed, still covered with a coarse woolen blanket, half blocked a door that led out to a small balcony. It smelled musty.

"Who lives here?" Biki asked.

Rawk wandered around the room. There were some clothes in a chest at the foot of the bed. Mementos were crowded onto a shelf above. "It belonged to Galad, the man who is buried with your husband."

"Oh."

"You can stay here if you like."

"But..."

"Galad had no family, so I claimed his things when he died." Rawk shrugged. "It isn't as if they were free; he'd barely started paying this place off."

Biki looked around, tears welling up in her eyes.

"I am living with Harper."

"The editor of the newspaper?"

"Yes."

"But that isn't a permanent thing, is it? No offense, but Harper would probably like to get his place back. You can't stay there forever." *No offense?* When had he ever been worried about offending a dwarf?

"But I can't afford to stay here. I only get a few hours of work every week."

Rawk cleared his throat and looked at Sylvia for a moment. She was staring at him, surprised look on her face. Rawk looked away. "Just pay what you can afford at the moment, if you feel the need to pay something. We can work the rest out later. And I might be able to help with the money thing anyway. You used to work in taverns, didn't you?"

"Yes."

"Well, go up to the *Hero's Rest* and talk to Travis."

"They won't let me work up there."

"Tell him I sent you."

"I don't know if I *want* to work up there."

Rawk shrugged. "It's up to you; I'm not going to argue about it. Just think of your daughter."

"I am always thinking of my daughter."

"Of course. I didn't mean..." Rawk looked around. Sylvia was still staring. She seemed even more surprised than she had earlier. "Anyway, I've got a big day tomorrow, I imagine, so I should go." He crossed the room and gripped the door handle.

"Thank you, Rawk. It isn't something I would expect from..."

"From a human? From me?" Staring at the back of the door, he gave a small shake of the head. "I don't suppose you would. I wouldn't either."

"Thank you."

"If there's stuff in here you don't want, just sell it. Keep the money."

"I couldn't."

"I don't need it, Biki. I wouldn't even notice the difference." He started to open the door. "I will see you at the *Rest* tomorrow, Sylvia?"

"Yes."

Tewsday

RAWK HAULED HIMSELF OUT OF BED with a groan. Now he had all the aches and pains of his trek through the forest lying over the top of his usual complaints, though he wasn't sure where one lot ended and he other started. He almost wished for the numbness of the last couple of days. The unicorn wound on his chest was burning and he couldn't even see it beneath Sylvia's bandages. Travis handed him a cup of tea.

"That's the *lorsie* one?" Rawk said when he'd taken a sip. "What did you do to it?" He sat down on the chair and sighed as if he'd just finished another long walk.

Travis smiled. "You said it was too bitter so I just added a little bit of honey."

"Well, it's good." He took another sip then put the cup down on the floor so he could pull on his boots. "How's things going in the cellar?"

"Well, most of the stuff is cleared out, thought the ostler's yard isn't looking so good."

"A great man once told me that tidying up isn't just about moving the mess to a different place."

Travis ignored that. "Apparently the dwarves are ahead of schedule. There's a hole in the wall out onto the street and they've dug about half way down to the cellar. They'll finish the digging today and should be able to line the hole. Gabbo isn't sure if they'll get the stairs done though because he's waiting on some bigger stone blocks to come from..." Travis' brow furrowed as he tried to think. "Well, the location doesn't really matter, I suppose."

Rawk nodded. "It's going well, then?" He took up his cup again. It was still early in the morning, so he hadn't made his way down for breakfast, but he was the tea was doing a great job of waking him up.

Travis looked away.

"What?"

"Kalesie says that if she has to listen to one more dwarf song she's going to have at them with a rolling pin."

"She'll get over it." He knelt on the floor and pulled the chest from beneath his bed.

"You really think so? She says it's going to take a week to get the smell out of her clothes."

Rawk winced.

It was Travis' turn to say, "What?"

"A dwife is probably going to be coming around to talk about a job." He started going through the weapons in the chest. But all he did was make a lot of noise without really seeing anything.

"A job? At the *Rest?*"

Rawk could almost see Travis readying his rolling pin. "Biki has worked in taverns before. Both in the tap-room and the kitchen."

"I think it's a terrible idea, Rawk. Nobody wants to have a dwarf serving them their lunch. Or cooking it."

"Then they can go somewhere else."

"You're willing to go broke because of a dwarf?"

"Her husband was killed saving my life, Travis."

"And she's going to kill your business."

"That won't happen. I still live here. I still eat and drink here just about every day." He finally saw the sword he was after and pulled it from amongst the mess.

"What are you doing with that piece of rubbish? Where's *Dabaneera.*"

"*Slade* isn't rubbish." It was close though. He'd only kept it for sentimental reasons. He looked at the blade and wondered if he even had the energy to get it cleaned up properly. "And *Dabaneera* is in the Old Forest, marking the grave of a dwarf."

Travis was staring at the horrible blade as well. He sighed. "What's this dwife's name? Biki? Do I have to fire someone?"

"Of course not. We're going to need staff for the basement."

"Sylvia is down stairs again," Travis said as he opened the door. "I'll suppose you want me to let her sit in the taproom tomorrow."

"I doubt she'll want to."

"There are better swords down stairs, you know. A whole room full of them."

Rawk watched Travis leave. He knew he was right, but sometimes that didn't matter. For one thing, he didn't want to walk down to the basement and then spend half an hour searching for a likely candidate. And secondly, the idea of *Slade* just felt right to him. He hefted the weapon again and made his way down stairs.

–O–

"Where do we start?" Rawk asked, looking up and down the street as if some brothels might appear in a nice orderly line. Most of the brothels he knew didn't do anything at all in an orderly fashion.

"Let us visit some of the cheaper places first," Sylvia said.

"Why?"

"It will be cheaper to buy information there."

"Have you done this type of thing before?"

Sylvia gave him a look. "I merely think about things before I act, Rawk. You should perhaps try it some time. Or are you on a first name basis with the madams so we can get the information for free?"

"Oh, very funny. I'll have you know it has been a long time since I've needed to know any of that type of woman."

"Well, I hope you brought some money then."

"This way."

Rawk might not have visited brothels but he spent enough time walking around the city that he knew where many of them were. The first was not far away, a few streets away from the main road that ran down the spine of Two Watch Hill. It didn't look too bad from the outside. The exposed timber frames of the wall looked like they'd been painted just a week ago. The plaster between the fames was clean and smooth. There was a balcony on the second floor, presumably where the women could display themselves to the passers—by, but it was a bit early in the morning for that type of thing. The street was all but empty anyway, so they would have been wasting their time. A sign above the door, freshly painted too, gave the name, 'The Birds and the Bees'.

All the money and time had been spent improving the outside of the building. Inside hadn't been painted for at least a decade. They'd probably left it that long because they'd first have to clean and that wasn't on their list of things to do.

"Is this cheap enough?" Rawk asked.

Rawk thought Sylvia probably wrinkled her nose, but he couldn't tell through her scarf.

The sound of Rawk's voice disturbed a woman sleeping in a chair in the corner of the room. She twitched and snorted and blinked slowly towards consciousness. When she saw she had company she pushed herself to her feet and ran her fingers through her long, rat's—nest hair. She smoothed what little clothing she was wearing and searched her arsenal for the right kind of smile. "Good morning to you, sir and madam. My name is Lapa."

Rawk nodded. "Good morning."

"Is that you Rawk? I never thought I'd see you in here." Lapa smiled some more. "You've come to the right place though. You won't find any establishment more discreet than ours." She looked Sylvia up and down. "Will you be requiring just the one girl this morning? And we have special rooms available. I can offer discounts given the time and all."

"We don't need any girls."

"Well, I don't know where Gus is at the moment, but I'm sure I can find him."

Rawk was dubious that Gus even existed. It seemed to him that Lapa intended go out through the back door and enlist the services of the first man she found on the street.

"No, Gus won't be need either. We're actually after information."

"That will cost you."

Rawk heard Sylvia mutter, "So much for discretion." The sorceress was still looking around the room in distaste, probably cataloguing diseases.

"We can pay."

"How much?"

"Depends what you have to say. We are looking for a one armed elf woman."

Lapa sniffed, then shook her head. "Not seen anyone like that 'round here."

"You're sure?"

"Positive. Not likely I'd forget that."

"You see everyone who comes through?"

"Everyone."

Rawk fished a five–ithel coin from the pouch on his belt and handed it over. "You know how to find me if you see a one armed elf."

"Of course. But I'd better get more than five ithel if I do."

–O–

Rawk stepped out of the door of the *Purple Lavender* and took a deep breath of the fresh air. It had been the worse than the other four they had visited, and if Falling Leaves was frequenting the place she would probably die of half a dozen diseases before they found her. He couldn't believe any would–be customers would be brave enough to move beyond the stinking, cramped foyer. Sylvia still hadn't come out and he was wondering if he needed to risk his life and mount a rescue. He didn't get the chance to make the decision, either way.

"Rawk!"

Rawk looked around and saw a soldier striding towards him. "Waydin. Just the man I didn't want to see."

"You think I'm thrilled to be out here looking for you? I've checked all your usual places."

"Well, next time check some unusual ones too."

Waydin looked at the *Purple Lavender*. "Unusual? I usually cross the street just so I don't have to walk past the door of the *Lavender*. I didn't know anyone ever actually went in there."

Rawk shrugged. "It's cheap."

"No, it isn't."

"And how would you know that, if you've never been in?"

"Lunch."

"They serve food? I wouldn't eat in there."

"With Weaver."

"Oh, right. Really?"

"Yes. Today. At the *Iron Clock* over on Bay Road."

"Really? He couldn't give me any more notice?"

"I've been looking for you since the start of my shift."

"Tell him you didn't find me."

The look on Waydin's face suggested that wasn't going to happen.

"Tell him I've got syphilis. And gonorrhea."

"Now that I could believe." Waydin glanced at the brothel again. "But Weaver pays my bills, so if he asks I'll tell him I passed on the message. What you do with the information is up to you."

"Thanks a lot."

"Just doing my job." And he wandered away. Apparently his job didn't need to be done quickly.

Sylvia came out of the *Purple Lavender*. She partly unwrapped her scarf from about her face and took a deep breath. "I didn't think he was ever going to leave."

"He'll be back."

Sylvia looked a bit worried.

"Not now. But some time. He always comes back."

"So are you going to lunch?"

"Weaver doesn't go away either."

"How could you possibly eat any more? You have visited more bakeries than brothels so far."

"Each bakery seems to have one special pastry that only they do. I don't want to miss something." Rawk looked around. "Maybe we can do one more before I have to go."

"One more?"

"Brothel, not bakery."

"If we must."

They made their way around the side of the hill. Rawk avoided two stories and a friendly young lady who was shopping for her mother before they found another brothel.

The sign above the door announced, *The Velvet Strumpet.*

Sylvia grunted and Rawk had to agree.

"If there is one piece of velvet in this entire place, I'll eat my hat," he said.

"You do not have a hat."

"Well, no. I had to eat it when Travis knitted me a pair of socks."

"Perhaps you should offer to eat your socks next time."

"Have you smelt my socks?"

Sylvia raised an eyebrow.

"Come on."

The *Strumpet* didn't even have a verandah. The door led directly from the street into a long, dimly lit hallway. Timber frames were visible and the plaster between had been painted with all sort of suggestive designs. There were no doors for almost fifteen yards.

"They probably just closed in a laneway," Rawk said. He looked up at the ceiling but couldn't see much. Sylvia was still walking so he hurried to catch up. When they finally reached the foyer, the light wasn't any better. Neither was the artwork from what he could see.

"This may be too cheap, even for Falling Leaves," Sylvia said, looking around in disgust. "Well, we are here now, I suppose."

Maybe the dimness was a ploy so the customers couldn't see what type of vermin were lurking in the corners. Or maybe it was so they couldn't see the women. There were five of them in the room at the moment, though only two were likely to notice that anyone had entered. The others were entertaining themselves on a tattered divan in the corner. If it was for show, then it was a noisy show that Rawk really didn't want to see.

A few seconds passed and nobody came to talk, so Rawk cleared his throat loudly. Then he sighed and called out. "Ladies." The two unoccupied women and one of the others turned to look but they didn't really look interested. It was surprising any of them answered to 'Ladies'. Eventually, Rawk went to the divan, grabbed the dress of the only woman who was dressed, and pulled her onto the floor.

She shrieked and tried to bite Rawk's leg. He gave her a bit of a kick and backed away.

"What do you want?"

"I'm looking for someone, a one armed elf woman."

"No elves work here."

"Not a worker. A customer."

"How much is this information worth to you?"

Rawk pulled out a five–ithel coin. It was probably a couple of days work for women like these.

One of them got up off the divan and sauntered over to take to money. "I ain't seen nobody like that."

"Of course you haven't. Anyone else?"

"No one armed elves here. I'd remember that."

"Very well. Thank you for your time."

"Who are you then? You work for Prince Weaver?"

A voluptuous, dark haired wild–woman on the divan looked at Rawk properly for the first time and pulled herself up straighter. "That's Rawk, that is."

The woman one the floor stopped snarling for a moment and tried on a smiled that was even scarier. "You want a freebie, darlin'?"

Rawk grunted. "I've brought my healer, and I still wouldn't touch you."

"Well, there's no need for that, now is there."

"Thank you for your time, ladies."

Rawk gave a dramatic, ironic bow then strode out into the narrow hallway in an equally dramatic fashion. He was so pleased with himself that he didn't notice the men coming the other way until he had taken half a dozen steps. Then, for a moment, he was so annoyed for not noticing that he didn't notice the long, curved dagger that man at the front of the line was carrying.

"Path."

Sylvia still hadn't notice. "What?"

The hall was a good place to fight. There were at least four men in the line but they would only be able to come at him one at a time. The trouble was, Rawk knew the man would be on him before he had time to draw *Slade*. So he pushed Sylvia back the way they'd come followed behind, drawing his sword as he went.

He stopped just through the door and turned to fight. It wasn't ideal; he just had to be pushed back a little and the followers would be able to join in. But he knocked aside the first, experimental attack and ran the man through before he had time to sum up the results of his test. Then next in line was a short, solid man with a scar on his cheek and a smile touching his lips. He would not make the same sort of mistake.

"Not bad, old man," the stranger said, standing in the doorframe. He shifted his grip on his short–sword. "I'd offer you a job, if you weren't about to die."

"Offer me a job?" Rawk shook his head. "You aren't from around here, are you?"

"I've just come in from Habon a couple of days ago."

"Well, I'm Rawk. You may have heard of me."

The man gave it some thought. "No, I don't think so." He shrugged. "My name is Franas."

Franas attacked before he'd finished uttering his name. He came in hard and low and normally Rawk would have stepped back, but that would have let more men through so he held his ground, merely lifting his front leg and letting the sword whistle harmlessly beneath his foot. He was too off balance to counter though, so the opportunity slipped by.

"Don't get ahead of yourself, Franas," Rawk said, holding back a grunt as his sore knee protested. He blocked another attack, but only just, and knew he wouldn't be able to hold his position for long.

He took the chance to look back over his shoulder. Sylvia was watching from the far wall, close to the only other door in the room. Good.

Then next time Franas attacked, Rawk slid the blade aside, then turned and ran, as much as his knee would allow. Franas was surprised enough to hesitate for a moment and that was all that was needed.

"Go, Sylvia," Rawk said. She stood for a moment, then opened the door and preceded him through. "Keep going."

"Where?"

But there was only one way to go. To the right was a plaster wall, to the left was a long hallway with doors off just the right hand side.

Rawk pushed on the first door, but nothing happened. Then he pulled and the door squeaked open. It couldn't go the other way because the room beyond was hardly bigger than the bed it contained. It was occupied by a man and a woman. Neither seemed to be enjoying themselves all that much. Rawk held his breath against the stench of mold and something even worse and quickly pulled open the next door. He discovered a large bald man snoring loudly.

"Are you trying to find a hiding place or a defensible position?" Sylvia asked.

"I'm trying to run."

But he turned to fight. Three men came through the door but only one at a time could get to him; he had the whole, long narrow hall behind him this time. All he had to do was last long enough to make use of it. But thankfully, Franas had somehow ended up at the back of the line. The first man was younger and bigger. He had red hair and a missing tooth.

"Franas sent you out in front, did he?"

Red grunted.

"Was he too scared?"

Rawk battered away a flurry of attacks, trying not to move too much lest his knee betray him completely. Red was at least twenty years his junior and much too fast. He might have been better than Franas. Rawk took a stinging cut across his shoulder. He deflected another blow and took the flat of the blade on the side of the head. He retreated slightly, half stumbling, and shook his head to clear it. And he barely deflected another blow before somehow finding the focus to get back into the fight. Not that it would do him any good. His ears were ringing and his arm was aching. He was getting slower by the moment and it wouldn't be long.

Red lunged forward and all Rawk could do was lean out of the way. The bandage around his chest saved him from another long, painful slice. He was sure he wouldn't be so lucky next time.

"What's going on out here?" The big, bald man from the side room wasn't snoring any more. He pushed open the door angrily. It slammed into Red, bounced off his forearm and went back to strike Snorer in the nose.

Rawk slashed wildly in the ensuing moment. He wondered if he had the energy to do more than draw blood, but *Slade* bit deeply into the other man's side and he gave out an anguished scream.

"Stay in the room, sir," Rawk said. "It isn't safe out here." The next distraction was as likely to kill Rawk as anyone else.

Sword back at the ready, Rawk took a deep breath and quickly wiped sweat from his eyes. He resisted the urge to retreat even a step. The body on the floor would hamper the next man to come. Hopefully. He calmed his breathing and stood waiting. Blood was trickling down his arm.

And in death, Red did help. The long fingered hand clutched at the next mans breeches as he tried to advance. The stranger looked down for just a moment and Rawk lunged. If he missed he would have died himself, he was sure, but *Slade* slid between two ribs and slurped back out again as the dead man fell backwards.

Franas stopped a few paces away. "So, why do you think I would know you, old man?"

Rawk shrugged.

"He is a Hero, Franas." A sorcerer came through the door, smiling. "And not just any Hero. Rawk is one of the great Heroes. Possibly the last of the great Heroes."

"Queel?" Rawk said. Queel had been pasty and pale the last time Rawk had seen him and it didn't look like he'd been out in the sun since. Unfortunately, that didn't affect his magic. "This week is turning into a bit of a reunion, but all of the sorcerers from my past are ending up dead, and I'm still here."

"Perhaps. But you didn't actually kill any of them, did you? I her Frixen even managed to out run you before he met his demise."

"Frixen is dead too?" Rawk said. "Well, the day just keeps getting better. And now I get to kill you, though I should have done it years ago."

"Of course you should have, Rawk. But you never were the brightest, were you. And now you've taken to listening to Silver Lark as well, apparently, so it's all down hill for you."

"At least I have a hill to go down, Queel. You worthless little life has been all one endless plain stretching from horizon to horizon. The only way you'll get any lower is when you get buried." Rawk smiled but he couldn't see anything to be happy about.

"Come, out of the way, Franas; I will handle this myself."

Franas' lip twitched but it seemed he was being paid very well for he gave a small nod. "What about the bitch? You said she was a sorcerer."

Queel looked at Sylvia. "How the mighty have fallen, Silver Lark. I didn't imagine it would ever come to this, for you of all people."

"Why would I be different to anyone else?"

"But you are different, aren't you. Does Rawk not know?"

"It is not his concern."

"It will be in a moment."

Rawk watched as Queel started to mumble and wave his hands. He didn't think his amulets would do much good.

"This is the bit where you do your thing, Sylvia." He shifted his grip on his sword and looked back at the elf.

"Get down, Rawk." She started mumbling as well.

Rawk saw the look in her eyes and wasn't about to argue. Ducking, he tried to cover his head but almost managed to take off an ear with his sword. There was a rustle of clothing, the sound of footsteps, then Rawk saw Sylvia fling her hands forward. A moment later, Queel screamed. He clutched at his face, screamed some more and tore at his eyes, as if there was something he really didn't want to see. But he didn't die, so Rawk ran him through and it seemed he was doing everyone a favor.

"Can you just kill him next time?"

"You let me worry about what I am doing."

"Right. Of course. Because it doesn't concern me at all."

Franas wasn't keen to take up the fight.

Rawk shifted his grip on his sword. "Are you coming?" he asked the man.

Apparently he wasn't.

Sylvia called out instead. "We have to go, Rawk."

"What?"

"Balen is here. He's building a *hagakim.*"

"What?"

"He needs to be able to see us and the range of the attack is not extensive."

"What?"

"Run."

Balen came through from the foyer. "Oh, Sylvia, you spoil all my fun." The sorcerer smiled.

"Apparently there's no way out down there," Franas said to the sorcerer.

"Thank you, Franas."

Down where, Rawk wondered. He took the risk of looking over his shoulder. Sylvia was running down the narrow hall, holding her robes up away from the floor. "Path." Rawk started to run as well, though apparently there was nowhere to go. He went through the end door just behind Sylvia, almost running in to her. Balen was striding down the hallway, in no hurry at all.

Rawk slammed the door and looked around. The room was an office that looked much like the foyer in terms of size and design. The pictures painted between the wall frames here were of flowers and birds. There was no other door and just one small skylight that was well out of reach, even standing on the desk and the chair.

Rawk closed his eyes, trying to breathe, trying to think. He walked his mind through the streets and the alleys around the building, getting his bearings. "I know where we are," he said eventually.

"I did not know we were lost." Sylvia was breathing heavily as she searched through her pockets.

There were two sections of wall that were different to the rest. The whitewashed plaster was attached to the face of the timber frames, instead of being set back inside. Rawk took up the chair and hit the wall. The plaster cracked. Another blow and a large chunk fell away revealing the woven timber strands inside. He went at it faster then, hammering as quickly as he could. He could imagine Balen advancing down the hall. Or perhaps he was changing his spell and wouldn't need line of sight at all.

When Rawk concentrated on his task again he noticed that a couple of the strands had broken. After that, things started to fall apart quickly. The chair. Rawk's shoulder. The wall. After a couple of more blows, the chair broke completely and Rawk went to work with his boot. It was only a couple of seconds before there was a hole big enough to crawl through.

Behind him, the door exploded. Shards of timber slashed through the room.

Rawk pushed Sylvia through the hole he had made in the wall as Franas edged into sight, sword ready, looking for trouble.

Rawk wanted to escape as well, but there was no time. He realized he was still holding the leg of the chair, though there was no longer any chair attached. He threw the timber, hoping to slow the other...

Franas was caught by surprise. The leg crashed into his face and he fell to the floor screaming. The broken, jagged end had pierced his eye and he was holding the gooey remains in his hands, as if pushing it back in would help. Rawk froze for a moment, but the thought of who might come through the door next pushed him into motion. He followed Sylvia through the hole and out into a narrow alley. His shirt snagged for a moment, but he tore it free and jumped painfully to his feet. He was raced along, trying to catch the elf. In some places, he had to turn sideways to fit between the close−crowding walls. Rubbish covered the ground. Water dripped down from leaking pipes.

Rawk almost ran out of the alley and into the street at the end. But he managed to stop in time and tried to compose himself. He took a deep breath and stepped out into the open. Sylvia was standing on the other side of the street, half in the door of a shop and half out. She visibly sighed with relief when she saw who had come out behind her. Rawk gave her a small nod and was almost hit by a wagon when he stepped away from the wall.

"Watch it there."

Rawk looked up at the driver and gave an apologetic wave. "Sorry. Been a long day."

"Long day," the man laughed. "It isn't even lunch time yet."

"I'm just praying I can make it that far." He managed a smile and waved the man on. When the wagon had passed he checked the traffic and limped across to Sylvia. He climbed the three stairs slowly, painfully and leaned against the wall by the door. "Should we run a bit further?" He rubbed his knee and drew in some deep breaths.

Sylvia shook her head. "They will not confront us here. It is too risky."

"Are you sure?"

"Why do you think they waited until we were inside the worst brothel in Katamood?"

"They wanted to celebrate when they were finished?"

Sylvia gave him a withering look. "Yes, I suspect you are correct."

"I normally am. Just ask Travis." Rawk drew in another deep breath and noticed a little girl watching him from in front of the next shop. When they made eye contact she shyly walked over and stood examining his boots.

"Can you tell me a story, Mr. Rawk, sir?"

"Well, I..." Rawk was saved the effort of either an excuse or a story when the girl's mother hurried from the bakery and came to take he hand.

"You can't wander off like that, Chamay. You don't know who's about."

Balen stepped out of the alley, looking slightly surprised. He dusted off his shirt and looked around.

"Yes," Rawk muttered, "you don't know who might be about."

For a moment it looked like the sorcerer might not notice them, but he saw them and glared in their direction. Sylvia stepped out into the open. She had her hands in her pockets, like she wasn't worried at all, but her stare could have wilted a cactus.

Rawk thought he could feel the tension in the air, but maybe it was just the midday glare giving him a headache.

Balen looked away first, then wandered off like there hadn't been a staring contest at all. Sylvia sighed and slumped down on the top stair.

"That went well," Rawk said.

"I suppose you are right, we are alive, after all."

"You could take Balen."

"You really don't know much about magic, do you?"

"Well... Travis is collecting lots of books for me to study."

"He is?"

"Yes, I've got a library and everything."

Sylvia raised an eyebrow. She was very good at it.

"I've got a book shelf."

"Fighting against magic with magic is like fighting with a two-handed war hammer while wearing a hat that keeps falling over your eyes. If you want to see what you opponent is doing, you need one of your hands to lift your hat and the hammer is useless. Otherwise, you are swinging blindly."

Rawk grunted. "You need a rapier."

"Why didn't I think of that?"

"Should we have followed Balen?"

"No, he will be watching for us. And you probably need to go and find Weaver."

"Is there a record for the most whore houses a man has visited in a day?"

"Ask Weaver's tax collector— he probably holds the record."

"I can't get out of it, can I?"

"I don't know how it works."

"It doesn't. Not any more." Rawk sighed. "Come up to the *Rest* later this afternoon and I'll show you my library."

"I hope that isn't a euphemism."

"It's about this big." He held his hands about a foot apart.

"You may need a bigger library than that to impress me, Rawk, but I shall come and look anyway."

"Hey, I thought the size of the library didn't matter. It's the quality of the books that counts."

"Keep telling yourself that."

He laughed. "I think I've had enough of that kind of thing for today."

"It was all down hill after the *Birds and the Bees* wasn't it."

"Yes, it was. I'm sure you have some patients you can see or something for a while anyway."

Sylvia shook her head. "I sent Clinker around this morning telling everyone I would be busy for a couple of days."

"What if they're dying?"

"Well, it will not do them any good knocking on my door if I'm not there. Their time will be better spent finding another healer."

"Well, I may have to come and see you later for something to get this smell out of my nose."

"I will be out of stock by the time I am through using it myself." She looked him up and down. "Do you need assistance with anything else? Are you injured?"

Rawk catalogued his new pains. "Nothing serious," he said eventually. "A few cuts and slices that I can handle."

"If you are sure."

Rawk nodded and watched as Sylvia rewrapped her scarf tighter around her face again. "That looks good," he said.

She eyed him suspiciously.

"I mean it."

"Well, thank you, I guess. The scarves started as a method used to protect laborers from sippon pollen but became both fashion and symbol over the centuries."

"Sippon pollen?"

"It grows in my mother's village. It is not just a drug; it can be used for many things."

"If you say so. Anyway, I've got to go find Weaver; he's probably already ordered potato stew for me."

–O–

Rawk sat down with a grateful sigh.

"Busy morning?" Weaver said. He was wearing a remarkably somber jacket with a wide brimmed leather hat pulled down low over his face. There was no wig or fake beard in sight.

"There's no rest for Heroes at the moment."

"I know. And I hear you're paying some to stand on corners and what–not waiting for trouble, instead of congregating in taverns where they can't help anyone."

Rawk shrugged. "It seemed like a good idea."

"It won't bring her back, you know."

"So I'm told."

"It's hard when you lose someone you love."

"I didn't love her, Weaver."

"You didn't? Then what's the problem?" The prince slapped Rawk's knee. "Stop wasting your money on these Heroes."

"Stop wasting money? People are dying." Rawk sat back, moving his leg so Weaver was forced to take his hand away.

"I know. I know. I didn't mean we shouldn't help people."

"I'm actually getting some more organized so they can cover south of the river as well."

"Now that's totally ridiculous."

"Who'll build your damn canal if all the dwarves are killed or hiding in their houses?"

"They think they know everything." Weaver pouted. "Let them come up with an idea for *this*."

Rawk watched the prince for a moment. "I'm sure they will. But until then, I'll pay for some Heroes to help."

Weaver shrugged. "So, what are you going to get for lunch?"

"You haven't ordered yet?"

"Of course not."

"Of course not?"

"I hear they do a great shepherd's pie here."

That was just organized potato stew. Rawk sighed. "That'll do, then. I still need more fruit too."

Weaver made a signal and Rawk turned to see a big, lumbering man rise from a chair and make his way to the bar to order. Rawk had never seen him before.

"Who's that?"

Weaver waved his fingers. "Bocco. Or Bocca. Or something. He's new. I'm not sure if I like him much; I don't like his attitude."

"Maybe he doesn't like being a waitress."

"Too bad for him."

"Well, he'll be happier tomorrow when you send him out to find the sorcerers," Rawk said.

"What?"

"You're supposed to be taking over the search for the sorcerers tomorrow. Remember?" Rawk cursed himself silently. If he'd kept his mouth shut Weaver might have forgotten all about it.

"Oh, right. Yes. Of course."

Rawk shrugged. "I can keep going if you want."

"No, that's all right. It's about time I took control."

"Then I think I'll move *all* my Heroes south of the river tomorrow."

Weaver narrowed his eyes. "The people won't like that."

"I'm sure my men will just get in the way; you're taking control, remember?"

The prince's thoughts quickly turned back to more important matters. "It's going to cost me a fortune."

Rawk shrugged. "The money isn't important."

"Not until you don't have any."

Rawk pulled out spoon. "There will always be things that are more important than money." He polished the metal, then the bone handle.

"Like love?"

"I didn't love her."

"I know, but..."

"Yes, Weaver, like love."

The pies arrived and Rawk got to sit quietly and eat after having gotten in the final word. It wouldn't last, of course, but he could enjoy the moment.

When he was done, Rawk sat back and waved for the waitress so he could get some fruit.

"So, how *is* you search going?" Weaver asked when they were alone again. "Find *any* sorcerers yet?"

"As a matter of fact I have."

The prince looked a bit surprised. "Really?" He chewed on his fingernail for a moment.

"There was magic flying everywhere. Ladies diving for cover. Children screaming."

"Just like old times."

"Not quite."

Weaver's eyes narrowed. "How so?"

"Well, I didn't kill them."

"You didn't?"

"No. I asked them some questions, then let them go."

"No, you didn't."

"Yes I did."

"But I heard about Valo."

"What about him?"

"You killed *him*."

Rawk sighed. "He died of a heart attack. I just happened to be there."

"Really? So, do you have any information I can pass on to Ramaner?"

"No."

"That isn't helpful." Weaver tapped his fingers on the table for a moment. He glanced at the door. "Anyway, I should go and do some work, I suppose, get Ramaner organized and what−not."

"I suppose. I need to get my men organized as well."

"You're wasting your money." And Weaver left, having gotten in the last word.

Rawk started peeling an orange.

−O−

Rawk saw Fabi sitting on a porch, taking slices off an apple with a huge hunting knife. He wandered across to the big black man and sat down by his side.

"I thought you were going to come and have a drink with me," Rawk said.

Fabi chewed his apple for a minute, staring out at the customers rushing between the large, dusty stalls of the grain market. "I went up there twice, but you were always out somewhere. I even found out where one of your regular lunch spots was but you weren't there."

"Oh. Sorry."

A wagon creaked by. It was piled high with bulging sacks that left a musty smell in their wake.

Fabi shrugged. "Women will do that to you." Then he looked embarrassed. "I'm sorry about Maris."

Rawk watched as he took another slice from the apple.

"Anyway, boss, what can I do for you?"

"Boss? You aren't one of Frew's guys, are you?"

"Yes."

"I thought I told you to get a different job."

"You did. And I did. But the merchant I was working for up and died after only a week."

"You let someone get to him?"

"Of course not. I think he was 120 years old or something. He died in his sleep."

"A shame."

"Yeah. So anyway, here I am."

"Here you are. But I'm getting everyone to go over to the south of the river as soon as possible. Everyone who isn't already there. I was going to tell Frew but I have no idea where to find him."

"I think he's down near the river somewhere. He thinks there will be more action down there, for some reason."

"Well, he's got more information than me."

"That's what I thought; he's just hoping. We'll be meeting tonight at the Veterans' Club. I can pass on the message, if you like."

"You don't mind working down south?"

"That dwarf..." Fabi scratched the side of his nose, looking embarrassed.

Rawk nodded. "I know. His name was Jargo."

"Jargo?"

Another nod. "His wife and daughter are going to be staying in Galad's old room."

"The one he was buying?"

"Yes. I'm buying it now."

"I think he'd like that."

Rawk laughed. "I'm not so sure. He didn't like dwarves much at all."

"Me either."

Rawk sighed. "Me either. But they aren't so bad, really." Rawk was going to say something else. He was going to say, *You know, some of them are all right,* but a scream from the other side of the market robbed him of the opportunity. He looked at Fabi. Fabi looked at him. And they both jumped to their feet and hurried against the sudden tide of the crowd. They rounded a blue striped awning that was missing a pole at the corner. They dodged past barrows of rice, between stacks of corn and bags of flour. A barrel of wheat had toppled over sending a dune of golden grain across the walkway. Here, they skidded to a halt in an oasis of calm.

The exot was fifteen feet tall and as ugly as a Maltessan sailor. Its blue feathers, from hands to huge shoulders, were covered in blood. The sword and shield were painted scarlet as well. Whatever had supplied the blood was no longer in evidence. The creature looked around with cold, black eyes.

Rawk looked at Fabi. "There's only one," he said. "I think you should take it."

Fabi looked at him.

"You wouldn't want to have to split your claim, would you?"

"I'm not a greedy man, Rawk. I like to share."

"I thought you were going to say that." Rawk took a deep breath and drew his sword.

"What the hell is *that*?"

Rawk looked the creature up and down. "I don't know. I've never seen one before."

"No, that sword. It's terrible."

"Oh, right. It's *Slade,* the first sword I ever had." Why hadn't he gone down to the cellar to find a better sword like Travis has suggested? "Yes, it looks terrible, but it's actually pretty good."

"Well, it had better be."

A small crowd was starting to gather at what it thought was a safe distance, but Rawk had to wonder if anywhere in the city was safe.

"Any ideas?" Fabi asked. He had his own two handed sword out and had moved a few paces to the side.

"Kill it quick."

"I like the sound of that plan. Details would be nice though."

"There's supposed to be details?" Rawk licked his lips as he examined the creature, trying to imagine a weakness. "I should point out that my plans haven't been working out all that well recently."

"You're still alive."

"Yes. I suppose."

"Come on then."

Rawk really didn't want to attack, but he wasn't going to have a choice. He looked at his sword. He *really* didn't want to attack. The blade was shorter than he was used to. The hilt felt strange in his hand, heavy. But Fabi was circling around further, slow and watchful, his own sword at the ready. With a sigh, Rawk went the other direction.

The creature sprang towards him, swinging its sword in a complex pattern. Rawk froze. Then he tried to follow the blade's movement. All within a moment. He set himself, breathed, let himself go, and blocked. Once, twice. He danced away, hand aching, arm shuddering from the blows.

Fabi came in from the other side. He was fast for a big man, but the exot turned and used its shield to knock aside the first attack. It spun around to counter and Rawk shook off his pain to move in behind. The creature was expecting that, waiting for it, and came back around, sword flashing. Rawk ducked. He tried to attack a feathered leg but he slipped on the spilled grain underfoot and missed. He ended up on one knee and might have ended there permanently but Fabi was lunging in. His attack was deflected again. He grunted and backed away but the creature was focused on him for the moment.

"I can't get close, Rawk."

"Path, damn it." Rawk's arm was still dull from the blows he'd taken earlier. His knee ached. He put his hand on the ground to steady himself, to rise to his feet, and felt the grain beneath his fingers.

Fabi feinted and backed away some more. The exot turned back to Rawk and charged.

Rawk pushed himself to his feet, and flung a handful of grain. He wasn't sure if the distraction worked for he was already diving forward, low to the ground. He jarred his shoulder when he landed, rolled, and slashed.

Contact. Rawk came to his feet and ran, continuing in the same direction, trying to put some distance between himself and the danger, expecting a sword in his back at any moment. He saw Fabi going past him, heading the other way, and managed to stop. When he turned around, he saw his companion ramming his long sword up under the exot's rib cage. He twisted the blade before pulling it free and danced away to avoid being crushed.

The creature died silently, which was about the most horrible thing Rawk had ever heard in his life. A life and death battle was not supposed to evaporate quietly like that. The passing of life on the point of a sword was supposed to be a noisy, screaming affair. But the fight was over and that was that, apparently.

Rawk sat down in the wheat as the crowd started to emerge from amongst the stalls. The cheering grew as a trickle of blood started to follow the straight lines of the cobbles, moving slowly towards the buildings beside the market.

"We should remember that," Fabi said, coming to slump down by Rawk's side.

"Remember what?"

"A lot of these creatures may not have seen some of the things that we think of as pretty basic."

Rawk grunted.

"Throwing something in its face. We wouldn't fall for something like that."

"Maybe. Or maybe it was allergic to wheat."

"What?"

"Never mind."

It was getting hard to ignore the noise from the crowd. Rawk sighed and managed to get back on his feet without looking too much like an old man. He smiled and raised his sword. People rushed forward to ask him questions and slap him on the back. He wanted them to go away. They wouldn't. He knew they wouldn't, even if he asked. At least they weren't throwing nuts.

The exot continued to bleed.

Rawk wondered how he would feel if he suddenly found himself on a strange world. Would he assume the locals were friendly? Or would he be a bit concerned by all the shouting and screaming and running? Would he try to talk to the people who came along and attacked him? Or would he defend himself first and try to work out what was going on later?

Rawk answered some questions but the crowd could tell he really didn't want to be there. A few of them at the back continued to shout but most fell to a confused, uncomfortable muttering.

"I must be going," Rawk said eventually. He gave a half–hearted wave and pushed through the crowd with Fabi following behind. Out in the clear, he stopped to breath. The crowd was dispersing, disappointed by the strange end to the event. One man stared accusingly at Rawk as he wandered away, muttering to himself and shaking his head.

"I killed some little hairy thing yesterday," Fabi said. "It had big claws and teeth but was as slow as winter in the north. But when I was done, the crowd kind of wandered away without saying much at all."

"They see exots being killed every day now, just about."

"But you turn up and they're all over you."

Rawk nodded. "I know."

"Where are you headed?"

"I'm going home. I'm sore and tired. I don't know how much longer I can keep up."

"You're getting old."

"I'm already old. The trouble is, I'm running out of time." He got his bearings and started for home. "You can keep the whole claim."

Rawk walked slowly up the hill and nobody bothered him. Perhaps people didn't want him to drop dead while they were talking to him, as if they might be to blame. When he reached the *Hero's Rest* he looked at the new doorway. Gabbo was standing nearby, leaning on a mallet and looking pleased with himself.

The dwarf smiled. "Rawk. We're done."

"Everything?"

"Yes."

"So, I can go down there?"

"If you want."

Rawk did want. It looked great. Not only had they made a door through the stone wall, they'd added a fancy, carved timber doorframe and a solid, iron bound door. He went over and opened the door. It swung open silently to reveal a yard of passage then a polished stone staircase. A small building had been constructed to protect the stairs from the elements.

"You don't do things by halves, do you?"

"Never." Gabbo cleared his throat and looked around. As ever, where ever Rawk went there were people following and watching. They still weren't actually talking to him though and now that he was talking to a dwarf they were stating to look a bit confused. "Do you know where Travis is? I had a friend make something and I wanted to show him. It's kinda just a sample of Feb's work." The dwarf picked up a hessian–wrapped bundle that was leaning against the wall and held it out. It was almost a yard long and heavy.

Rawk removed the wrapping and discovered a sign carved into a slab of same timber as the doorframe. "THE VAULT".

"Grint told me the reason for the stairs so if I can just get Travis to tell me the name I can have a proper one made up. If he wants." He came around to examine the sign himself.

Rawk smiled. "How much does something like this cost?"

"Feb's just starting out and would be pleased at the exposure, if people just go around mentioning his name."

"Well, personally, I think this is a perfect name. I like the double meaning; a basement and a safe. I think Travis will love it too." Rawk looked around too. "I think it would be best to put it on then wall now, that way Travis can get a proper feel for it." And it was free.

Rawk looked at the doorframe again, smiled and made his way down the stairs.

Things were moving along nicely down there as well. There was a small stage being built in one corner and a completed bar in another. There were already five ale barrels lined up in racks, waiting to be tapped. A couple of workers were arranging tables and chairs.

"Rawk?" Travis came from the hallway, carrying a couple of more chairs. "I didn't expect to see you back so early. How is your investigation going?"

Rawk grunted. "I had to stop so I could have lunch with Weaver."

"Right. How is *he* doing?"

"Crazy as ever."

"I knew *that*." Travis handed his two chairs to a passing worker. He continued once the man had moved away and was talking to someone else. "So, are we serving food down here?"

"That would make things difficult, wouldn't it? Getting the stuff down from the kitchen and all?"

"Yes."

"Then don't worry about it. There's more money to be made in ale anyway." Rawk started towards the door Travis had just used. "Sylvia will be here soon. Send here through to my office."

Travis just grunted in reply.

In the office, Rawk sat down and put his feet up on the desk. It still wasn't very comfortable, but he stayed where he was and examined his library. It had grown considerably since he'd last been there. It looked as if Travis had cleared almost every book out of the Tapalar mansion. Two entire shelves were full now and one level of the third as well. Some volumes were so big they could not stand upright, others would get lost in your pocket if you weren't careful.

Rawk got himself upright without tipping over his chair and collected a book of a more regular size. It turned out that *Fire Magic of Southern Tharpin* was all about cooking spells. Or spell that involved cooking. Or...

"*THRICE BOILED WATER— SILVER.* You will need. One copper pot filled with water. One ring of pure silver. One piece of cured leather. One stone from a peach. Place the stone in the pot and set on a fire. When the water has boiled, remove the pot and allow to cool. Remove the stone by hand and replace with the leather. Return to the fire to boil again. Repeat the process a third time with the ring."

"Thrice boiled water?"

Rawk looked up and saw Sylvia standing in the doorway. "You know of it?"

"Of course."

"Does it work?"

"If you are attempting to make the worst soup in the world, yes, it is fine."

"What is it supposed to do?"

"It was used as the basis for many spells in traditional Tharpinal magic. There is also Golden Thrice Boiled Water and lead and..." She waved her hand. "There are probably hundreds more for all I know but there were about ten common ones."

"So they don't do it anymore?"

"Of course not. That book must be hundreds of years old if it is taking the subject seriously."

Rawk looked at the cover and shrugged. "Somebody called Talamar Haf wrote it, that's all I know."

"Haf?" Sylvia suddenly looked interested. "Really? That *is* impressive." She came into the room for a closer look and noticed the shelves for the first time. She changed direction and headed towards them instead. She scanned the titles for a moment then pulled one of the larger volumes out. She ran her hands over the leather cover and opened it up to read a few lines to herself. She tucked that volume under her arm, as if unwilling to let it go, and pulled out something else. She put that one back, though somewhat reluctantly, and found another that she liked the look of.

"So?"

She managed to turn away from the books for a moment. "I must say, Rawk, I was skeptical, but..." She held up the first volume for him to see. "This one here is almost two thousand years old. You could buy Weaver's palace and he would still have to give you some change."

"The *Rest* has a better view."

Sylvia sighed. "Your library is very impressive, Rawk. It is not often a man downplays his attributes." She pointed out another book. "This one opened up a whole new area of magic. Jacob Madacan was a genius."

"I got that one especially for you."

"But where did you get them."

Rawk hesitated, but Sylvia couldn't really tell anyone, even if she wanted to. "The Lady Tapalar was studying magic, amongst other things. Not to do, you understand, just to know. She collected these for years. I even got some for her, when I was traveling around. Just random selections, of course; I had no idea what was what."

"Can I take some of these?"

Rawk rose to his feet and went over to look at the shelves. He ran his fingers over one of the spines. It was one that he had bought. He could remember because it had been damaged in a tavern fight when he was returning home. "I would rather you didn't," he said. He looked at *Fire Magic of Southern Tharpin*, which was still in his hand. "Well, you can take this one. And you can come and read them any time you like. I'll get Travis to get you a comfortable old couch and all, if you want."

"I guess that will have to do. I shall start with this one."

"Do we have time, do you think?" Rawk asked, looking at the book. "Ramaner is going to be sending out the City Guard to look for the sorcerers tomorrow."

Sylvia examined the book as well, then glanced up at the shelf. "I'm not sure if I can visit any more brothels, Rawk. And most of the sorcerers I know are smart enough to either avoid detection or leave.

Rawk didn't want to start with the brothels either. And it was only a couple of hours before dark anyway. They would lose a lot of that just finding the first place. He sighed. "Very well. Tomorrow then."

"Tomorrow."

Sylvia nodded and when it looked as if she was going to sit on the floor, Rawk motioned her to the desk and the chair. "Thank you." A moment later, her head was buried in the book and Rawk left the room without her noticing.

In *The Vault*, Grint was near the stage, talking to a woman that had to be a carpenter, as some workers set up the last of the tables. There were seats for about fifty people, which would do nicely if he could charge them a couple of ithel just to get in the door and then sell them lots of ale. He watched the men for a few more minutes as they cleared away some mess. Some of them were muttering about taking orders from a dwarf and continually cast dark glances towards the front of the room. The carpenter obviously wasn't all that happy either. She had her arms crossed and never seemed to do anything more than shake her head. Eventually, Grint shook his head too, threw down a sheaf of papers he was holding and stormed up the stairs to the street. The workers laughed and the carpenter collected the pages. Rawk wondered over to her.

"What was that all about?"

The woman looked up, surprised. "Rawk?" She looked around as if someone might be playing a joke on her. She was blonde haired and freckled, under the dirt and sawdust.

"Yes. Did my disguise not work?"

Her mouth flapped while she looked for an answer.

"What was that all about?" Rawk repeated.

She looked at the stairs recently used by Grint. "The stage is too small, apparently."

Rawk looked at the stage. It wasn't huge, though surely big enough for a couple of stools.

"He's a bloody dwarf. How much room does he take up?"

Rawk didn't point out that Grint, like most dwarves, was no skinnier than humans, just shorter.

"He says they might have more than a couple of people up there occasionally."

That seemed fair enough. "And you think they won't?"

"Well..."

"So you don't actually know?"

She pursed her lips and looked at Rawk as if she suddenly didn't know who he was.

"He's a dwarf, so I imagine he gave you detailed plans for what he wanted."

She waved the papers at him. "Of course."

Rawk took them from the carpenter and flicked through a couple. The third one showed the stage with measurements clearly written. He looked at the stage. "You stage does seem quite a bit smaller than the one in the plans."

The woman shrugged. "Great Path, it isn't much. A couple of foot, at most."

"You don't even know the dimensions of what you've built?" Rawk shook his head. He imagined that if he went and found Gabbo, the dwarf would be able to tell him every detail of the stairs: run, riser height, tread size and possible even the weight of each stone block used. Rawk handed the pages back. "I don't imagine you'll get paid if you don't do the job you were hired to do. Grint may be a dwarf but Travis isn't."

The woman looked at Rawk some more. "Well, I'm done for the day. The damn dwarf and his stage can wait until tomorrow." She stuffed the pages into her toolbox, threw the remaining tools on top and joined onto the end of the line of workers who were making their way up the stairs.

Rawk looked at the stage.

"It looks pretty good." Travis was striding towards the bar with a crate of tankards in his hands. He dumped his load then came to look more closely.

"It's too small."

"What? Who says?"

"Grint."

"What does he know?"

"He knows a bit about stages, I would think."

Travis looked. "There's plenty of room for a couple of stools."

"What about five stools? Grint and Celeste can't sing every night, much as I would like them too. Maybe we need to organize some other acts to play a couple of nights a week as well."

"Why can't they play every night? We're paying them enough."

"Grint gave her plans. If the stage isn't the same as the plans by tomorrow afternoon, pay the woman a couple of ithel then get a dwarf to come and do the job."

Travis started laughing, then seemed to realize that Rawk was serious.

"They aren't worth the trouble, Rawk. If people hear about all the dwarves you've got working here they'll stop coming."

"No, they won't. They'll just pretend the dwarves are slaves working for their betters and think it's a great idea."

It looked like Travis would say something else, but apparently he thought better of it. He shook his head instead and left.

Five minutes later, Rawk was sitting on the edge of the stage, watching as the last of the workers finally finished up and left via the stairs. Grint came the other direction with Celeste trailing behind. One of the men bumped the dwarf and some others made comments to Celeste. They weren't nice.

"Rawk," Grint said, putting down the bag that held his drum.

"How is it all going?"

"Seems to be going well enough, I suppose."

Rawk raised an eyebrow. He wasn't sure if he got it exactly right, but the dwarf seemed to get the idea.

"It's all these bloody humans," he said.

Rawk wanted to raise his eyebrow again, but he didn't think he could get it any higher. That left jumping the one eyebrow down then up, or raising the other as well. "Really?" he said.

Grint seemed to realize he was talking to a human. "It isn't *all* the humans, obviously." He cleared his throat. "The woman building the stage has no idea. And the workers..." he looked over his shoulder at the stairs.

"The stage will be finished tomorrow, or we'll hire someone else. A dwarf. And the workers..." Rawk shrugged. "I dare say they are laborers because nobody is willing to give them a job where they actually have to think. I think they're done anyway."

Grint and Celeste looked around the room.

"It's looking good," Grint said.

Rawk started to nod but didn't like the look on Celeste's face. "You don't like it?"

She shrugged, then shook her head. "It's very... stark."

"Stark?"

"Bare. Grey."

Rawk had another look. She was right. There was just stone and timber. He hadn't really given a thought to *decoration*. "Will it matter?" he asked. "It will be dark and..." He glanced at Grint, but the dwarf look as unsure as he did.

"It won't be completely dark. And lamps may well accentuate the starkness."

Rawk still wasn't sure. "Well, you can be in charge of un–starking it then. Do whatever you want. I'm sure you'll do a great job."

Celeste ducked her head and blushed. "I'm not sure if..."

Grint grunted. "Then next time don't say anything, sister."

"No," Rawk said. "It's all right if you aren't sure. Talk to Travis and..." He tried to think of who else might be able to help with something like that. "Go and talk to Yardi at the *Keeto Alata* offices. She knows everything. And if she doesn't she'll know someone who does. Don't let Hurno bully you."

Celeste looked up and gave a small smile. "I'll go tomorrow."

"Good. I'll be trawling through brothels again tomorrow, I expect. I'm sure Yardi will have something to say about that. What are you two doing back here now anyway? Isn't it time to go home?"

Grint pulled out his drum. "Normally I'd be putting down tools now and getting ready to go somewhere to play. We aren't used to going home at this time of the day. And we want to test the place out anyway."

He took a chair up onto the stage and started to play his drum while Celeste wrestled her mandolin out of its case. Rawk watched for a second, then found a second chair and put it on the stage for her. A minute later, she was playing as well and Rawk was reminded why he was going to all the expense and trouble of getting the room set up. The sounds drifted around the big room, questing into corners and swirling around the tables and chairs.

Rawk found a chair for himself and sat down. He almost closed his eyes but instead watched the flash of Grint's stick and the dancing of Celeste's fingers on the strings. He listened as they moved seamlessly from a Kenkonian gig to a Redami lullaby to a Habonian dirge. They did it all without words, with just a glance.

Rawk sat for ten minutes, not moving. He would have stayed frozen for even longer, but he heard a noise behind him and turned to see Sylvia standing near by. He looked at her for a moment but she didn't say anything, so neither did he.

The music continued to fill the room.

Wensday

THERE WAS A KNOCK AT THE DOOR. Rawk stayed silent, hoping whoever it was would go away. The knock had been so timid that he doubted whoever was out there really wanted to come in anyway. The knock came again, no louder than before, then the door started to slowly open.

After a moment, Biki stuck her head through the gap and looked around.

"Hello," Rawk said, rolling over to the edge of the bed.

The dwife jumped and almost dropped her tray. "Rawk. Hello. I wasn't sure if..."

"Well, I'm here." He rubbed his eyes. "I was up late last night though, so I probably won't be in the best mood. You started working this morning?"

"Yes."

"And Travis is already sending you up to my room?"

She looked up but didn't say anything.

Rawk nodded. "I don't think he likes you much."

"Why?"

Rawk shrugged. There had never been a dwarf in his room before, male or female. The ones who'd worked on the shower room had all come up via the back stairs. He'd made sure of that. And now... He gave a laugh. "Travis thinks I will see the error of my ways when there is a dwarf in my actual room, doing things."

"He thinks you will have me fired because you don't want a dwife in your room? Even though you suggested that I work here?"

"Something like that."

Biki stood silently and looked at him.

"You're waiting for me to tell you to leave?" He rubbed his scalp. "I may not have any dwarf friends, Biki, but any fool can see that when a dwarf does something, they do it properly. I could have some human in here, bumbling around doing stuff, but you'll do it well, you do it without all the fuss, and then you'll leave me to sit and drink in peace."

She gave a small smile and but still didn't move.

"You have jug of tea there?"

"Yes. Whatever that is."

"And a cup?"

"Yes."

"Well, just set it down, then pour me a cup." Rawk looked around and realized that there still wasn't a table in the room. "On the bed will do." He watched her as she worked. As if to prove him right, everything was done precisely, each movement, each task, as if it was the most important in the world. And when she was done, she quietly slipped out the door.

Rawk closed his eyes and breathed in the fumes before taking a small sip. And when he was done with the tea he was going to do some exercise and have a shower. After that, he would be ready to face the day. Perhaps. He didn't know how many more brothels he could visit.

"As many as it takes," he said. He took another sip, then collected some clean clothes and set them on the bed.

—O—

Rawk took a deep breath. He closed his eyes and leaned against the wall just down the road from the day's fourth brothel.

"Are you unwell?" Sylvia asked, shading her eyes against the morning sun. She had not unwrapped the scarf from her face, as if it might protect her from the *Blue Deng* as well as Weaver's spies, but her eyes showed concern.

"I'm fine. I was just wondering how many of those women actually want to be in there."

Sylvia looked back at the *Blue Jasmine*. "I would think that none of them want to be in that place at all."

"I don't mean that place in particular." He looked back too. It was one of the worst places they had seen. Not only was the building about to fall down, but the women inside acted as if they would welcome the release. "I mean all the whores in all the brothels. How many of them would prefer to be washerwomen? Or servants?"

"I know what you meant, Rawk. My comment stands. Though after a while, many of them probably tell themselves that selling their body to strangers is an easy way to make money."

"Killing exots is easy too," Rawk said. He catalogued his aches and pain as he rubbed at his sore knee. "Come on, there's another place not too far away."

There was a group of children watching from nearby. One of them finally worked up the courage, with the help of her friends, and crossed the street.

Rawk held back a sigh. "Hello."

"Hello." She glanced back over her shoulder. "Can you tell us a story, Rawk?"

The other children were poised, ready to rush forward like a charging army. Rawk shook his head. "Not today, I'm afraid."

The girl's shoulders slumped.

Rawk tried to think of a likely story. He gestured to Sylvia. "My friend needs my help doing some very important work."

"Are you fighting monsters?"

"Sort of. We're fighting sickness."

"But that's silly. You can't fight sickness; you can't see it."

Rawk smiled. "Just because you can't see it, doesn't mean you can't fight it."

The girl stood there looking, waiting for more.

Rawk looked around for an example. He could see Clinker standing near a strange contraption of timber and gears and a big wire brush. He was fiddling with some bolts and appeared to be muttering to himself. Graffiti on the wall behind him proclaimed, *The tide is ever rising—Words of Wisdom.*

"See the boy?"

The girl wrinkled her nose. "The dwarf?"

"Yes."

"What about him?"

"You could go and talk to him."

"Why would I do that? I bet he smells."

"To fight the things you cannot see."

"Can he see them?"

"Yes, he can, though he probably doesn't realize."

There was a pause. Rawk thought the girl was thinking about what he had said. But, instead... "So, you aren't going to tell us a story?"

"No."

She shook her head and went back to her friends.

"You will lose followers if you talk like that, Rawk. Those people who throw walnuts at you do not want philosophy."

"Well, too bad for them."

"Come, let us continue."

They had barely taken a step when they heard a scream.

Rawk stopped and looked around, unsure where the sound had come from. Sylvia pointed.

"Are you sure?"

"Yes."

Rawk drew his sword and ran. Down a street with rough, uneven cobbles underfoot and walls looming on either side. At the next corner he stopped again. Sylvia caught up to him before he decided on the next direction to take. He didn't let her catch her breath, running again, shouting at people to get out of the way. Ahead, there was as small square with a stone cistern in the middle. Women from the apartments probably used it for washing clothes, though it was really for drinking. Nobody was there now. There was a splash of watery blood, or bloody water, on the ground.

Shifting his grip on *Slade*, Rawk examined the square. There was nothing there. No people, no exot. Just a quiet expectancy.

"It's in the cistern." There was a woman looking out of a second story window. Her face was white, her hands shaking.

"What is it?"

The woman shrugged.

Rawk sidled up towards the low stone wall to get a better look. A creature lunged at him, surging upwards, bringing with it a wave of water that almost knocked him from his feet. He stayed upright, staggering back. The thing landed half in the water, half on the cobbles. It was a long snake of a thing as thick as Rawk's torso with a line of barbed fins right down its back.

"Great Path." Rawk looked at Sylvia. "Can you..." He thrust his fingers towards it.

"What?"

"Do some magic stuff?"

"No."

"Of course not." Rawk looked at the creature's hide. It looked like it was covered in scales, though if it was they were so close together that getting a blade between might well be impossible. Especially if the blade was a chunky as *Slade*. "So, what do I do?"

"Now you wish to think about things and make plans?"

"Well..."

"It has no arms or legs Rawk. How hard can it be?"

It sounded good, but Rawk doubted it would be as simple as strolling in and stabbing it in the eye. These things generally weren't. "Path." He took a step in and watched as the exot reared up, showing its dagger long teeth and long forked tongue.

"Wait," Sylvia said.

"What?"

"I think I have heard of these. They are poisonous."

They generally were. "So don't get bitten?" He had already been intending to avoid that if he could.

"No. It secretes a poison. If it touches you..."

"Great." Rawk needed a longer sword. He always needed a longer sword these days, even when he had a longer sword. He looked around but couldn't see anything that would help. Apart from the exit. The only other thing was a plant in a pot, like in Yardi's office. With no other options, Rawk backed up, sword at the ready, and grabbed the stem of the plant. It was heavier than expected and once he had it, he still wasn't sure what he was going to do with it. Sylvia was watching.

There was really only one thing he could do with the plant but he wasn't sure what the result would be. He moved back in. When the creature lunged forward again, Rawk threw the pot and the plant. His aim was off, but that didn't matter because the exot snatched it out of the air with a viscous snap of it's jaws. Except it wasn't quite what it was expecting. And in the moment while it masticated and gave it some thought, Rawk raced forward as fast as his knee would allow. It wasn't very fast. When he was three paces away, he threw *Slade*. It didn't feel right to throw a sword, but it worked. The ugly, heavy blade buried itself in the creature's eye and stayed there. Black blood gushed forth, spraying onto the cobbles, and Rawk danced away, staying clear just in case it was dangerous as well.

"That was not very heroic, Rawk."

"What? Now you want me to sword fight a snake—lizard thing. Yesterday you were telling me I should retire." He looked at the exot. It was still thrashing about on the ground. He wasn't quiet sure how he was going to explain the creature to Weaver's secretary. Surely it must be worth quite a bit though. He sat down. He wanted to rub his knee but Sylvia was watching him. "I knew there was a reason I didn't get a decent sword yesterday. I think I need a proper one now though."

"What, *now*?"

"Well, what if we get attacked again?"

Sylvia sighed. "Is there anywhere near here that you can get one?"

"Well, let's head towards my usual smith and visit some brothels on the way."

"Very well."

Rawk trudged back the way he had come, trying to gather his thoughts and remember where he had been heading before the diversion.

$$-O-$$

Rawk had tried to be as efficient as possible as they made their way down the hill towards the river, but it still felt as if they'd walked for twenty miles and he'd already thought of another three brothels they'd passed within a couple of streets of. And the quality of the establishments left a lot to be desired. The women and men in the places they had visited most recently made the company of the snake–exot thing seem like a pleasant way to spend the morning.

Denu's Nest was a tall, narrow building on an even narrower street down near the river. The sign above the door was graced with elegant, curling red letters and there was a small, blue bird perched on the 'T'. The front porch was tidy. There were curtains in the windows. Overall, it and looked quite a bit more inviting than the previous places. But Rawk didn't think anything could make him want to enter another brothel at any time in his life.

"Can we stop for lunch?" Rawk asked.

"We have barely started."

"Maybe you don't need lunch— look at how skinny you are— but I certainly do. It's got to almost be noon."

"You have already visited two bakeries."

"So."

"We are here now. Let us just check this one then find something to eat."

The inside of *Denu's Nest* lived up to the standards set by the exterior. The foyer had a large, expensive looking rug with a striking design and tasseled corners. There were tasteful paintings on the wall above chaise couches. There were several women sitting around chatting, but they were all fully clothed and seemed to be in possession of all of their teeth. There was an ornately carved desk in the back corner with an old woman writing in a ledger. She looked up when they entered, and purposefully closed the book. She wiped the nib of her pen and set it down on top. Then she adjusted her perfectly coiffed hair, and rose gracefully to her feet.

"Good afternoon, Rawk. I would never have thought to see you here, but I am honored."

"Are you, Denu? Well, sorry, but you shouldn't be honored. This is the sixth place I've been to today."

"Seventh," Sylvia said as she unwrapped her scarf for the first time that day and took a deep breath. Obviously this place met with her approval.

Denu smiled. "Then you truly are a great Hero. A god amongst men."

Rawk couldn't help but smile back. "You make sure you tell that to everyone who comes in."

Sylvia sighed. "Denu, we apologize for coming in like this, but we are looking for a certain person."

"I am not sure that I can help you."

Sylvia looked around the room then motioned over to the desk. She followed the other woman over and Rawk trailed behind. In the relative privacy offered by the distance, Sylvia whispered, "I can understand that your reputation would depend on a certain amount of discretion."

"Indeed."

"So I will rely on your discretion now... The ohoga portals that are admitting the exots to our world are being opened by sorcerers."

"Surely not. Does Prince Weaver know?"

Rawk thought he should help. "He does know, but has been trying to keep it quiet. So, Sylvia and I are here, doing the work he would do himself, if only he could. Though he may be taking a more direct hand in events as of today."

"Prince Weaver has done everything for Katamood. I can remember when..." Denu looked around. "Well, we do not need to speak of that."

Sylvia nodded. "The sorcerers are letting the creatures through for reasons we do not know. All we do know at this stage is that innocents are dying. And we have one clue. Someone saw a one armed woman, an elf..."

Denu's hand went to her throat, clutching at a necklace she wore.

"You know this woman?" Rawk asked. He wanted to grab her but thought it might be counter–productive.

"I don't know if..." She glanced at the ledger.

Rawk did too. Then he put a hand on the woman's shoulder. "This is a fine establishment, Denu. We would not ask you to do anything to risk your reputation but this is important."

"Perhaps later today... But no... I cannot tell you anything."

Rawk cleared his throat. The woman wanted to tell them something, but also wanted to be able to deny everything. He gently pushed her towards the women on the nearest couch. "Perhaps you could introduce me to some of your ladies, in case I..."

"Yes, of course." She nodded and willingly moved away from the table. "Even if you do not visit us again, you could perhaps make comment to others on the quality of the establishment and the ladies working here."

"Of course. Who is this lovely lady?"

He was introduced to three women, all of them beautiful and well spoken, before Sylvia rejoined them.

Rawk kissed the hand of the final whore and thanked her, then turned to the madam. "Thank you for your time, Denu. I am sorry you were unable to help us, but I was very impressed with your business and will spread the word whenever I am able."

"Thank you, Rawk. Willing customers are easy to find. Ones that can afford my girls are a different matter."

"The pleasure is all mine, Denu." Rawk kissed Denu's hand as well. "If I ever get lonely, I know where I will come." He looked the woman up and down. "Did you once, perhaps…"

Denu blushed. "Not for many years, Rawk."

Rawk smiled and let Sylvia draw him towards the door. Before she exited, she paused to tie her scarf, tucking in her long hair and adjusting the folds carefully.

"So?" Rawk said as they finally stepped outside.

Sylvia looked around. "I cannot be sure, but it looks as if Falling Leaves has an appointment at dusk today."

"You can't be sure? And I can't believe you have to make an appointment at a brothel, even one as nice as *Denu's Nest*."

"I cannot be sure, because I cannot be completely sure what name Falling Leaves is using. And you probably only have to make an appointment if you have tastes as unusual as hers."

"Oh."

"But there is an appointment for someone named Rilliona, which is an old elvish word meaning 'hidden power', which would be just like Falling Leaves."

"But Rilliona is an actual name. There could really be someone with that name."

"As I said, I cannot be sure. No other names caught my attention."

"So, we come back at dusk?"

"I believe that would be the best plan off attack. In the interim, I must go and speak with someone."

"So we'll meet back here?"

"An hour before dusk, just to be safe?"

"Right. I'll see you then."

Rawk was going to get himself a new sword. Hopefully something better than *Slade*. Looking around to get his bearings, he spied Clinker lurking in the shadows at the mouth of an alley.

"What are you doing there?" Rawk asked.

The lad came out into the open. He shrugged. "I saw you and Sylvia and was just wondering..."

"You were following us?"

Clinker nodded.

"You don't want to know what happened to the last dwarf that followed me."

Clinker looked a bit confused. "He's over there."

"What?" Rawk looked where the lad was pointing. There was a dwarf sitting on a step a few buildings down. He looked like he was just relaxing, but he had a pen in his hand and a thick wad of paper in his pocket. He had a wooden box, about the size of a hatbox, by his side. A moment later the dwarf was on his feet and walking quickly away. "Who was that?"

Clinker shrugged. "I don't know his name."

"How long has he been following me?"

"Longer than I have."

"Well... Great."

"What are you and Sylvia up to?"

"Nothing. And I'd appreciate it if you didn't go talking to anyone about it."

Clinker gave that some thought. "I'm going to tell people that you aren't up to anything? Who'd want to listen?"

Rawk looked down the street to where the other dwarf had gone. "A lot of people, apparently."

"All you humans are a bit strange today."

"We are?"

"Yeah. Some kids talked to me before. Asked all sorts of weird things."

Rawk smiled. "They did? Like what"

"They asked if I could see sickness."

"What did you say?"

"Of course I can't."

"Do you know what a metaphor is?"

"Yes. Sort of. Not really."

"Well, it doesn't matter."

"Strange."

"Has Thacker given you a proper job yet?"

"No. But I get lots of work anyway."

"What was that thing you were working on earlier?"

"What thing?" He seemed to be blushing.

"The... thing." Rawk gestured vaguely, as if that might help. "The wooden thing with the brush."

"It's supposed to scrub the graffiti off the wall."

"Supposed to?"

"It doesn't work very well."

"Why not?"

Clinker shrugged. "The brush scrapes the wall, but not hard enough. I have to try some stuff."

"Surely Thacker has people who do that kind of thing."

Clinker nodded. "Thacker doesn't know about my machine."

"*Your* machine?"

"Yes."

"You made it?"

"Kristun helped me with some building. It was a bit hard."

"Kristun?"

"Not Kristun ga Lund; he's a tanner. Kristun ga Meyer. He's an engineer but does some inventing and stuff too."

Rawk shook his head. "Right. That's why I was confused." He had no idea about any of them. "So, do you know any blacksmiths? I need a new sword."

The boy gave it some thought. "I know lots, but I don't know who's the best. You should ask Thacker."

"I should, shouldn't I?" He had enough time. Just.

"Don't tell him about my machine though."

"I promise." He looked around for a goat cab but before he spotted one of them, he spotted a bakery.

–O–

Rawk sat with a grizzled, old dwarf on one side and a too-skinny elf on the other. They both seemed as nervous as he did, but for them, it probably didn't have anything to do with the contraption they were riding in. He examined the city outside as he had the first time. It was as amazing now as it was then. Crowds bustled about, seemingly much happier than the human crowds on the far side of the river.

As the tram rounded a bend, Rawk looked forward and saw Thacker's offices, clinging to the wall of the valley. And, coming down the stairs, was Sylvia.

"Path." Rawk sidled over to the other side of the carriage, watching the elf as she went to stand beside on the little raised dock. As soon as the tram hissed and screeched to a halt, Rawk jumped down to the road on the other side. He almost fell, but didn't have time to stop. He hurried towards the thickest clump of people before realizing they were all dwarves and he would stand out like a... well, like a Hero in a crowd of dwarves. He hunched his shoulders, as if that would help, and turned to see if Sylvia had seen him. The tram was already pulling away, clanking and rattling, sending out a stream of smoke, and the elf was reading from a scrap of paper. She didn't notice anything much at all. Nodding to a dwife, Rawk hobbled across the road to the offices. The foyer was empty again. It felt strange to just march up the stairs, but he didn't see that he had a lot of choice.

Two dwarves were guarding the door to Thacker's office again. They were smiling when Rawk stepped out into the open, but quickly put on their serious faces and stood up a little bit straighter. Rawk recognized one of them from his previous visit.

"Rawk?" the dwarf said.

"Yes, hello, Rake. I was hoping to talk with Thacker."

"Ummm..." Rake looked at his companion, who shrugged. "Sure. I suppose." He opened the door and stepped aside.

"Thank you."

Thacker was sitting with his feet up on the desk. He had a tankard of ale in one hand and a newspaper in the other. "Rawk? What are you doing here? You just missed your partner."

"What did she want?"

"She... Well, you know." He tried to get his feet back on the floor, but with his hands full it wasn't easy. He eventually gave in and put down his drink. "She just needed to check up on some things. How about you? What can I do for you?"

"Well..." Rawk knew that dwarves made the best swords; they made the best everything. And he had used dwarvish swords before. But he had never asked a dwarf for a sword. He'd never spoken to a dwarf about swords. Before a few weeks ago he had barely spoken to dwarves at all.

"Come on, out with it. I'm extremely busy."

"I've gone through three swords in the last few weeks." That actually wasn't very fair on the swords. Only one of them— the best of them— had actually failed. "So I need to know where to go to get another."

"I heard about *Kult* and *Dabaneera*. What happened to the other one?"

"*Slade* is covered in something horrible and smelly that I don't want to touch."

"Fair enough. But as luck would have it..." He hauled himself onto his feet, as if he'd been working hard all day, and made his way to a table against a side wall. He took up a cloth wrapped bundle longer than he was tall and offered it to Rawk.

Rawk took the bundle and it was immediately obvious what was inside. He folded back the cloth to reveal the three swords. They were all approximately the same length and they were all well made and straight, but that was where the similarities ended. Rawk placed the swords on the desk and picked up the first. It had a thin, single edged blade with no adornments. He waved the sword experimentally and placed it carefully on the table. The next was overly ornate with a laminated blade and half a dozen jewels on the guard and pommel. He tested that one too, before taking up the final blade. And as soon as he touched it, he knew it was different. He glanced at Thacker and saw the dwarf smiling.

"The first two were swords Rezik had lying around his workshop. The last one, he made especially for you."

"But..." Rawk moved away from the table so he could move through some simple forms, spinning around the room until his knee almost gave out on him.

"Perfect, right?"

"Yes."

"*Kult* and *Dabaneera* weren't made by masters, but they were good swords made by talented smiths. And swords like that always get their specifications recorded at some stage. It might not be when they are made, but dwarves like to know the details. If you get a sword sharpened by a dwarf, he'll take enough measurements to recreate the sword if he wants. A good smith can tell a lot just by looking. He can tell even more just by picking the sword up. And that sword there is a combination of *Kult* and *Dabaneera.*"

"It's astounding."

"Rezik is about the best there is. He's also a friend of Biki's. He heard what you did for her."

"It was only two days ago."

"No, you went to see her three days ago to tell her what happened. Most humans wouldn't have even done that."

"You couldn't make this sword in three days."

"Well, you know how dwarves are when get an idea in their head..."

Rawk spun the sword around to look at the other side of the blade. "I want this sword. How much is it?"

Thacker shrugged. "It's a gift from Rezik."

"No." He shook his head.

Thacker's eyes narrowed. "Pardon?"

Rawk cleared his throat. "I've just got this thing recently about paying people what they are worth. Somebody made a timber sign for the *Hero's Rest* as well. I want him to send a bill."

The dwarf nodded slowly. After a moment, he made a note on a sheet of paper on his desk. "I'll find out about the sign."

"Gabbo knows who it is. He told me the name, but I can't remember." Rawk looked at his new sword but was thinking about Clinker and his wall—scrubbing machine. Could the dwarves make machines that made fighting easier? Was there something they could build so he wouldn't need a sword at all? He glanced at Thacker but didn't say anything. "I guess I should go. Sylvia and I have plans."

"Plans?"

"Not like that."

"Of course not."

Rawk sighed. "Read tomorrow's newspaper."

"They won't be having one tomorrow."

"Why not?"

"They don't have them every day."

"Oh. Right. Anyway, make sure they send the bills."

Thacker gave a salute from his chair but didn't otherwise move as Rawk rose to his feet. But once on his feet, Rawk didn't leave.

Thacker sighed. "What is it? I won't tell anyone."

"Do you know Juskin the bookseller? He's over near Mount Cheese."

"Of course."

"Well..." Rawk cleared his throat. "He's got these things that he puts on his eyes."

"Spectacles."

"Right. Yes. I think that's what he called them."

Thacker wrote down an address on another piece of paper. "Go and talk to Gessup. He's still perfecting the idea, so it may take him a while."

"Thank you."

−O−

"Is that her?" Rawk pointed to an elf woman striding down the street. He heard Sylvia sigh and turned to look at the elf.

"Does she have one arm?"

"Well... Yes, actually... And another one."

"When I see her, I shall let you know."

"What if you don't see her though?"

"The door is not that big, Rawk. I doubt she will slip through without me noticing."

"I just want to be sure."

"Well, can you please be sure in a more quiet fashion."

"It that her?"

"Rawk, I... Yes. Yes ,it is."

"Huh."

"I would have noticed her in a moment."

"So now what do we do?" Rawk looked up and down the street, wondering if the sorcerers were now hunting in packs, waiting around corners to see if any of their friends were attacked. But Shef hadn't known who Falling Leaves actually was. It was only coincidence he had recognized the others that he already knew.

"We wait."

"Great. So, do we wait here? Or do we go in so we can keep an eye on her?"

"You want to go into the brothel and watch Falling Leaves to make sure she doesn't slip out the back door?" The elf raised an eyebrow.

"Something like that." He smiled at Sylvia. "It would be interesting to see what all the fuss is about."

"I think not. It is much smarter to stay here."

"Since when have I ever done the smart thing?" But he waited where he was, hand on the hilt of his sword.

"You have a new sword?"

"Yes. It's called *Kaj*. I named it after the wolden wolf I killed outside the city. The duen's pet. And it may well be the most magnificent sword I have ever held."

"It doesn't look all that special."

Rawk glanced at his weapon, wondering if he should be offended. "No, it doesn't, does it? But I suppose I don't look all that special, either." It was just his luck to get such a magnificent weapon when he had already retired. Perhaps he should have talked to some dwarves years ago.

Sylvia laughed. "I guess looks can be deceiving then."

Rawk turned to look at her. "Are you saying something nice about me?"

She looked away for a moment. "You are not all bad, Rawk."

"Why, thank you."

−O−

Rawk grunted. "We wouldn't have had to wait this long if Falling Leaves was a man." It seemed they had been waiting outside *Denu's Nest* for half the night though it was probably barely two hours. Rawk was starting to wonder if they should be watching the back door. He was also wondering if he should go into the bakery for another pastry. He could smell the preparations for tomorrow's bread. The baker and his assistants were all laughing and singing.

Sylvia grabbed his shoulder. "There she is."

He looked up and saw Falling Leaves sauntering down the stairs of the brothel, looking very pleased with herself. She paused in the flickering illumination of a street lamp, looked each way along the street, then started to make her way up the hill.

"So what do we do now?" Rawk asked, rising to his feet.

"We follow her, obviously."

"I know that. But, do we confront her and force the information out of her?"

Sylvia just looked at him as she started to follow.

"What then?" He cast a longing look back at the bakery then hurried to catch up.

"We follow to where she is staying and see if we can find the note saying where the meeting is."

"That's your plan? That's at least as bad as any of my plans. We don't know that there is a meeting."

"There must be soon."

"Yes, because cabals of evil sorcerers keep to exacting schedules."

"Let us just follow her."

"Will she recognize you?"

"Of course."

"Even with the scarf?"

"Yes."

"Will she attack us?"

Sylvia hesitated and shrugged. "Perhaps. She was always a little bit crazy."

"Then maybe we should..." Rawk didn't know what they should do. He thought about it as he continued to trudge up the hill. "Clinker."

"What."

"Over there." He hurried over to the young dwarf.

"Hello, Rawk."

"Hello, Clinker. Are you following me again?"

"No."

Either he was getting better at lying or he was telling the truth. "Anyway, I have a job for you."

"What?"

"See the one armed elf?" Falling Leaves was visible up ahead, just turning a corner.

"Yes."

"Do you think you can follow her without being noticed?"

"Why?"

"So Sylvia and I can follow you without being noticed even more."

"Of course I can." Clinker gave a nod, scooped up his satchel and ran up the hill.

Of course he could. Rawk was going to shout a warning to be careful, but that would have been about the most conspicuous thing he could do himself. He just hoped the lad knew what he was doing and signaled to Sylvia to keep up.

At the corner he could see Clinker at the *next* corner, standing on some stairs and looking in the dark window of a closed shop. A moment later, he glanced at Rawk, turned and made his way along the side street. Hurrying up to the corner, Rawk glanced in at the shoes the boy had been examining and saw a pair of boots that he liked.

In this manner, from corner to corner, watching out for the boy, they made their way around the side of Two Watch Hill, staying a few blocks up from the edge of the river. It was almost twenty minutes before the rhythm of their journey changed and when it did Rawk was not quite sure what to do. Clinker was standing just up the street, leaning against a lamppost and going through his satchel. So he waited where he was, Sylvia close by his side, buffeted by the last of the day's traffic.

"What do you think is happening?" Sylvia asked.

"I'm not sure. I'll go and see."

Rawk sauntered up the street, looking around and trying to look casual. He pulled out a coin as he approached the boy.

Clinker didn't look up. "I lost her."

"What?"

"One minute she was right there and the next... I couldn't find her at all."

Rawk looked around, as if he might see what the boy could not. "Which way was she heading?" he growled, putting the coin back in his purse.

Clinker shrugged. "I don't know."

"Well, you're no bloody help, are you? I'll do it myself next time."

"Sorry."

"Sorry doesn't help. You have no idea... Bloody dwarf."

He saw Clinker watching him, tears in his eyes. "Get out of here. I have to work out what I'm going to do."

Clinker hurried up the hill without looking back, satchel clanking all the way. Rawk went the other direction.

"He lost her," he said, leaning against the wall near Sylvia.

"What did you say to him?"

"Nothing."

"He's just a boy."

"He said he could do it. And now we have no idea where Falling Leaves might be. This was our best chance."

"That may be, but you cannot blame Clinker."

"Of course I can."

It looked as if the elf would argue the point, but she sighed and looked around. "Perhaps she lives around here."

But around here smelled like moldy leather and the only accommodation, as far as Rawk knew, was taken up by the leather workers."

Rawk looked around as well, reigning in his anger. "I don't know. Maybe there's another brothel around here." But he knew there wasn't. The closest one was a few streets over. They had visited it the day before.

"So what do we do now? Wait again?"

"No, let us continue a small way to see what we can see."

They walked fifty yards up the street, trying to remain inconspicuous. That wasn't really possible, but Rawk did his best to appear unapproachable.

When they reached the next corner, Sylvia held out her hand to stop Rawk. "Wait."

Rawk looked around. He looked around some more. "What?"

"Magic."

"Really?"

"Yes."

"I don't see anything."

"Obviously not."

"But..."

Rawk almost yelped as Sylvia grabbed his shirt and started to pull him towards the side of the street. Which was probably where they should have been in the first place, instead of standing around in the open with nowhere to hide if it was needed. They hid in the shadows of the recessed doorway of a leather dying shop. And they waited.

Rawk scanned the street. He saw the usual gaggle of people, most of whom, thankfully, weren't taking any notice of the people lurking in the doorway. His tightened his grip on *Kaj*'s hilt and exposed and inch of blade. He licked his lips. And he didn't relax until Sylvia sighed and shook her head.

"She is gone now."

"Gone? She who?"

"Falling Leaves."

"She was here? Just now? Did she see us?"

"I do not believe so."

Rawk stepped back down into the street and looked around some more. There were not that many people so he was sure he would have seen Falling Leaves if she had just been standing around.

"She was using a cloaking spell."

"What does that mean?"

"It is a spell that makes it hard for people to notice you."

"So... she was using magic to hide herself?"

"Is that not what I just said?"

"Could you see her?"

Sylvia shook her head. "I could feel the magic, that is all."

"And it's gone now?"

Sylvia sighed.

"So, what do we do?"

"I do not know."

"How many brothels did we visit? And now we've lost her." He looked up the street where Clinker had gone and had the horrible feeling he'd also lost someone else.

A priest paused nearby and turned to look at hem. "Have you given yourself to the Great Path?" the man asked.

Rawk grunted. "Bugger off, you old fool."

Sylvia touched his arm. "Come, let us see what we can see. There are still traces of the magic..."

Rawk followed silently as Sylvia walked slowly up the street with her eyes almost closed. She mumbled to herself and Rawk tried to steer her around the traffic after she bumped into a young woman and a merchant with a tray full of pies. He couldn't make out what she was saying, but it put his nerves on edge anyway. And just when he was about to ask what was going on she gasped and stopped so quickly she almost fell over.

"It is gone."

"What is?"

"The magic. It cut off as if..." Sylvia shook her head. "It cut off as if a magic shield had been lowered. But that isn't possible."

"It isn't?"

"Well..."

"So nothing? No clue?"

She shook her head again. "No. I am a sorry. She could be in one of these building around here or..."

"Damn it. I am never going to get the stink of those brothels out of my hair." He turned and stalked away down the street without looking back.

Inevitably, Rawk ended up at the Armory but, of course, Celeste and Grint weren't there. Instead, there was a woman with a fiddle and a squeaky voice. There were only ten people in the audience and it looked as if the only reason they were there was because they were too drunk to leave. Rawk intended to join them. He sat in his usual table at the front of the room and it felt as if everyone was watching him. He thought he could hear them muttering, wondering why there were still exots in the city, why there were still sorcerers. And Rawk had no answer for them, apart from, *I'm too old. I don't know what else to do.* He ordered an ale and drank it down without even noticing the taste. He did the same with a second. And after just four songs, third drink half finished on the table, he pushed himself to his feet, wavering for a moment, before heading for the door. He seemed to bump into all ten people on the way.

"Shut up," he shouted to one man who complained at the treatment. At least he intended to shout, but it came out as nothing more than a slurred mumble. "Shut up."

Outside the door, he leaned against the wall. His head was spinning and the staircase looked unusually long. By the time he made it to the top, he was almost crawling. "Three ales and I'm drunk," he thought. It wasn't even three. Two and a half.

"Excuse me."

Somebody pushed past. He didn't even see them, apart from their red, pointy−toed shoes.

In the main bar he ordered another drink but took it out into the hallway to get away from the noise. That left him with the mural. A painted soldier was eyeballing him from the back of a horse, wondering why he was here, instead of out finding the sorcerers. He swore at him too, but he just kept watching.

With a grunt Rawk took his ale into the refectory, hitting the doorframe on the way through and leaving a puddle on the floor. The room was half full but the rumble of noise seemed much less offensive than it had in the bar, so he squinted around blearily looking for somewhere to sit. He finally spotted a vacant table, but he was distracted from his mission when he heard someone call his name. He started looking again, wavering where he stood, and eventually saw Thok. The other man's face wasn't much more than a blur, but his size made him hard to miss. Rawk made it to the table and managed to pour himself into a chair without spilling any more of his drink.

"You're drunk," Thok said.

"Perhaps."

"No, I'm pretty sure."

Rawk waved the comment away and took another drink.

"What's the occasion?"

"Why do I need an occasion?" Rawk leaned forward. "What are you eating?"

"Stew. And I know you don't normally drink, so something is going on."

"I'm getting old." He spun about in his seat and looked back towards where the pots of stew filled the end of the long room with clouds of mist. They seemed a long way away.

"It's your birthday?"

"No. It was just a comment. There are sorcerers in the city that I can't find. And there are exots that I can't kill."

"There always were."

Rawk narrowed his eyes.

"You knew there were sorcerers hiding in Katamood, didn't you? You knew where Sylvia was. Did you really think you knew about *all* of them?"

"Well..." Rawk tried to get his head around the conversation. He took a sip of ale, though he doubted that would help at all.

"You can't do everything, Rawk. You never could."

"I could too."

"Right. That's why Galad had a mushon skin cloak and you didn't?"

Rawk had turned his back on tackling a mushon and Galad had finished the job. "You know about that?"

"Of course. Not everyone believes *all* your tales."

"They do. They should." Rawk wanted something to eat. "One mushon out in the forest doesn't matter. Sorcerers making unicorns appear in the middle of Katamood does matter."

Thok nodded slowly. "No war is more devastating than a personal battle."

"What?"

"The thing right in front of you regularly stops you from seeing the bigger thing behind."

Rawk squinted some more, trying to see his meaning this time. He couldn't squint enough for that. "Do you always talk like this?"

Thok laughed. "I'm not talking like this. You're just drunk."

"That's all right then. I though I was losing my mind."

"Not tonight."

Rawk sighed. "I'm getting old, Thok, and very soon the people are going to notice. They are going to see an exot get away from me. They are going to hear about the sorcerers and wonder why I haven't handed them over the Weaver."

"And then you can retire."

"I already retired."

"Then what is the problem?"

"Unicorns and sorcerers."

"That is quite a problem to have."

"I killed the unicorns, and things only got worse."

"Just do what you can, let the rest sort itself out. Or not, as the case may be."

Rawk finished his drink. "I don't like to fail."

Thok shrugged. "Then don't try."
"I need something to eat." He made his way to the stew via the common room.

Thersday

RAWK LAY IN BED, blinking against the light and listening to the boots thumping up the back of his head. They were very loud. Too loud. His head pounded with each step. When the noise became too much, he groaned and swung his legs over the side of the bed. He was at least half way when Travis came through the door, two steps ahead of Ramaner. Waydin was close behind as well, with three other guards.

Rawk rubbed his eyes. They felt like they were too big for his head. And there was still way too much light. He squinted against the glare and groaned. Sitting up hadn't made him feel any better. It hadn't made anything feel any better. "I'm not sure the two seconds warning helped all that much, Travis, but thank you."

Travis gave a nod, but didn't leave. It looked like he was there to fight, if need be.

"What's the problem, Ramaner? Apart from the fact that your wife slept with me twenty years ago." He closed his eyes and decided he was never opening them again.

"Another sorcerer has turned up dead. You wouldn't know anything about that, would you?"

"You are correct. I don't know anything."

"The name Falling Leaves doesn't ring a bell? One armed elf woman?"

"Of course it does. I never said I didn't know anything about sorcerers, just not newly dead ones." He opened one eye.

"So you knew Falling Leaves?"

"Not personally. I've never spoke to her but I spent the last two days looking for her. How did she die?"

"You killed her."

"Wait, you are accusing me of murdering a sorcerer?" Rawk laughed. That was a bad idea. He closed his eye again and waited fir the spinning in his head to slow down. "First of all, no. And second of all, sorcery is illegal. And, by extension, being a sorcerer is illegal. I have been doing my job as a Hero, searching for sorcerers so I can stop them from killing innocent people and destroying the city with exots. Weaver knows this. I told him. And he had stopped talking for a moment, so I know he heard."

Ramaner grunted. His hand flexed on the hilt of his sword. "If you had stopped to think for a moment, you could have let her live and asked where the others are. But you are not capable of stringing two thoughts together, are you?"

"What others? How do you know there are others?"

His knuckles turned white on the hilt of his sword. "There are always others."

"Well, where did you find Falling Leaves?"

"Why?"

"So I can go and look for clues."

"Clues?"

"Yes, clues. Clues that might point me towards all these other sorcerers you're so worried about."

"Weaver has order me to send out the City Guard."

"You're a day late."

"We will take care of this, before you force all the sorcerers into hiding."

Rawk was going to say that they were already in hiding, and had been for years, but he didn't get the chance.

"You make sure you keep out of their way or you *will* be arrested and I don't care what Weaver says."

Rawk watched as the Guards followed him out. When they were gone, he turned to Travis. "What's for breakfast? Food is supposed to be good for hangovers, right?" The conversation had made his head pound even worse than before; all the shouting had bruised his mind.

"I'm not sure we have *that* much food."

Rawk rose carefully to his feet.

"Where are you going anyway?" Travis asked.

"To look for sorcerers, obviously."

"I think Ramaner was serious."

Rawk started walking and didn't say anything. At the door, he stopped to lean for a while.

"I'll have lunch ready for when you get down stairs."

"Did I miss breakfast?"

"Not yet, but at the speed you are going..."

"Shut up. I'm fine." He pushed himself upright, wavered for a moment, then made a heroic dash for the stairs.

When he was done eating, Rawk was feeling slightly better. At least until he stood up again. Then he was feeling decidedly worse. He thought of sitting back down but knew he probably wouldn't get up again until lunchtime. He sat down again and watched as Kalesie cut some vegetables and shouted orders at the helpers. All of them except Biki. Kalesie completely ignored her. The dwife worked anyway, silently taking tasks given to others and getting the job done. And Rawk might have stayed there, except the all shouting and the clanking was worming its way into his head and bouncing of the inside of his skull. He got to his feet, promising to never drink again, and went to sit at the table outside the back door.

The ostler's yard was still shaded and the cool, quiet settled his head enough for him to wonder what he was going to do. Valo, Shef, Frixen, Queel and Falling Leaves were all dead. The only other lead they had was Balen, and it was unlikely he was going to come out of hiding now. He thought perhaps he could find Waydin to ask what he knew, but Waydin was never going to cross Ramaner with the mood the General was in at the moment. And he didn't know who else would...

Except... Rawk grunted. There were probably dozens of people who could tell him where Falling Leaves had been found. He could probably step out onto the front porch right now, miles from where it had happened, and find someone who had heard a rumor about the death.

"Path, damn it." He just wanted to sit and do nothing for a while. He signed and headed down to the office to collect *Kaj*. Biki had left the kitchen and was now cleaning the *Vault,* wiping down tables and singing quietly to herself.

"Good morning, Rawk."

"Something like that."

Biki's eyes narrowed. "Are you sick? You look a bit green."

"Yes, fine, thank you. I just drank too much." Which didn't take much. "Did you come down here for a break from Kalesie?"

"I am used to that kind of thing," Biki said quietly. "Perhaps it was to give her a break from me."

"You could go home. You seem to be here more often than not."

She hesitated for a moment.

"What is it?"

Biki shrugged. "Some of the people living in the building..."

"Oh." Rawk shook his head. "Well, there isn't much I can do about that, really."

"I know. I didn't expect you to."

"Of course. Except..." He smiled. "You'll be home this afternoon?"

"I could be."

"Great. I'll send someone down to see you."

"I don't want to cause trouble."

"It's no trouble."

"What do you mean, you'll 'send someone down to see me'?" She looked a bit worried, but Rawk just smiled. That made him feel better than all the food.

He was still smiling when he crossed the weapon room. Sylvia was sitting on the couch, concentrating on a book, when he entered the office. She was worse than Biki.

"Did you sleep here?"

"Of course not." She glanced up. "What are you smiling about?"

"Biki is worried I'm going to send down some muscle to have a word with the old lady who lives across the hall from her."

It seemed to take a moment for that to register. "Pardon. Are you unwell? You look a bit green."

"It doesn't matter." Rawk looked around for *Kaj*. It took a moment for him to realize that the sword was hanging on the wall. Travis had obviously been busy again. His head spun as he reached up to collect it. He wondered if there was any point taking it. He doubted he'd beat Clinker in a fight at the moment, and the weight on his hip would probably mean he would spend the morning walking around in circles. But he put the belt around his waist and tightened it more than was necessary. "So, are you ready?"

"For what? I am not going to start visiting brothels again."

"That would be pointless. Falling Leaves is dead."

Sylvia looked up properly for the first time. "What? When did this happen?"

"Last night obviously."

"How do you know?"

"Ramaner told me. He wouldn't tell me anything else though."

"So..."

"So we're going to find out where she was killed and go and have a look."

Sylvia looked confused. "How will we find out?"

"We'll ask."

"Whom shall we ask?"

Rawk shrugged and regretted it. He held his hand to his head, as if that would stop the spinning. "Doesn't matter. I reckon it will take us about five minutes." He started towards the door but noticed the tea jug on the table at the back of the room was sending out a think drizzle of steam. "Did you make some tea?"

"Travis brought it in."

"Give me a minute then." Rawk poured himself some tea, added honey. For a moment he closed his eyes and breathed in the steam, then took a small sip.

"That is what saved you, you know."

"The tea? When?"

"With both the smoking man and Mistletowe."

"How?"

"Antioxidants."

"In the tea?"

"Yes. Lots of them."

"Really? Huh. I knew it was good to drink."

"Yes, but perhaps the word is trying to tell you something."

"It normally is."

"Twice in the last few days you have been afflicted with something that should have paralyzed and killed you."

Rawk took another sip, only half listening.

"Perhaps it is a metaphor for your life. You have stagnated. You are not going anywhere."

He gave a slow nod. "Maybe. But I'm not paralyzed any more, am I? I've made some new friends and opened a music venue and... And I've retired."

"Who are these friends?"

"Grint and Celeste. And Clinker. And you."

"Really? These friends seem a lot like your retirement."

"That's not nice." Rawk took a couple of more sips of tea then put the cup down on the corner of the desk. "Come on. We don't have all day."

Sylvia put down her book and started working on her scarf.

–O–

Rawk wanted to catch a cab, but their destination was not all that far away so he headed across the road and down the hill towards the forest. They were going down the steepest side of Two Watch Hill, so there were hardly any horses but the foot traffic was bad enough. The crazy angle made Rawk feel as if he was continually falling, and he wasn't sure that he was going to be able to get up again afterwards. He wished he'd brought a hat to keep out the early morning glare that struck like lances between the buildings.

They had been walking for just a few minutes when Rawk noticed a noise above the general murmur of the city. Shouts and cheers. And heckling. He laid a hand on Sylvia's arm, drawing her to a halt as he looked around and tried to gauge the direction of the sound. Soldiers came into sight, ten men coming from a side street with all the elegant precision of a herd of cows. They came closer and Rawk knew it would look suspicious if he and Sylvia turned around to walk the other direction. So he waited where he was hoping they walked on by.

"Ho, Rawk."

Rawk sighed and waved to the soldier in the front. "Lakin. How goes it? What are you up to?" His heart was racing like he was about to fight a dragon.

The captain stopped and his men came to a ragged stop behind him. "Weaver has got us out looking for sorcerers." He took off his plumed officers helmet and tucked it under his arm.

"Has he? He said he was going to be starting south of the river."

Lakin shrugged. "I think most of the troops may be over there but... Well, here we are."

"Indeed. Will ten of you be enough?" He knew he shouldn't be getting into a conversation with him, but he still didn't want to just walk away.

Lakin looked at his men, as if he hadn't considered the possibility of failure previously. "I should think so."

"I've seen sorcerers face entire armies." He hadn't, not on their own, but Lakin didn't need to know that.

"Yes, well surely someone like that wouldn't be hanging around here."

"I keep getting told that Katamood is the center of the world. Lines of power meet here or something."

"Who told you that?"

"Valo, Frixen, Mistletowe."

Lakin looked suspicious. He pulled at his nose. "You know they're all dead, right?"

"Of course. I obviously spoke to them before they died though. And I didn't kill any of them, before you ask."

"Right."

"And, just a question. How will you know a sorcerer when you see one?"

"I have an amulet. It glows when there is magic nearby."

Rawk swallowed. "Really?"

The captain pulled the item in question from his pocket and held it up for Rawk to see. There was a gem in the center of a four—pointed star. Nothing was glowing.

Seeing the thing wasn't working, Rawk started to relax. "So... You just walk around until it starts glowing."

"Yes. It can even detect magic for a few days after its gone."

"How can you see it in your pocket?"

Lakin didn't say anything.

"And then you knock on doors and ask people if they are sorcerers?"

"The gem glows brighter the closer the magic is."

Rawk glanced at Sylvia as she adjusted her scarf, then back at the gem. "All right then. Sounds like you've got it all under control."

"Of course."

"Good luck with it, though hopefully you don't find all of them or you'll put me out of business."

"I thought you had retired."

Rawk shrugged. "I have and I'm the busiest I've been in years." Rawk clapped his hands together. "Speaking of which, I've got work to do and so have you."

Lakin nodded and jammed his helmet back on, looking as if he was embarrassed by the ridiculous item. He gave a salute, as if to emphasize the point, then marched off with his men behind.

"You did magic two days ago, so I guess their amulet is useless then."

"I guess so. Most amulets are. Let us continue before we are found by soldiers who are not so friendly."

The street where they had lost Falling Leaves was much busier than it had been the previous night. Two wagons had come together in the middle of the road, wheels locked in some strange, unsolvable puzzle. While the two human drivers argued, getting louder and coarser by the minute, traffic accumulated around them. Pedestrians could easily fit by on either side, but a lot chose to stay where they were and watch the excitement and that just added to the chaos. Rawk winced at the commotion. The tea had not helped as much as he had hoped. His head was throbbing again and the sun made his eyes ache and now this... He wasn't about to tell Sylvia though.

"Where do we start?" Sylvia asked.

Rawk shrugged and looked around. There was a bakery not far away. He managed a smile. "Right there," he said.

Sylvia sighed and shook her head. "Do you still do the exercises you told me about? At this rate you will be huge by the end of the week."

"I've walked around this city a hundred times in the last few weeks. I'll be fine."

"What about your hangover?"

"I'll get something with fruit in it. That will give me the anti—poxi—thingies."

"Antioxidants."

"Yes, them."

As they walked up onto the small porch at the front of the bakery, another woman was coming out. Rawk stopped when he saw her. The woman was wearing a scarf, wrapped around her face and head, covering everything but her eyes. It was all a bit of a mess, but was obviously an imitation of Sylvia's headwear.

The elf stopped by his side and gasped.

Rawk gave the woman a nod of greeting and gestured to her scarf. "You need something longer," he said. "And you actually start around the neck to hold it all in place." He'd seen Sylvia wrap her face often enough that he knew approximately how it was done.

The woman glanced at Sylvia and hurried away.

"She was a southerner, I am sure."

"Yes."

"And a human."

"Yes. I'm guessing someone copied the scarf off you, Sylvia, because they saw you with me over the last couple of days. You've started a fashion trend."

"I do not want to start a fashion trend. The scarf is a tradition that goes back hundreds of years."

"Well, if everyone is wearing one it will make you less conspicuous."

The elf turned to watch the woman but she was long gone, lost in the crowd.

In the bakery, Rawk picked some long thin thing with berries and fresh cream and while the mustachioed man counted his change asked, "Did you hear about the woman who was killed near here last night."

The man handed over the money and shook his head. "I heard about it, but I canna tell you any details."

"Oh. Well thanks." Rawk nodded and took a bite of his food as he turned to leave. He stopped and looked back. "This is good," he said around a mouthful. Then he followed Sylvia back out onto the street.

"So this is your plan?"

Rawk was still eating, so he nodded.

"I see no more bakeries in the area."

He gave her a look and headed towards the next shop. The old lady behind the counter tried to sell Sylvia a pink, lacy dress and talked for five minutes about the horrible details of the murder before finally admitting that she didn't actually know anything at all.

A cooper in the next building kept working as Rawk asked his question, nodding slowly. "I heard," he said, working at bending a stave. "Don't know much, but Ben Balkam says the City Guard were all over the warehouse next to his shop this morning."

And it only took him a second to get to the point; Rawk liked him. "And where's Ben's shop."

"Next left up the hill. About fifty yards down there."

"And what does Ben do?"

"He's a shoemaker."

Rawk thanked the man and hurried back out onto the street. The wagons were still exactly where they had been, though the two drivers had stopped arguing with each other now and were arguing with the dwarves who had taken it upon themselves to actually try to sort out the problem. They were working at the wheels while the men swore at them and threatened to hit them with their cargo if they didn't keep their dirty dwarf hands off. The dwarves carried on and Rawk started pushing his way through the still growing throng of people. Sylvia stuck close behind.

They found the shoemaker easily enough and waited behind an old lady with what seemed to be a hundred pairs of shoes to be repaired. As she put each pair up onto the counter she introduced them with a short history and a detailed description of the owner and how the need for repair came about. Rawk tried to be patient but his hand twitched on the hilt of his sword. He wondered if he could claim she was an exot, trying to make him die of frustration.

"This pair," the woman said, carefully placing a pair of old felt slippers beside the boots, "belonged to my daughter. She used to wear them all the time, but only when she was at home. She never used to walk anywhere.

She danced. Danced while she was cooking and cleaning and... But then she got pregnant and her man left her and she died when the baby came." The woman fingered the hole in the bottom of the shoe. "The baby died too, of course."

There was a moment of silence after that as the woman reminisced and everyone else waited rather awkwardly. When the silence continued the cobbler cleared his throat. "I'll see what I can do for you. I will need a few days though."

The old lady gave a small nod then wandered out onto the street as if she didn't know where she was or where she was going.

"Well," Rawk said as he stepped up into her place at the counter, "that was a nice way to start the day."

The other man nodded, looking from Rawk to Sylvia and back again.

"Are you Ben?"

A nod.

"I'm Rawk—"

"Of course."

"—and this is..." Rawk looked at Sylvia with her face still cover with her scarf. "Anyway, to continue the cheerful proceedings, I need to ask you about the woman who was killed near here."

"I don't know anything about it."

"The cooper said it happened in a warehouse near you."

"Macco? What would he know?"

"He knows how to repair barrels, I imagine."

Ben smiled. "Barely."

"So, he says you saw all the soldiers loitering last night."

Ben started taking the shoes down off the counter and putting then into wooden boxes. He glanced up at Rawk and motioned with his head. "Five doors down that way, I think. This side of the street."

"You are a good man, Ben. If I ever need shoes repaired..."

Ben nodded and continued with his work as Rawk and Sylvia headed out.

"Told you," Rawk said.

"Yes. I know."

The warehouse was easy enough to spot but the main front door and the door into the office were both locked and didn't even move when Rawk gave them a nudge.

"What did you expect?" Sylvia asked.

Rawk went to the corner of the building and down the alley at the side. It was wide and clean, as far as such things went, and obviously much used. There were three wagons, all full but with no horses in sight, waiting to be unloaded. And there was a small door being guarded by a dwarf.

He watched them coming for a moment, then smiled. "Rawk." He gave a nod. "And Sylvia, I assume."

Rawk nodded as well. "Hello. Do I know you?"

"No. I'm Herron Mer Gal"

"Right. Good to meet you then, Heron. So, what are you doing?"

"Guarding the door."

"So this is where the woman was killed? Nobody's allowed in?" He glanced through the door and saw half a dozen more dwarves standing around, talking and arguing.

"Well, it's not so much that they aren't allowed. It's more for their protection."

"So what are they doing? Cleaning?" Rawk asked.

Herron glanced inside as well. "They will be soon. It's a mess in there. Not pretty."

"Well, we need to go in," Rawk said.

"I think we will be able to handle it," Sylvia added. "We have both seen a lot of blood and death, in our different ways."

"I don't..."

"You said that we were allowed," Sylvia reminded him.

"Well, nobody has said that people *aren't* allowed, but I'm not actually sure that that's the same thing."

"You know what Sylvia and I are doing?"

"Your investigation? Of course. Everyone does."

Rawk motioned inside. "Well, that woman in there is our one and only way forward. This is the only chance we've got to find out who is opening the portals."

"So, it wasn't her?"

Rawk glanced at Sylvia. The elf answered. "She was a sorcerer, but she was only one member of a group. We need to find the rest."

"So we need to get in there and look before your friends clean up some of our clues."

"Nobody has said that we cannot," Sylvia said.

The dwarf let out a huff of breath and stepped out of the way. "I'd better not get into trouble," he muttered.

Rawk clapped him on the shoulder as he passed. "I'll tell them I had to threaten you."

Five steps into the warehouse, Rawk stopped. He swallowed and suddenly discovered that his hangover had fled, washed away in a sea of blood and gore. He looked at Sylvia.

Sylvia had stopped halfway through unwrapping her scarf from her face. Her mouth was uncovered. It was open. "That," she said softly, "is a lot of blood."

Rawk examined the scene again. "Yes, it is." It wasn't that the blood and the spilled entrails made him ill, but it was an unexpected sight in the middle of the warehouse.

Falling Leaves was laying in the middle of a large open area with piles of wool bales making walls on two sides. Eight dwarves were gathered around a table near a narrow walkway towards the front of the building. There was a strange conglomeration of rusting machines against the far wall. Apart from the body and the blood, it didn't look like the location for the doing of evil deeds.

"Is opening the portals evil, do you think?" Rawk asked Sylvia. "I mean, if you leave your door unlocked at night, are you a bad person, or is the thief who takes advantage of the situation?"

"They are inviting the thieves in, Rawk."

"But are they really? Do you think they really know what's on the other side? They are probably letting through as many nice fluffy creatures as horrible ones."

He turned and saw Sylvia looking at him.

"I mean, obviously, whoever did this isn't the nicest person you'll ever meet..." He cleared his throat. "Let's find out who's opening the portals and stop them, shall we."

One of the dwarves was coming over to them. He was the biggest dwarf Rawk had ever seen. It looked like he could lift horses if he wanted to.

"Morning. What are you two doing here?"

Sylvia finished unwrapping her scarf. "Good morning, Yed. We have come to have a look at this place before you do your work. The woman is Falling Leaves, a sorcerer who is involved in the opening of the ohoga portals."

"Falling Leaves? You don't say. At least you saved us from spending a few hours looking for her arm."

"The stump of that arm has healed," Rawk said, "I'm sure—"

"I was joking, Rawk."

"Oh. Right." Rawk looked at the blood. "My mind is on other things."

"I can understand that." Yed looked as well. "Look, I can give you about fifteen minutes, at best. This place is going to stink like a slaughter house if we don't get moving."

Sylvia nodded. "Of course. We shall examine the body first so you can get that away as soon as possible."

"Excellent. Thacker wants his surgeons to take a look."

"I imagine so. Has anyone touched the body? Have the walked out to it?"

Yed shook his head. "We've only been here about five minutes. We've just had a quick look around and were trying to work out how to go about things. I drew the short straw, so I'll be going out there soon enough."

"I thought you were in charge," Rawk said.

Yed laughed. "Kings soon lose the respect of their soldiers if they aren't willing to lead them into battle occasionally."

"I guess so."

Rawk followed Sylvia towards the body, being careful to find clean, dry patches of floor to place his feet, which became more difficult with every step. And with each step it became harder and harder to ignore the smell. It became harder and harder to ignore the naked body. When he got there he stopped for a moment. He was going to take a deep breath to calm himself, but thought better of it. The taste of death was unlikely to calm him at this point. He crouched down to look.

There was a gaping hole in the stomach and another in the chest. "So, I guess this isn't a *Fiddernich*."

"No. No it is not."

"It's hard to believe that someone who removed a heart without leaving a wound then turned around and did something like this."

"I agree, the change does seem incongruous. Each of these methods of killing is frightening in its own way but the two of them together? I imagine the minions are petrified, not knowing what to expect."

"I guess." There were sigils, or something similar, scrawled in blood on Falling Leaves' legs and arm. "What do those words say?"

Sylvia gathered herself and examined the marks as well. She mumbled to herself for a moment. "*Hadaven, mulkern, grech.*"

"Really? I wouldn't have expected that here."

"You know of the *jakanini?*" She sounded impressed.

"Of course not. I have no idea what you are talking about."

Sylvia sighed. "It is part of an ancient curse from the northern regions of Nern."

"And it's normally painted on dead people?"

"Yes."

"So, what's missing?"

"Pardon?"

"Well, surely there must be another word to go on the fourth limb."

She looked impressed again. "Yes, there is. But the four words mean 'Your soul to never'— which basically means 'go to hell'— and the word 'to' is missing. I would not think that was significant."

Rawk tried to think about what it might mean. After a minute he sighed. "You're probably right. Whoever did this wasn't leaving a message. Not for us, anyway."

"The violence is the only message here."

"So, was it done with magic? Or just with knives?" Rawk looked at the wounds for the first time.

Sylvia did too, tilting her head to the side and pursing her lips. "I wish Thacker had sent a surgeon... I think it is a knife; it seems to be an actual cut."

"So, not helpful then. It could be any sadistic bastard, really."

"Indeed."

Rawk stayed where he was, staring at the body, wondering if there was anything he could decipher. But the longer he looked, the less he saw. Apart from the blood and gore. That wouldn't leave him alone. Eventually, he rose to his feet and made his way over to where the dwarves were watching. They were standing by a trestle table near the gap between the bales. "Have you had a look around this place?" Rawk asked.

Yed shrugged. "The lads had a bit of a wander around but didn't find anything significant. No bloody knives or signed contracts or anything like that, if that's what you were hoping."

"I *was* hoping, to be honest." Not that he knew what he would do with the knife if he found it. Rawk looked around, as if he might see something from where he was that the dwarves has missed. He didn't, of course. "Has anyone talked to the owner? Did he know people were using his warehouse?"

"He came around a bit earlier, very surprised and annoyed, and we sent him on his way. He didn't know anything. That's what he told us, anyway."

"Of course."

"Have you finished here? I've really got to get started."

Rawk looked at Sylvia and the elf nodded. But she turned to Yed. "The surgeon will be looking at the body today?"

"We'll be sending it straight there."

"Who is it?"

"Hani Mer Habaonet."

"Thank you. I may go and see her, to see what she finds."

While Yed started his work, and Sylvia watched on, Rawk started to move away. As he headed towards the table, he passed a couple of dwarves going the other way with a big bag. He nodded a greeting but kept going to the workers that remaining behind.

Rawk watched for a moment. "So, none of you found anything unusual around here?" Perhaps if he asked the question enough times someone would change their mind. They were starting to ready themselves too. They donned aprons and gloves and took tools from bags. There were old rags and scrubbing brushes, shovels and scrapers. And there was a crate with glass jars full of clear liquid and another one full of empty jars. There was a half eaten pastry on the corner of the table.

"Nothing particularly strange stands out," one of them said. He glanced out at the floor of the warehouse and gestured vaguely at the body and the blood. "Except that, of course."

Rawk sighed. "That's what Yed told us. I was hoping you might have thought of something though."

"Sorry."

One by one, they moved away until there was just one left. "I'm not quite sure how I ended up in this line of work," he said as he examined a scrubbing brush critically, as if a patch of rotting skin might still be stuck on there from the last job. "My father was a boilermaker. He had an apprenticeship lined up in his workshop and everything." The dwarf grunted. "But I wanted to explore my options."

"Well, it seems that stuff like this is just another day at the office. For some of you at least."

He looked out at the floor again. "Not this. Nobody can get used to this."

Rawk gestured to the pastry on the table. "Somebody can."

The dwarf shook his head. "That isn't ours. It was here when we got here."

"Oh. Sorry."

And the dwarf sighed and moved out onto the battlefield where his companions were already hard at work.

Rawk stared absently at the pastry, trying to keep his mind away from the mess behind him, wondering what he was supposed to do next. Falling Leaves was their last lead and if they didn't find something soon then the City Guard would continue their trawl through the city. Sylvia would not be safe. Probably lot of other innocent people would not be safe either, even those who had nothing to do with magic.

He was not sure how long he stood there, staring, but a thought eventually struck him. He stepped forward and crouched down near the table.

"So, who owns this," he muttered to himself. He poked the pastry with his finger, then flipped it over. Then he nodded with satisfaction, wrapped it up in the brown paper, and put it in his pocket. When he turned around he discovered Sylvia standing close by. They stood silently and looked out over the blood and gore for a moment.

Sylvia sighed. "I am afraid this is a dead end," the elf said. "I am not sure what else we can do."

Rawk grunted. "One of the sorcerers lives on the eastern slopes of Two Watch Hill," he said after a moment. "Somewhere near Picamoko Square."

Sylvia looked at him. She blinked. "Do you make this nonsense up on the spot just to vex me, or do you plan it all out before you leave home in the morning?"

"Planning is too much like work; I like to be spontaneous. Come on."

"Where are we going?"

"Picomoko Square. I thought I said that."

"So we just go and stand in a random corner of a random square and hope this sorcerer turns up? That seems even less likely than trawling through the brothels."

"The trawling worked, didn't it? But, no, we don't just stand in a random corner. We stand in the corner nearest to the Moko Bakery."

Sylvia hurried after him. "What?"

"The bakery. We were there on Sunday just between the *Golden Fetch* and the *Randy Bride*. Or..." He wasn't *exactly* sure which brothel they had recently left or which they were heading towards in their search for Falling Leaves, all of the establishments had merged in his mind, but he knew the bakery. And he knew the apple slice he had eaten. And he most definitely knew the pastry he had eaten afterwards.

"I refuse to continue..." Sylvia had to rush to keep up.

Rawk silently listened to Sylvia all the way across the city. She didn't stop talking. She went around in circles, from "Where are we going?" to "If you don't tell me what is happening I am going to go home." It wasn't a very big circle.

When they reached Picomoko Square, Rawk stopped to get his bearings, then headed for the bakery down near the Maple tree in the corner. When he climbed the stairs, Sylvia stopped in her tracks and also stopped talking. But just for a moment.

"You are going to the bakery? You really came here to buy food?" She looked even more exasperated with him than usual.

"Come on," Rawk said, motioning her through the door. "You've come this far..."

"I am not hungry."

He pulled the wrapped pastry from his pocket.

"What is that?"

Rawk didn't answer. He went up to the counter and put the pastry down as the baker came out from the back room sending out a cloud of flour as he dusted at his apron.

"Good morning, Rawk," he said.

"Good morning."

"What can I do for you?" He eyed the pastry.

"Do you give refunds?"

The man didn't reply.

"Sorry. That was a joke. But you did make that, didn't you?"

The man dragged the item in question closer. "I reckon so. I don't know of anyone else that makes them."

"What's the yellow stuff called again?"

"I call it custard."

"Right. It's good." Rawk tried to gather his thoughts. "So, anyway, I guess you sell a lot of them?"

"Of course."

Rawk sighed. "Of course."

"What is happening, Rawk?"

Rawk turned to Sylvia. "This pastry was in the warehouse. The dwarves didn't take it."

"I wouldn't sell to a dwarf."

Rawk turned to glare at the man. "So if a dwarf walked in here and tried to give you money for a loaf of bread you'd send him away?"

"Well..."

"That's what I thought. Give me another one of the custard things." He fished around in his belt for some change, and turned to back to Sylvia when he had the pastry. "I remembered the custard from when we were here the other day. You should try some, by the way." He took a bite.

"So you are suggesting one of our sorcerers came here before going to the gathering."

"What sorcerer?" the baker asked.

"Exactly."

"So, do we start knocking on random doors, hoping they are home?"

"Of course not, that could take all day and we don't want them to know we're onto them."

"Unlike Shef?"

"Shut up."

"So, what is your plan?"

"We find a nice shady spot and sit down to watch."

"And this will bring quicker results than the door knocking plan?"

"Perhaps not quicker, but less strenuous. And there will be less chance of them slipping past us while we are knocking somewhere else."

"Who says they live in the area and were not just passing through? And who says they will be back?"

"They'll be back. You really should try the custard."

"I really do not have time for this nonsense."

Rawk shrugged as he licked custard from his fingers. "Suit yourself. I'm going to find somewhere to sit down."

—O—

Rawk leaned back and watched the latest batch of children run off after the latest story, though he was sure he'd seen one of the girls earlier in the day. Beyond them, near the edge of the square, a dwarf on stilts was lighting the lamps.

"You know I was there, do you not?" Sylvia said.

"Where?"

"I was in Lasket about three days after you left."

"Were you following me?"

"That is unlikely, Rawk. I generally tried to stay as far from you as possible. I was heading north, to Hula."

"Oh. So..."

"So I know there was no Merdule warrior. There was no *Flail of Destruction* and there was no princess."

"Who says?"

"The villagers."

"Well, what would they know? Most of them had never been more than two miles from the Lasket in their lives so they wouldn't know a Merdule if he was breathing garlic in their faces." Sylvia raised an eyebrow and Rawk shrugged. "Nobody wants to hear the truth."

"But perhaps they should hear it anyway. If Heroes keep telling their admirers that dwarves are less than human then why would they ever think otherwise?"

Rawk closed his eyes and didn't say anything for a long time. "Is there a rigid standard against which we should judge people, do you think? Or can we only judge them for the moment and the place that they inhabit?"

"What do you mean?"

"Twenty years ago it was acceptable to hate dwarves..."

Sylvia watched critically as another woman walked past with a scarf around her face. "As it still is."

Rawk waved the comment away. "So, if someone lived back then, are they a terrible person for hating dwarves?"

Sylvia gave a slight shrug. "I do not know. Perhaps we can only judge ourselves. Perhaps it is just about balance."

"How so?"

"When you looked at dwarves you expected their respect, but did not offer them respect in return. When we fought at Maradon you cast your stones onto the King's side of the scales without even considering the peasants."

"So I was a bad person?" He hadn't felt like a bad person at Maradon. He'd thought he was doing the right thing.

Sylvia shrugged. "I am a healer, Rawk, not a philosopher. But I will say this... All those years you were trying to kill me, I was never convinced you were actually evil, merely stupid and misinformed."

"I'm not sure if that's a compliment or not."

"It is neither compliment nor insult. It is just the way things were."

"I don't agree with slavery," Rawk said, "but Kenkona has been carried on the backs of slaves for hundreds of years."

"So, do you forgive the nobles of Kenkona because that is the moment and the place that that inhabit?"

Rawk shook his head.

"Then I suspect you have your answer."

Rawk nodded. "Bree— Lady Tapalar— hated dwarves. She would cross to the other side of the street to avoid them, unless they were working for her. Then she just ignored them for the most part."

"As did you, Rawk."

"Perhaps we were merely misinformed about that as well."

A sewer was inching it's way across the square, bright red safety markers standing guard as dwarves hacked at the ground and hoisted load after load of soil up into waiting wagons. It seemed that they could do that sort of work all day. A priest, dress in the orange robes of the

Great Path, was watching them critically, staring as they sweated and sang their work songs.

And...

A portal opened behind the priest. Rawk surged to his feet, *Kaj* hissing from the scabbard. People parted before his shout and, after a moment of confusion, they fell in behind as he raced across the square. But by the time he reached the portal, nothing had happened. No creatures had emerged. Nobody had died.

Rawk stood in front of the grey shimmer–in–the–air, sword ready, heart racing. And still nothing happened. And just when he was beginning to think there was no danger at all, a dozen creatures came through, all in a rush. They had two legs and two arms, and ran upright, but their skin was grey and bald and they were only three feet high. Then twenty or thirty more came through, running hard, some looking back over their shoulders. A large group of them paused for a moment to look around, but then they ran again, disappearing into the crowd. And a moment later, there was a dragon. The creature was as big as an ulifant, but fast and fierce, loud as a dying horse. It was past Rawk before he could even think and snatched up two of the staring spectators with huge, clawed hands. A moment later it was send up a storm of dust as it beat its wing furiously and heaved skywards. Its outline was visible against the stars of the swarm as it flew over the top of Two Watch Hill and headed towards the Old Forest. And the creatures it had pursued were gone as well, disappearing into the city.

"Why didn't you save them?"

Rawk turned and looked at the priest. "Excuse me?"

"You stood there and..." The man saw the look on Rawk's face and fell silent. It was a bit late for that.

"Why didn't I save them? Why didn't *you* save them?"

"Because—"

"You could have said a prayer, surely. The Great Path would have swept down from heaven like he always does and... Oh, wait, that's right, the Great bloody Path never does a damn thing. He sits back and waits for men to do all the work."

"The Great Path—"

"Go to hell."

Rawk strode away, pushing through the stunned crowd, back towards Sylvia was waiting silently. She had started to follow his original mad dash, but had not gotten very far.

"Are you all right?" she asked as Rawk approached.

He nodded. "Which is more than can be said for those other two."

"Indeed. There was nothing you could have done."

Rawk grunted. "That's not what the priest thinks." He looked back over his shoulder. "How can an all powerful god have anything to do with that? I mean, life is so damned random and complicated. Those two people were walking through the square doing some shopping, then the next minute they were dragon food."

Sylvia nodded. "What of the other creatures? Have you ever seen them before?"

"No. And I doubt I will see them again. There was not a warrior amongst them."

"You do not fear them then?"

"No. They'll hide for a while, then get the hell out of here once they realize what it's like."

"I suppose..." Sylvia stopped and looked around. She adjusted her scarf. "There."

"What?"

"That man with the beard. He is a sorcerer."

"Are you sure?"

"Of course I am sure."

The man in question went into the bakery and emerged a few minutes later with a small, paper-wrapped parcel.

"Come on then. We'll follow him home then we can..."

"We can what?"

"I don't know. We'll beat some information out of him."

"If he does not know the location of the next meeting, or the identity of his co–conspirators, then what can he possibly tell us?"

"You think too much. Let's worry about all that when the time comes."

"Of course. A sound plan."

"Shut up."

The sorcerer had left the square and was going around the back of Two Watch Hill. The Old Forest slowly crept in to view to the West and, to the North, farmland stretched away as far as the eye could see. The streets were starting to go quiet with the coming of night. Hawkers chased last minute sales and workers headed for home.

"He must really like those pastries," Rawk said. "He goes a long way just to get them."

"That sounds a bit like someone I know."

"Really? Who's that?"

After a few more minutes the man turned down the hill towards Grand Smelling, a small district filled with cheap warehouses and second–rate craftsmen.

Rawk had a sudden thought. "He isn't heading for home. He's heading for a meeting right now."

"Two nights in a row? Surely not."

"Why not? Do you know something I don't?"

"I know how hard it is to do complex magic."

"Well, you don't have to get smart about it." But Rawk was sure he was right. It was the same type of area they had found Falling Leaves that morning. He took a few more steps. "Where did he go?"

"He is cloaking."

"That isn't what I asked."

"He is approaching the building over there. I believe he intends to go inside. Yes."

The building in question looked like it was about to fall down. One end of the porch drooped badly and the windows were all boarded up.

"Definitely a meeting." Rawk put his hand on *Kaj*, feeling the way the hilt seemed to fit perfectly. He looked around and continued down the street to the building.

"What are you doing?" Sylvia whispered fiercely.

"They are in there opening portals that will let creatures through to our world. Those creatures will most likely kill people."

Sylvia grabbed his arm. "We cannot just march in the front door, Rawk. We must think." She looked around, then pulled him towards a narrow alley down the side of the building.

"Who says going in the back door will be any better? One of them is probably leaning against the back door plotting something."

"Let us see what we can see."

Not far away, a board had fallen away and a dark window that stared blindly over the rubbish. A few yards beyond that was a narrow, warped door.

Rawk found a half rotten crate and placed it carefully under the window. He tested to see if it would hold him, then climbed up to peek inside. For a moment he couldn't see anything, but his eyes slowly adjusted and he peered into the gloom. After a moment he sat down on the crate and quietly cleared his throat.

"What did you see?" Sylvia's face was hidden in shadow. The light from the street did not reach them.

"Well, I saw Balen and the guy we were following."

"That was all?"

Rawk winced. "There may have been a couple of others."

"A couple?"

"Three or four others."

"Three or four?"

"Or five." Rawk jumped when a noise erupted from further down the alley. A rat or a cat or something similar. He breathed. "They were standing around in the dark with their hoods up."

"Five others? Apart from Balen and the other one?" Sylvia glanced at the window. "We need to get help, Rawk."

"Help? From who?"

"Well... Weaver?"

Rawk sighed. "Weaver may well help, but I can assure you that it wouldn't turn out the way we expect. And besides that, it would be an hour before he could get here with some people. This little meeting will be over by then and the sorcerers will melt back away into the city. We'd have to start searching all over again. Again."

"When they leave we can follow one of them. We could go back to our original plan."

"And how many innocent people die because we let this meeting go ahead tonight?"

"So, let me see if I am correct... You are suggesting that we charge in there to fight seven sorcerers?"

When he thought about it, Rawk realized it didn't seem like a good idea at all. He couldn't back out now, though. "Of course," he said. "Unless you can come up with a better plan." He hoped she could.

"Any plan would be better than that."

He heard a voice inside. It was deep and muffled and sent a shiver down his spine. He stood back on the box and tried to hear what was being said but could not get more than an occasional word. He climbed down and looked at Sylvia again. "We could surprise them. I can probably get to a couple of them before they even know we're there." He couldn't stop himself.

"I hope you are joking, Rawk."

Was he joking? "We have to do something. If we wait until they start their spell then they won't be able to sense whatever you're doing, right?"

Sylvia gave a small nod.

"Great. So, we wait for the right moment, then I'll charge in and distract them some more while you..." Rawk waggled his fingers in the air. "While you do your thing."

Sylvia started to say something, but paused. She cocked her head to one side. "They are starting."

Rawk got back up for another look. Everyone was standing in a circle, arms crossed over the chests, heads bowed.

"There are seven people in there." Sylvia said. It sounded like she was going to say more, but when Rawk looked back at her, her face was pale.

"What is it?"

"There is one who has no magic at all, and another who has more power than I have ever seen."

"So there are only six sorcerers? It's getting better all the time."

"Pardon?"

"What does the powerful one look like? I'll attack him first."

"Rawk, you cannot. He will kill you with a thought."

"Or rip my heart out without leaving a mark?"

"Yes."

Rawk swallowed and licked his lips. He was pretty sure Sylvia couldn't see him. "So we just let a man who can do that run around free?" He was starting to get the feeling that the elf wasn't going to be able to talk him out of anything at all. She was supposed to be smart; surely she could come up with something.

"Rawk..."

"Yes?"

"I need to tell you—"

The box collapse under Rawk and he fell on the ground in a heap. It was embarrassing. It was loud. He jumped back to his feet, cursing his knee, and looked around. There were voices coming from inside, talking, asking what was going on.

"Do we run?" He asked Sylvia. He hoped she said yes. It seemed that he would either die in a few seconds or the sorcerers would scatter and he would never be able to find them again. Neither option was something Rawk could live with. Especially the first one.

For a moment Sylvia said nothing. "Balen has recognized me."

"What?" But the details didn't matter. Drawing *Kaj*, Rawk raced to the door and shouldered it aside. He ran into the building and found himself surrounded.

Rawk lashed out at the nearest figure and was rewarded with a scream of pain. He pulled *Kaj* free of the tangle of robes and flesh, and spun away painfully into a barely noticed gap. He slashed low as he went, missed, and kept going into the corner.

Someone was on him with a sword. That wasn't supposed to happen. He pushed the blade aside as his knee locked completely for a second. He got a cut across his arm and swore as he grappled with the stranger. Shoving, pushing. Searching for an advantage. The smell of garlic on the other man's breath. That certainly didn't help. Rawk ducked away to try and get a moment to think.

A voice hissed out of the darkness, colored by magic. "Leave him. We go."

Rawk winced as he changed course to attack a sorcerer. It took a moment to work out that it was a woman, standing with arms raised in front of her. Rawk hesitated, considering the rules for killing unarmed women, then ran her through before common sense fled completely.

He looked around, scanning the darkness to see if he could find who ever had spoken, but the swordsman was right on him, giving him no time. There was a glimmer in the darkness, and Rawk ducked. A sword hummed overhead. He slashed but was moving away again and was never going to hit his target. He found himself close to another sorcerer though, the bearded man they'd followed, and elbowed him in the stomach instead. He would live but probably wouldn't be doing much for a while, apart from trying to breathe.

With the wall at his back, Rawk paused to catch his own breath. His knee was aching. The old wound on his left arm was aching as well, for some reason. His heart was beating like Grint's drum. And he thought he could hear a sorcerer muttering the beginnings of a spell. He looked around, wondering what Sylvia was doing to help.

But there was nothing he could do now, because the swordsman was heading towards him, coming out of the darkness like a ship out of the mist. A pirate ship with a pointy prow and evil looking...

Rawk gasped. "Ramaner?"

The general smiled and spun his sword in his hand. "Who did you expect, Rawk?"

"Well... I hadn't *expected* anyone to be honest." Rawk looked around, wondering if Ramaner was distracting him from a different attack. He finally spotted the only sorcerer who was calm enough to think. Balen was in the corner, building a spell. That was Sylvia's problem. He took a deep breath, wiggling his leg slightly to test his knee, and concentrated on Ramaner.

There was another flurry of swords that Rawk barely survived. Ramaner was about twelve years his junior and it showed. Rawk really did feel like an old man. He was half a second behind. The blows on his new sword shook him. But he did survive and smiled, for show. "I'll have to tell Weaver what you've been up to."

"Weaver isn't here, Rawk. I've waited a long time for this day."

"You're still angry that I slept with your wife ten years ago? She wasn't even your wife."

Ramaner's lip twitched. "It meant so little to you that you can't even remember when it was? It was eighteen years ago."

Rawk shrugged. "I didn't know if you were talking about the first time or the last."

The general attacked, but it was a sloppy, wild effort that Rawk easily avoided. He smiled as he suddenly saw his opening, probably the only chance he had.

"Come away, General," the sliver of voice said again, like a knife blade pressed against his cheek.

Rawk tried to ignore it. He licked his lips. Breathed. "It's been a while since I talked to Nelly. Perhaps I should go visit her after I've finished here."

Ramaner charged in. He was snarling like a wild animal. His eyes were fierce. Rawk fended away a few blows then attacked, pushing back, almost all the way across the room to where Balen watched. The sorcerer threw a spell of some kind that crackled past Rawk's face, making his skin tingle and his eyes ache. His momentum was lost and the general seemed to regain some composure.

"I intend to kill you, Rawk, but that is not my revenge."

Rawk nodded. "Well, your revenge was worthless, Ramaner. I didn't love Maris. Her death was pointless, and it hurt—it still hurts—but not like you were hoping. I will not be eating away at my soul in twenty years time."

The general laughed. "Maris? Of course she doesn't matter. I took my revenge soon after you earned it. Why don't you have a think about what else happened about eighteen years ago?"

"You expect me to remember something from eighteen years ago?" Rawk was going to raise an eyebrow but he almost lost it instead as Ramaner came at him. He ducked, too late, and stumbled as he backed away. He wiped blood away from his forehead. He was going to be having trouble seeing soon enough.

"I stole something from you, Rawk. Just like you stole something from me." Ramaner's smile was a sick, twisted thing.

Rawk almost dropped *Kaj*. He gripped the hilt of the sword tighter as he tried to think. As he tried not to think. "You killed Lady Tapalar? You killed Bree?"

Ramaner smiled some more.

Rawk felt sick. He swallowed. "And it made you feel better? It makes you feel better every day? Was it worth it." He hesitated for a moment, thinking of Bree, thinking of the tales he had told in her parlor, telling her of the world she would never get to see because of who she was. There was often an evil general. The general always died. Rawk felt the old coldness settling in his chest again. Bree's death had hurt him once, but it couldn't any more. Not like Ramaner was hoping. It was obvious the general's anger was making him lose control, but Rawk found himself focusing. He found his whole world narrowing to the tiny space surrounding his opponent. He could hear each breath and see each twitch. "I won't go to see Nelly after I kill you, Ramaner, because I would just be disappointed. Being with her would just remind me how far above every other woman Bree stood. Nelly is nothing compared to Bree. You are welcome to her memory for the last minutes of your life. I don't want her."

"Don't you ever—"

Rawk attacked this time, pushing hard, gritting his teeth at the burning in his knee. *Kaj* flashed about his head, a strip of polished moonlight. He followed Ramaner across the room, but with each step, Rawk could feel a pressure growing in his head, a warmth in his cheeks. He risked a look around and saw Balen not far away, waving his hands in a dark corner, working hard at his magic.

Rawk stumbled. He felt a searing pain across his arm as he struggled to regain his balance.

There was someone else still in the room. Most of the sorcerers seemed to have fled, but a big fat man stood silhouetted in a doorway, as still as an icy winter night. His robes seemed to suck the light away.

"You will not escape this time, Rawk." Balen shouted around his spell.

Rawk had battled sorcerers a hundred times before— it was no different to fighting a warrior in a lot of ways— but Ramaner turned to see what was happening. Rawk ducked a distracted swipe, tucked his shoulder and rolled. When he came up onto his knees, he thrust his *Kaj* forward. He watched it slide between the younger man's ribs and held the pose for a moment, forming the story in his head as Bree smiled and clapped, playing the part of a giddy noblewoman. And he almost lost his sword as the general toppled over. But the story wasn't done.

Balen's spell reached a crescendo.

"Sylvia," Rawk called.

What was she doing?

Then there was a moment of intense light and Rawk thought it was all over. But it was Balen who died. Thunder filled the room, filled Rawk's head. And Balen was thrown across the room. He hit the wall with a thud that splintered the rotten timbers, and slid down to the floor.

Rawk struggled to his feet. His ears were ringing, drowning out the sound of his racing heart. He looked around for the fat man, wondering if he had another fight left in his arms and legs. But there was nobody there. Rawk felt the stranger had drifted away like mist on the wind, but he'd probably just left.

He took a breath. Then another. The air tasted strange, but it felt good none–the–less.

Someone touched his shoulder and he jumped. Sylvia.

"Thank you," he said.

"That is all right." She started looking at the worst of his wounds. They all hurt, but Rawk already knew that none of them were fatal.

He gestured towards the remains of Balen. "I didn't think you were going to do anything."

Sylvia grimaced and poked at a long cut on his chest. She started to say something. Stopped. "The other one has gone."

Rawk looked to the door where the fat man had watched. He nodded and took a deep breath. "You scared him off."

"I don't think so. He was..." She shuddered and didn't say anything more.

"Well..."

"Indeed." She looked him up and down. "You look like you could do with some assistance."

"Thank you." He leaned on her shoulder as she helped him towards the door. "It's a long walk to your shop."

"I will take you to the *Rest* then go for my supplies."

"You could have helped sooner."

Sylvia sighed. "How many times must I tell you, it is not that easy as that?"

"Nothing is ever easy, apparently." He stopped to looked back over his shoulder. Three dead sorcerers, which meant three more had escaped. He just hoped they were too scared to show their heads again, though he doubted that would be the case with the fat man. And Ramaner. He really hadn't expected *that*.

"Do you think Ramaner was in charge?"

Sylvia looked back at the general for a moment too, lying in a pool of thick, liquid darkness. "Perhaps."

Rawk felt the elf shudder and decided that she was probably correct. With the things she said, and the things she left unsaid. He tried not to think about the fat man because he really just wanted to go home and sleep.

She continued. "I believe we may have broken their power though. At the very least it will take some time for find sorcerers to replace those they have lost in the last few days."

"So, you may someone knocking on your door very soon. It's a bit insulting that you weren't offered a job in the first place, really."

Sylvia ignored the comment. "What will you tell Weaver?"

"I was hoping you'd tell him."

"That sounds unlikely."

"That's what I though. I think I might retire and not worry about it."

Faraday

RAWK WOKE UP when the door opened. Weaver stood outline in light for a moment, then stepped into the room.

"What the hell happened, Rawk?"

"When?" He tried to get his head around the morning, but it would probably take more than a couple of seconds, especially with Weaver glaring at him.

"When do you think? Last night. You were see coming out of building down in Grand Smelling."

"Right. Of course. Well..."

"Ramaner is dead. Did you know that?"

"Yes."

"What happened?"

"I killed him." He pushed himself upright and sat on the edge of his bed. He was bandaged in six different places and each of them seemed to hurt more than they had when he went to sleep.

"What? I can't just let that—"

"Why do you think it was my fault?"

"Because..." Weaver paused, drew in a breath.

"That's right, Weaver. He hated me much more than I hated him. You know that I was looking for sorcerers."

"Ramaner was, too."

"Ramaner was?"

"Yes."

"Personally? Out there looking for sorcerers?"

Weaver chewed on his bottom lip.

"After dark."

"What are you saying?"

"I know you liked him, Weaver, but he was with them. He may have even been the one running things. I think it was all some sort of elaborate plan to finally get his revenge on me."

"That's ridiculous."

Rawk shrugged. "Perhaps."

"He was with sorcerers?"

"Yes. There should have been three of them there."

"Lakin said there were others there. He didn't say they were sorcerers."

"Well, I don't imagine they were wearing badges or pointy hats with stars on them or anything."

Weaver slumped down into the chair. "You killed three sorcerers?"

Rawk nodded.

"What did they look like? Did you know them?"

"Only Balen."

"Only Balen? Nobody else? Well, right then. Right." Weaver slapped his hands on his knees. It looked as if he as going to get up, but didn't. "As long as you are all right and all that."

"I'll live."

"Good. I suppose you want me to pay you for three sorcerers."

"Just add it to the account."

When Weaver left, Rawk just wanted to stay where he was, but he knew he'd go crazy sitting around in the one small room all day, so he pushed himself slowly to his feet and found come clothes. Ten minutes later, he was in the kitchen reached the hallway at the bottom of the stairs and went to see if there was anyone working in the Vault. Grint was there, sitting on the edge of the stage, looking around.

"What are you doing here?" Rawk asked the dwarf. He sat down at the table closest to the door, not sure he could make the trek all the way across the room.

"Just one last check before or first performance tonight."

"Tonight? Already?"

Celeste came down the stairs from the street, struggling to carry large stained glass window. Rawk tried to get up to go to help, but if she was struggling he thought he would collapse under the weight. Grint hurried across and would have beaten him anyway.

"What the hell is this?" Grint asked as he took the window off his sister and leaned it against the wall.

"Decorations. There are another eight in the wagon upstairs."

"Decorations?"

"Yes. We need to build a box around them so we can put a lamp inside and hang them on the wall."

Rawk nodded and smiled. "I like it."

Celeste jumped slightly. "I didn't see you there, Rawk. Should you be out of bed?"

"Yes. Why? What do you know?"

"I was talking to Sylvia when she came in earlier."

"Sylvia was in?"

"She is still in your office, I think."

"Oh."

As if to prove the point, Sylvia appeared in the doorway, book in one hand, cup of tea in the other. "You should not be out of bed," the elf said.

"Yes, but..."

Celeste gave him an *I told you so* look. "And if you wear yourself out today, you will not be able to come tonight."

"Don't worry, I'll be here."

Grint gave a grunt. "You may be the only one. The word on the street isn't promising."

But Rawk smiled. "You're a dwarf, Grint; nobody is going to admit to anything. But the people who used to see you at the Armory will come to watch. And others will come eventually." He glanced at Celeste. "And they don't have to cheer, or tell you how wonderful you are. As long as they turn up and hand over their money, right? That is the real indicator. Let's just wait and see."

Grint grunted again.

"They'll come," Rawk said. "And they'll keep coming though it may be a while before they talk about it with their friends." He glanced at Celeste, then at Sylvia. "People can change, it just won't happen instantly."

—O—

Keep an eye out for the continuing adventures of Rawk in
The Last Great Hero
Book 3:
An Army of Heroes

ABOUT THE AUTHOR

Scott J. Robinson grew up in a small town in rural Australia, the kind of place where you had to make your own fun. And, from a young age, his idea of fun was to create strange worlds and populate them with interesting people.

He now lives in a different small town, with his wife and three children, and still enjoys creating strange worlds. Though now, he actually finishes some of the things he starts. When not writing he enjoys photography and movies and recently retired from an amazingly mediocre cricket career.

For more information visit
www.tengama.com
or email
scott@tengama.com

Other books by Scott J. Robinson

<u>The Bygone Wars</u>
Book 1: Songs of Space and Time
Book 2: All the Wars of Heaven

Kim McLean is just another tourist visiting Sherwood Forest when aliens attack on the back of giant bats. She didn't think her day could get much weirder after that, until she follows an elf and a dwarf through a magical gateway to another world.

Then, as the endless alien hordes keep coming, she gets involved with bureaucrats and soldiers, governments and people who should know better, and she starts to wonder if her definition of weird needs to be revised.

All she knows for sure is that it's up to her to save the human race.

Travelling to distant worlds and different universes, she gathers strange companions and uncovers long forgotten secrets as she tries to end the death and destruction.

But the war was being waged long before Sherwood Forest was attacked and Kim soon suspects that they aren't even fighting the right enemy.

<u>The Brightest Light</u>

Kade was once the up and coming star of The Skyway Men, a ruthless criminal organization. Then he made one mistake. Then another. Then one too many. Lucky to be left alive, he was banished to a backwoods skyland that flew the quietest wind–lanes.

When he's finally offered another chance Kade can't believe his luck.

But ten years working a smithy and fixing crystal engines is a long time, and with a weapon like none other up for grabs, the stakes are higher than ever.

In a world of death and corruption, shady deals and dirty deeds Kade doesn't know who to trust. He doesn't know who's on which side. He doesn't even know which side *he's* on any more.

All he knows is that in a world of kill or be killed he suddenly isn't sure which is the better option.